The first bell rang.

Héctor's heart dropped.

He couldn't be late to homeroom. That would get him sent to Ms. Heath. So he slowly inched open the door, and, as naturally as he could, he slipped into the flowing crowd, bound for homeroom. He did not look back.

If he had, he would have seen that the door to the janitor's closet was no longer there on the smooth, flat expanse of wall.

Also by Mark Oshiro
You Only Live Once, David Bravo

THE INSIDERS

MARK OSHIRO

HARPER

An Imprint of HarperCollinsPublishers

Library of Congress Cataloging-in-Publication Data

Names: Oshiro, Mark, author.
Title: The Insiders / Mark Oshiro.
Description: First edition. | New York : HarperCollins, 2021. |
    Audience: Ages 8-12. | Audience: Grades 4-6. | Summary:
    Twelve-year-old Héctor Muñoz, fleeing from bullies, discovers
    a magical closet that not only provides him sanctuary, but also
    unites him with two other kids facing similar problems at their
    own schools, helping them find friendship and strength in each
    other.
Identifiers: LCCN 2021010296 | ISBN 9780063008113
Subjects: CYAC: Space and time—Fiction. | Friendship—Fiction.
    | Bullies—Fiction. | Gays—Fiction. | Belonging (Social
    psychology)—Fiction. | Mexican Americans—Fiction. | Middle
    schools—Fiction. | Schools—Fiction. | LCGFT: Novels.
Classification: LCC PZ7.1.O844 In 2021 | DDC [Fic]—dc23
LC record available at https://lccn.loc.gov/2021010296

Typography by Jessie Gang
22 23 24 25 26   PC/BRR   10 9 8 7 6 5 4 3 2 1
❖
First paperback edition, 2022

To all those
In the closet
On their way out
Living in their truth—

This one's for you

CHAPTER ONE

Héctor Muñoz glittered.

Literally. His mami glanced over at him from the driver's seat and smiled. "You're going all out, aren't you?" she said.

"I have to!" he said, smoothing out the wrinkles on his black button-down. "First day and all. Gotta let them know what they're in for."

She turned the car onto the wide stretch of Madison Avenue. The streets were so much bigger here than anything he was used to back home in San Francisco. Well, not "home" anymore. It hadn't been long since his family had moved to Orangevale, which was *definitely* not San Francisco.

He fell silent as his mother drove him to school. He wasn't going to tell her how fast his heart was beating, or that he missed his friends. That he missed being able to walk through the Mission to school in the morning. That he missed the corner market off Valencia where the man behind the counter always joked about Héctor being too young for coffee.

So he fiddled with the tiny stuffed Eevee on his backpack.

He zoned out while staring at all the strip malls and gas stations and drive-through restaurants as they passed by.

He flicked the tiny bells he had sewn into the top strap of his bag.

"You'll be fine, mijo," his mami said as they slowed behind traffic. When he glanced up at her, her eyebrows were raised in concern. "You just be your wonderful self, and it'll all be okay."

"You think so?"

"Depends on if your new classmates have any taste," she said in a faux serious tone. "You might just be too cool for them."

He laughed. "Oh, come on, Mami. You think that's true?"

She grunted. "Honey, the buttons on your shirt match the buttons on your shoes."

"True."

"And yesterday morning we saw a man wearing a cargo *vest* at the store."

He nodded. "Also true. I did not know a person could need so many pockets."

Mami turned off Madison toward the school. "What do you think he keeps in them?"

"Duh, Mami. His *hopes and dreams*."

They both laughed at that, and Héctor was thankful he could joke as often as he did with Mami. He relied on humor a lot because it just made everything fun. He looked more like his papi than his mami. She was a lighter brown and her nose came to a point, and her face was framed with long black hair. Héctor had the black curls, the dark-brown skin, and the wide nose of his papi—but he got his jokes from Mami. Definitely.

He hoped that his humor would get him through this day.

Because there it loomed, off to the right and at the end of the block.

Orangevale Middle School.

It was a single story. Sprawling. The green grass of the sports field stretched so far back that Héctor couldn't even see the fence on the other side of campus. Did it go on forever? Probably. Everything seemed to in this town. Long streets, an endless horizon, so much *space*. There were no buildings leaning up against one another, no growing and diving hills with homes that seemed like they were riding the wave of the earth.

Other kids were streaming up the steps into the school, and he took a deep breath. "I can do this," he said, almost to himself.

But his mami heard him. "I know you can," she said,

and then she reached over and grabbed his hand. "You're amazing, mijo. You're gonna make so many friends, and everyone is gonna love you."

"They better," he said, grinning. "I put on my best outfit for them."

"Go impress 'em," she said, then kissed him on the forehead. "Be the Héctor I know and love."

"It's a new stage," he said. "And this is opening night."

"That's a neat way to think of it," said Mami. "You gonna join the drama club today?"

"If I can find it," he said as he opened the car door and jumped out. "Papi is picking me up, right?"

She nodded, and Héctor blew her a kiss. He shut the door. She drove off.

And then it was time.

Héctor Muñoz stood at the bottom step, kids streaming around him and into the wide-open double doors. So. This was his new school. It felt even stranger that his first day here was at the beginning of October, too. No matter; he had to make a good impression.

So he joined the flow, and moments later, he was inside his new school.

The halls were bright, the tile shiny, and the echoes of voices and scuffling shoes bounced around him. The energy felt . . . different. It wasn't as loud here as his last school. No one was reciting a monologue in the hallway, or singing, or practicing a synchronized dance routine. There weren't any kids running with a giant canvas hoisted on their back. As he counted *six* kids wearing green cargo shorts, he deeply missed Tim and Sophia, his best friends back in the Mission. *I'll have to text them*, he thought, and he pulled out his phone.

"No phones out in the halls!"

The voice rang loud and clear, just off to Héctor's left, and he froze in place, long enough for someone to bump into his backpack.

"Out of the way," the girl whispered, and she looked over Héctor from head to toe, then shook her head, her blond curls bouncing back and forth.

Seriously? he thought. *Did she just judge my outfit?*

But he had no time to say anything. A woman stood tall in front of Héctor, her arms crossed in front of her, and she wore a head-to-toe gray outfit: gray skirt, gray blazer over a gray shirt, and a gray cloth headband pulling her brown hair back, with impeccably shined gym sneakers on her feet. Everything was perfectly matched.

"Young man, did you hear what I said?"

Héctor did, but he was still lost in all that gray. There was so much of it! Did she dress this way *every* day? He kinda respected that.

"Sorry," he said, putting his phone back in his pocket. "I'm new here."

She raised a brow high on her angular face, which only seemed to stretch it longer. "New?" she said. "Did you already go through registration?"

"Last week," he said. "Mami brought me in to—"

"Because there is an *order* to things here at Orangevale Middle School," she said, cutting Héctor off. "You can't just do as you please, young man."

"O-okay." He frowned. "I wasn't trying to."

"Did you read our handbook on student conduct?" Seemingly out of nowhere, she produced a pale pamphlet and held it out. "Perhaps you need a refresher."

He shook his head. "No, I think I'm fine, Ms. . . . Ms. . . ."

"Ms. Heath, head of campus security," she said, raising her chin higher. "And what is *your* name?"

"Héctor Muñoz," he said, beaming up at her.

There was a notepad in her hand. *Where did that come from?!* he wondered. *Where did the pamphlet go?*

She scribbled something down. "Hmmm," she muttered. "Well, off to homeroom. You do know where that is, right?"

"What did you write?"

"Mr. Muñoz, that is none of your business," she intoned, her voice dropping in pitch. "Please continue to class, and remember: here at Orangevale Middle School, we follow the rules."

Then she turned and walked off down the hallway, her gym shoes squawking loudly on the tile.

Well, that was odd, he thought. Why had she singled him out? Sure, he *was* new. Still, it wasn't the best start to his first day.

A bell rang out. It was flat, an even tone, low and boring. Ms. Heath was still walking away, so he peeked at his phone. His homeroom class started in five, and after that, he'd meet all his new teachers. All his new classmates. Maybe there'd be a kid obsessed with musicals. Or even someone who just liked drama. At this point, he'd take someone who had visited a thrift shop once in their life. He just had to find his people, right?

Héctor stepped into his noisy homeroom class, believing that it could only get better.

CHAPTER TWO

Well, Héctor thought, *this is worse.*

He stood with a yellow plastic tray in his hands, just beyond the end of the cafeteria line. He was ignoring the food *on* the tray; he wasn't even sure it *was* meat in the breaded patty that limply sat in one of the squares. His focus was on the long expanse of tables before him.

Héctor had only attended one school since kindergarten: Alta Vista Academy. And you didn't have to worry about where to sit at lunch when you were five. By the time that sort of thing mattered, Héctor had found Tim and Sophia. He'd discovered musical theater. He knew where to go!

So where did Héctor belong *here*?

This felt like one of those movies Mrs. López used to show in her Health Sciences class, as if Héctor was about to be taught an important lesson about friendship by an animated bird. *At least that would be more helpful*, he thought. He had *no* idea what he was doing.

The table of jocks was closest: all the athletes flocked to one another like they were their own species. There was no way Héctor would *ever* be caught there in his whole life.

The cheerleaders would probably be nice to Héctor, but that wasn't the right table, either.

There were the band geeks, their gear stuffed under the table in black hard-shell cases. Héctor internally sneered at them. It was silly, but there was a long-standing competition between band geeks and theater nerds. He was sure these kids were fine people! But it was the principle. Never! Never shall the two be friends!

A group of gamers were huddled around a Switch, but as Héctor watched, Ms. Heath swooped in like a hawk and confiscated it. As the kids at that table groaned loudly, the meme kids at the next table over took advantage of the noise to continue making videos on their phones or showing each other whatever new meme they found online. Clearly, they were much better at hiding their devices from Ms. Heath.

They still weren't right for Héctor.

He passed each table and observed for a moment or two, hoping that he'd see something familiar: kids practicing their lines; impromptu fashion shows; harmonized sing-alongs. But there was nothing of the sort. His heart raced as he passed by the comic book nerds, and then . . . that was it.

Héctor was at the back of the cafeteria, and there was

only one option: a mostly empty table with just five kids sitting at it.

Four of them were huddled at one end of it, and then, far at the other end, there was a lone kid with pale skin and dark hair and a skull T-shirt on. Héctor recognized it as a Misfits T-shirt. It was kinda impossible to live in the Bay and not know who they were.

The kids closest to him glanced up and examined Héctor head to toe. Then, a Black kid on the end, thick-framed glasses on his face, nudged the brown-skinned girl in a hijab next to him. They scooted over, and Héctor decided to take a chance. Where *else* was he gonna sit?

He plopped his tray down. "Hi," he said. "Héctor."

The boy with the glasses smiled at him. "Jackson," he said. "Well, my first name is Jeremy, but I go by Jackson." Then he pointed across the table. "That's Carmen."

Carmen waved. She was brown, slightly lighter in complexion than Héctor's deep brown, and he really liked how she did her makeup, with sharp eyeliner and red lip gloss.

"That's Taylor."

Taylor was abnormally tall and had dirty blond hair, and he looked just like a surfer, down to his sunburned white face. He flashed Héctor a peace sign.

"I'm Aishah," announced the girl in the hijab. "Welcome to the Table of Misfits."

Héctor laughed at first, then saw no one else was laughing. "Oh. You're *serious*."

"We are," said Jackson. "And not just because of him." He gestured with his head to the far end of the table.

"What's that kid's deal?" asked Héctor.

"That's Pat," explained Carmen. "He doesn't want to be friends with anyone."

Héctor let loose a chuckle, but cut it short when, once again, he was the only one reacting that way. "Oh. *Really?*"

Aishah nodded. "He *literally* announced it during lunch on the first day of school. He stood up on the table and just yelled at all of us."

"Said that we were all *beneath* him and that none of us were worth the time," Jackson added.

"Wow," said Héctor. "So, this is his table, then. Table of Misfits."

"Well, also, none of us fit in anywhere else, bro," said Taylor. His drawl was *absolutely* that of a surfer. "Like, I don't know if you know this about me, since you're new and all, but, like . . . I *surf*, bro."

"Really?" Héctor said, his voice shaking as he struggled to keep a smile off his face. "I couldn't tell."

"Totally," said Taylor. "And I don't know if you know this, either, but there's no ocean here in Orangevale."

Héctor glanced over at Carmen, who had her face in her hands and was shaking her head.

"Yeah, right, of course," said Héctor. "We're so far inland."

Taylor's mouth dropped open. "Bro. We *are*."

There was silence at the table as all of them stared at Taylor. *He is . . . a special person*, thought Héctor.

"Anyway," said Aishah, "Taylor isn't wrong. I'm the Black Muslim girl into art, and all the art kids think I'm pretentious."

"I'm starting a makeup history channel on YouTube," said Carmen. Then her voice dropped. "When I turn thirteen next year. My mom won't let me make videos yet, so the meme kids don't want me to sit with them."

"And I'm the band kid who doesn't fit in with the other band kids," said Jackson. Héctor heard a thump under the table, and he looked down at the hard trumpet case at Jackson's feet.

That was a surprise to him. "What do you mean you don't fit in?"

"I listen to a lot of reggae and first-wave ska," said Jackson, his face lighting up. "Like the *real* early stuff. Everyone else . . . well, they just want to compete, but I just wanna get better at the trumpet. And start a band!

Maybe bring about a new wave of ska."

"I wouldn't have guessed you were a band geek," Héctor said quietly. "They're not like you back at my old school in San Francisco."

And it was true; the band kids Héctor had known didn't seem to know any modern music aside from the covers they performed at school events. He wanted to ask Jackson about music, but Carmen changed the subject.

"Wait, you're from the *City*?" exclaimed Carmen. "And you ended up *here*?"

Héctor poked at the food on his tray. "I mean . . . yeah. My mami got a big teaching job here, so we just moved."

"Well, maybe you belong here with us," said Aishah. "You can definitely sit here every day." She paused. "If you want, of course."

He smiled back at her. "Yeah, cool," he said, and he tried the weird breaded patty.

Oh, he should not have done that.

His stomach rumbled as the others fell back into another conversation. Héctor tried to keep up, but he didn't know what they were talking about half the time. Still, he felt a warmth in his chest when Jackson said that he hoped to see Héctor again at lunch the next day.

It's a start, thought Héctor.

CHAPTER THREE

"Okay, so maybe it wasn't the *worst*," Héctor said over dinner that night. "Until I found out that there's *no drama club* at school."

"None?" Héctor's papi ran a hand through his hair, thick with coiled curls. "They don't do plays or anything?"

Héctor shook his head, then scarfed down the beans he had sopped up with his papi's fresh tortillas. "Nothing. At all."

Papi frowned, then looked toward Mami. "Lilliam, did you hear that? No drama, he says."

She clicked her tongue against her teeth. "I'm sorry, mijo," she told Héctor. "I didn't know that when we were researching schools. They told me they had a 'robust art department.'"

"I mean, they *do*, but not the kind of art I usually do," said Héctor. "Aishah says I should join Mrs. Caroline's art class with her, so I'll probably switch to that tomorrow."

"Aishah? ¿Quién es?"

Abuela Sonia—perhaps Héctor's favorite person in the world—sat at the head of the table, opposite him. She'd lived in Orangevale for most of her life, so she had spent a lot of time at the house helping them unpack the last two weeks. If he got his temperament and humor from Mami, and most of his looks from Papi, then his sense of style . . . well, that all came from Abuela. She'd been making her own clothing for years, long before Héctor was even born.

That evening, she was wearing a blouse she'd made of this strange fabric she found at a thrift store. It was a pale yellow with orange koi fish all over it, and it looked *incredible*.

"I met some kids today," Héctor said. "They invited me to sit at their table during lunch."

"¡Mira!" Papi said. "That's good."

"It's literally the table for the kids who don't fit in."

"Oh." Papi exchanged a quick glance with Mami. "Well, maybe those *are* your people. You know, forge your own path."

"True," said Abuela. "There's no one like you on this earth. Embrace that, papito!"

"And maybe this art class won't be so bad," said Mami. "We can look into an after-school theater program, but in the meantime, you can learn something else. You *have* always said you wanted to know how to paint."

He nodded at that, then wolfed down more of his papi's home-cooked meal, filling the pit in his stomach left by the mystery patties from lunch.

Héctor was still thinking about his mami's suggestion later that night when he sat in front of the family computer and called Tim and Sophia on video chat.

They both answered immediately, and just the sight of his best friends filled his heart with joy. Since they'd last talked, Sophia had just gotten her first set of Bantu knots. Four of them sat evenly over her head. Héctor screamed as she showed them off on camera. "Oh, they look *so* cute!" he said.

"They took way longer than I thought they would, so they *better*," she said.

"What's good, homie?" said Tim, and he flashed a toothy smile at Héctor. He could see the wall of musical instruments behind Tim: guitars and basses, some brand-new, some beaten up from years of live music, all of them belonging to Timoteo's father, who played in a Chicano punk band that was super famous in the Bay. "Please tell me you survived the move to Orangevale, and I'm not currently talking to your ghost."

"Well, you *might* be," said Héctor. "Would that change anything for you?"

"Nah. Homies for life."

Héctor reached out toward the screen. "I miss you

both so much," he whined. "It's so *hot* here. All the time."

"Boo, it's *October*," said Sophia. "How is it still hot there?"

"I think that this town is literally on the sun," said Héctor.

"That bad?" she said.

"It's . . . fine," he said. Then, "It's just very . . . different?"

That didn't really describe it, but how could he explain it? Life here was simply *off*, like he'd been thrown into a parallel universe.

"Come on," said Tim. "There's gotta be some bomb Mexican food out there at least. You know our people are everywhere."

"Maybe," said Héctor. "I just haven't found anything that feels familiar. I mean, it's only been a week, but still. Everything is so spread out here. And hot. Did I say it was hot here?"

"You did," said Sophia. "So it's permanent? You're really stuck there?"

Truthfully, Héctor was still entertaining the idea that maybe this wouldn't work out. Maybe Mami's teaching job would fall through, maybe they'd have to go back to San Francisco, and maybe Héctor's life wouldn't have to change.

"I don't know. I might be. We'll see."

Tim told Héctor about a ridiculous backyard gig his father played, and then the three of them got lost in all the gossip from Alta Vista Academy. Like how Nick Royce had been cast as the lead in the fall musical, and soon audiences would be treated to his loud sandpaper voice. They laughed together. Héctor showed off the outfit he was going to wear the next day: lavender pants, paired with an egg-white T-shirt and a silver chain. "It's like if the Rock was dating Prince," Héctor explained.

That made Tim and Sophia crack up. "Oh, I miss you, Héctor," said Sophia.

"Miss you, too," he said. "*Both* of you."

When he signed off, though, a creeping doubt slid up his chest. How was he ever going to keep up his friendship with Tim and Sophia if he could only see them through a screen? Well, he'd have to keep trying.

He glanced over at tomorrow's outfit, displayed on his bed. Yeah, that would impress someone. Right?

He wasn't sure who he was trying to impress.

CHAPTER FOUR

The next day, Héctor met with the school counselor, Ms. Milan, so he could switch to the same art class as Aishah. He was nervous when he stepped into her office, but Ms. Milan was warm and charming. She had light-brown skin and wore big hoop earrings that poked out from under her straight black hair. She told him that she was glad he was "showing initiative" by choosing to do art, and he told her the truth: he would prefer to do theater, and this was the next best thing.

"We haven't had a theater department in *years*," she said, her mouth curling down in a frown. "It just wasn't very popular."

"That's okay," he said, even though it wasn't. It just seemed like the right thing to say.

Ms. Milan smiled at him. "I really think you'll enjoy Mrs. Caroline's class. And if not, you do have another week to change your mind."

Throughout his day, Héctor couldn't ignore that everyone had started without him. He struggled to catch up with lessons that had already been taught, chapters that had already been read, discussions that had already been had.

Lunch rolled around, and the square of pizza he was given was swimming in oil. When he sat at the Table of Misfits, he saw that Jackson had dumped a pile of napkins on top of his pizza.

"Yo, what's with the food here?" Héctor asked. "It all seems . . . I don't know. Not that great?"

"That's an understatement," said Jackson, and he adjusted his glasses. "It's like an alien came to earth and ate pizza, and then described it to *another* alien, and that's what this is."

"Wait, *aliens* made our food?" said Taylor, his eyes wide.

"Oh, honey," said Aishah. "Your soul is too pure for this world."

"How's your second day, Héctor?" said Carmen.

"It's okay, I guess," he said. "Aside from the food."

Jackson raised a monstrous blob of oily napkins above his tray. "Yeah, this is *gross*."

"I switched to art," said Héctor, looking at Aishah. "So I'll see you after this."

"Yay!" Aishah said. "I promise you, you'll love it."

"Mrs. Caroline is the best," said Jackson. "If I wasn't allergic to art, I would be in her class, too."

"What do you mean by that?" asked Héctor.

Jackson did not get to say whatever was about to come out of his mouth. There was a loud laugh, almost more like a bark, that rang out behind Héctor, and he watched the color drain from Aishah's face.

"Oh no," she said. "He's coming."

In an instant, the others dropped their heads down and began to act like their greasy food was the most interesting thing in the world.

"Um . . . what's happening?" said Héctor.

"Hey, new kid!"

A hand clamped down on his shoulder.

Hard.

"No one told me there was a new kid here!" the voice continued. Héctor craned his head around and stared up into the face of a tall, lanky kid with blond hair and green eyes, his pale face slightly sunburned like Taylor's. "What's your name?"

Héctor looked back to the others at the table. None of them made eye contact with him or the boy who had strolled up to the table.

Oh, this seems bad, he thought.

"I'm Héctor," he said hesitantly. "You?"

"HECK-tor," the kid said, grinning.

Héctor winced. His name was pronounced wrong all the time, so he was used to telling people about the accent mark and the right way to say it. But suddenly, he wasn't sure this was the right time to correct anyone.

"Well, nice to meet you, HECK-tor." The kid stuck his hand out. "I'm Mike, and I'm going to be your best friend."

Héctor's mouth fell open a little. "You are?"

"Absolutely," he said. "I can tell you have style. You're unique. And I think you should join me and my friends at my table."

Héctor leaned to the side to look past Mike toward where he was pointing. Over near the table between the sports kids and the popular girls, there was a half cafeteria table with two other boys at it. They seemed deep in some discussion with one another, until they turned exaggeratedly and stared at Héctor and Mike.

Were they *laughing*?

"Think about it," said Mike, clapping his hand down on Héctor's shoulder. "You'd be a good fit."

He sauntered off. Héctor watched him as he sat down at the smaller table with his friends, then turned back to the Table of Misfits.

Aishah looked like she was going to be sick. Jackson was sweating, and Carmen wore a tight frown on her face. Even Taylor was avoiding Héctor; he furiously texted someone under the table.

"So . . . what's going on with y'all?" said Héctor. "Are we at a funeral or something?"

"Bruh, don't do it," said Jackson, standing up. His food wasn't even eaten, but he dumped it in the trash can at the end of the table. "It's not worth it."

"Don't do *what?*" Héctor asked.

"Mike is not your friend," said Carmen. "He and the Minions are the *worst*."

"The *what?*"

"The Minions," explained Aishah. "Carlos is the Mexican kid, Frank is the white one."

"Why are they named after those things from the *Despicable Me* movies?"

"They do whatever Mike tells them," said Taylor, brushing his blond hair to the side. "*Whatever* he says."

"So . . . what is he? Like, the school bully or something?" Héctor shrugged. "I've dealt with bullies before. They're all the same."

"Not him," said Carmen. "Trust us, there's a reason we're all at this table."

"He tries to be your friend," said Aishah. "Or at least that's what he was like to me."

"He did the same to me," said Carmen. "And he's nice and he's popular, and all the teachers here like him."

"So it seems like everything is fine, unless you know better," explained Taylor.

"And then he turns on you," continued Jackson. "He did that to me the first week of school. That's . . . that's *really* why I'm sitting here and not with the rest of the band."

"Because he makes you damaged goods," said Taylor, his head still drooping down over his phone. "No one wants to hang out with you anymore."

That made Héctor angry. "Well, I want to hang out with you," he said. "And I'll just stay away from Mike."

"Good luck," said Aishah, and the Table of Misfits finished the rest of their lunch in silence.

As Héctor watched Mike goof off with his Minions, his stomach twisted. He didn't like the way Mike spoke to him. Or the way he'd grabbed him so hard. He might have been desperate to find his place, but his gut reaction was to stay far, far away from Mike.

Héctor had no plans to stray from that.

CHAPTER FIVE

Unfortunately, Héctor didn't really have a choice about that.

He told Aishah he'd meet her in art; he wanted to get there early to introduce himself to Mrs. Caroline. So he drifted past Mike's table without a single glance. He paid Mike and the Minions no mind.

Héctor had just barely left the noisy cafeteria and stepped into the squeaky-clean hallway when he heard his name being called. Mike burst through the swinging double doors, his two friends trailing behind him. Carlos was short and stocky, and he wore tight blue denim jeans over pointy boots and a white button-down. He had a whole vaquero thing going on. Frank, however, looked just like Nick Royce, the sandpaper singer from Héctor's old school. Frank's dark hair seemed greasy, as if he never washed it, and his mouth was curled up in a snarl.

Héctor had a *plan*, though. Avoid and ignore, right?

But Mike reached out, grabbed at the sleeve of his shirt, and spun him around.

"Wait up!" said Mike. "Where you headed, friend?"

"Me?" Héctor pointed at himself. "You mean me?"

There was no one else in the hallway. He sounded ridiculous. *Nice job, man*, he thought.

"Of course I mean you," said Mike. "Tell me, Hecktor. You thinking of going to the fall dance at the end of the month?"

Héctor shook his head. "I . . . I don't know what that is. New kid, remember?"

Mike gently slapped Carlos's arm with the back of his hand. "How could I forget?" He laughed, and it did not sound friendly.

What is this guy's deal?

"Well, you should roll with my crew and come," said Mike. "We get all the attention from the girls. They'll be all over you!"

Ah. Héctor couldn't stop the grimace that flashed over his face. *He thinks I'm straight.*

"Yo, Mike," said Frank. "He doesn't seem that excited by your offer."

"Look," said Héctor. "I'm sure you're all nice, but I think you're barking up the wrong tree. I'm not really interested in girls. At least not like that."

"What does that mean?" said Mike, and he laughed. "Are you, like, *gay* or something?"

"Yeah. I am."

It was like all the air had been sucked out of the

hallway. Carlos's mouth dropped open, and Frank actually took a step back. *Why?* Héctor wondered. *They can't possibly be surprised by this.*

"What did you say?" asked Mike.

"I'm gay. Like . . . *literally* gay."

"Bruh," said Carlos. "What?"

"That's so . . . so *gay*," said Mike.

"Well, yeah, I hope so," said Héctor, chuckling softly. "Be weird if it wasn't."

But they didn't laugh.

They didn't smile.

Mike examined Héctor, like he was a specimen in a lab.

"You're serious," said Mike.

"I am," said Héctor. "I thought it was obvious?"

"So . . . are you saying *I'm* gay because I wanted to be friends with you?"

"What? No!" Héctor held his hands up. "What are you *talking* about?!"

"Did you say Mike was fine?" Frank said, and he covered his mouth like he was scandalized. "Wow, bro, did you hear that?"

"Shut up, Frank."

The playful tone in Mike's voice was gone, and a spike of fear rushed through Héctor's body. This had *never* been an issue at Alta Vista. Like a solid third of the theater department wasn't straight. Was it not like that here in Orangevale?

Everything around him told him this place was different: the wide, flat streets. The boring buildings. The lack of a theater department. And now, *especially* Héctor's clothing. He looked down at his lavender pants. Was anyone else here even wearing that color?

That spike of fear became a flood as Mike took an aggressive step forward. Héctor heard the Minions giggle, and he knew that he'd made a mistake. He shouldn't have said any of that.

"So, you like boys, then."

And Héctor knew he should have given Mike what he wanted, but when his mouth opened, the following words came out instead:

"Well, not *you*."

He immediately clamped a hand over his mouth. *Héctor, why did you say that?*

But Mike just smiled. It was one of those smiles that didn't reach his eyes. "Good to know," he said. "Where you stand, that is."

He patted Héctor on the arm. "See you around, *Heck*-tor."

Frank and Carlos trailed after Mike without another word.

Héctor remained motionless, and Jackson's words came back to haunt him:

"And then he turns on you."

Like a light switch. In one moment, Héctor had gone from potential friend to . . . what? What was going to happen next?

The end-of-lunch bell rang, and soon, other kids were bumping into him as he stood in the hallway. He shook himself out of his stupor and headed for art class, his nerves thrumming with energy. Had he just made everything *worse*?

He was lost in this thought when he stepped into Mrs. Caroline's class, and he nearly walked directly into his art teacher, a tall Black woman. She had a large yellow envelope held up in front of her and a big smile on her face.

"Mr. Muñoz, I assume?"

She had the most *killer* purple lipstick on, and Héctor realized that they kinda matched: she had on a white blouse and a grape-colored pencil skirt. Her curls were much more tightly coiled than his papi's, and they bounced as she walked toward him.

"Uh . . . yeah, that's me," he said, taking the packet.

"Fantastic!" she said, and she said it like she meant it, as if it truly *was* fantastic that he was now in her class. "I made you this little packet to help you catch up on what we've already learned. I'm very excited for you to join our artistic haven!"

Then she gestured around the room—which took Héctor's breath away. The entire ceiling was painted like *The Starry Night*, all deep blues and bright stars and flowing lines. Shiny gold streamers hung from each of the stars and the moon, and they swayed in the breeze of a small fan on Mrs. Caroline's desk. Each of the walls was covered in a different kind of art: papier-mâché. Oil paintings. And it was so much bigger than the other classrooms!

As the last few kids rushed to get to their seats before the bell rang, Mrs. Caroline gently guided Héctor to his, which was near her desk. "It's a lot to take in," she said. "I like to keep it interesting every year."

"This is *amazing*," he said. "I've never seen anything like it."

"And what would you like to do?"

The question caught him off guard. "What?"

"What kind of art would you like to learn about this year?"

He sat down and let his backpack slide to the floor, the bells jingling. His eyes jumped from one piece to another. "Did your students do these?"

"Everything," she said. "Even the ceiling."

"Wow." He cleared his throat. "I was sad because there's no theater department here, but . . . but I want to learn how to do *this*." He gestured about the room.

The bell rang, and the last few stragglers rushed inside to sit down.

"I think we'll get along well, Héctor Muñoz," she said, and then she winked at him.

She said his name *exactly* right.

CHAPTER SIX

Héctor was in a much better mood that night at dinner. It helped, though, that Papi—who loved cooking as much as Abuela did and generally handled all their meals—said he felt super lazy that night, so they'd just ordered pizza. Actually *edible* pizza, that is, which was also *way* better than Héctor had expected! Maybe Orangevale did have a few things going for it. Mami even said they might do pizza more than once a month because it was so good.

The next morning, Papi dropped Héctor off at school before he headed downtown to meet with someone about a blueprint he had designed. So he swung by Héctor's favorite fast food chain for a breakfast sandwich as a treat. The two of them sat in the family car in the parking lot of the school, eating them.

"Pizza last night, and then bacon, egg, and cheese sandwiches," Papi said. "I gotta get some actual green vegetables in you tonight."

"There was basil on the pizza last night, Papi," said Héctor. "That's, like . . . two vitamins, right?"

Papi laughed hard, a deep and hearty sound. "You truly take after Mami, mijo," he said.

"What can I say? She passed me all her funny bones, Papi."

His papi stuffed the last bit of his sandwich in his mouth. "Well, have a good day at school," he said. "And you know . . ."

He didn't finish the sentence at first. "Papi?" Héctor asked.

"You know, just . . . let me know if you need to talk about anything. About how school is going and stuff. I'm here."

Papi got all bashful then, looking out his window. Héctor smiled. His dad was like that sometimes. He didn't have a problem with his emotions, but unlike Abuela Sonia, who was incredibly direct and straight-forward, Papi seemed uncomfortable in moments like this. Héctor thought it was kind of adorable.

"I will," he said. He hopped out of the car and waved, then darted toward the front steps.

He was going to be fine. He knew it. That morning, he'd anticipated the heat this time and put on some gray shorts, a black V-neck, and some black Jordans. It was a simple, monochrome look, but it gave him confidence. There was nothing that could stop him if he *felt* good.

So he walked into school with a bounce in his step,

keeping rhythm to a song in his head. He thought of what he'd told his mami: This was a new stage. A new production. All these kids were just actors in a play, and now, it was time for Héctor to take center stage, to sing his big number. He grinned when he imagined what that would *really* be like. A big choreographed dance up the steps? Oh, if *only* he could do something like that!

I really wish there was a theater program here, he thought as he ascended up into Orangevale Middle School. Maybe he should ask Mrs. Caroline about starting one.

He was lost in thought when someone slammed into his shoulder.

Hard.

Héctor's backpack fell to the tiled floor, the bells on the top strap jangling as it did, and his stuffed Eevee went flying. He spun around and was met with the grinning face of Carlos.

"'Sup, Héctor," he said.

And before Héctor could mumble a confused reply, another shoulder slammed into him, and he spun in the opposite direction.

This time, Héctor nearly fell over, but he was quick on his feet. "Hey, watch out!" he said, but then he heard Frank's loud, barking laugh.

"You gotta watch where you're going," said Frank, and

Héctor didn't know how, but his hair looked even *greasier* today. Was his shower just a torrent of oil?

Héctor didn't have time to be grossed out by his own thought, because then Mike came through the double doors. There was a malevolent smirk on his face.

"Careful, *Heck*-tor," said Mike. "If you're just checking guys out all the time, you'll never see what's in your way."

Héctor sighed and reached down to pick up his bag. "I wasn't checking anyone out," he said, but he knew as soon as the words were out of his mouth, this was pointless. Futile.

"Oh, am I not good enough for you?" said Mike, faking outrage. "Did you just call me ugly?"

Carlos and Frank cackled behind him.

"No, I didn't—" Héctor began.

Mike advanced on him, and before Héctor could react, Mike reached out and flicked the collar of his V-neck. "Who wears shirts like this? That seems real fruity."

Héctor's heart raced, and his hand went to his collar, covering up his exposed skin.

"I tried to be your friend, you know," Mike said.

Now Héctor started backing up. He hated that this was his reaction.

Because he was *afraid*.

A nervous energy filled Héctor's chest as his back hit a

wall. "W-we can still be friends," he said, his voice shaking. It did not sound terribly convincing, and he knew that. But he had no idea what else to say.

"Maybe we should try again," Mike said, and he stopped advancing.

He stuck his hand out.

"A truce," he said.

"A truce?" Héctor repeated. "Meaning what?"

"Meaning we can be friends!" said Mike. "If you can outrun us."

Héctor's mouth fell open. "What?"

Mike lurched forward and Héctor's reaction was instinctual:

He *ran*.

Héctor had no idea where he was going. It was his third day here, and every hallway was like a new part of a maze. Mike and the Minions cackled behind him, and Héctor made the mistake of turning to see how far away they were.

Oh.

They were gaining on him.

Great! he thought. *What a great way to start the school year!* He flung himself around a corner to his left and—

"Mr. Muñoz, there is no running in the halls!"

He froze, but only for a moment. There, at the end of the hallway, was Ms. Heath.

Today, she wore all red. Literally, head-to-toe red tracksuit with a red headband and bright-red sneakers. (To himself, Héctor admitted what a *look* this was.)

She began stomping toward him.

He backed up.

Mike and the Minions were right there, around the corner he had come from, muffling their laughter, slowly creeping toward him.

Héctor panicked. He didn't want to deal with *any* of these people!

So he didn't really think about it. He darted to his right, lunged for the door in the wall, and opened it. He heaved his body into the darkness and slammed the door behind him.

The sound echoed in the small room, right alongside Héctor's heaving breath.

What are you DOING?! he asked himself. *They all saw you go in here. What's your plan? Hope that they somehow forget you even existed?*

Light from the hallway filtered through the frosted glass in the door, and Héctor stayed as quiet as he could. Soon enough, a tall shadow crossed in front of the glass.

"Boys, good morning. Have either of you seen Mr. Muñoz?"

That was Ms. Heath. Another blurred shape appeared, and Héctor knew it was Mike.

"No, Ms. Heath," he said, laying on an innocent tone *real* thick. Héctor rolled his eyes. He wasn't even a good actor!

"Well, get along to class, gentlemen," she said, and sure enough, Héctor heard their footsteps get farther and farther away.

But Ms. Heath stayed there. He saw her turn around a few times, then face the door. She tried the handle.

It wiggled.

Héctor's heart leaped into his throat.

But nothing happened. It didn't open.

Which made *no* sense. Héctor hadn't locked the door behind him. What kind of closet locked from the *inside*?

Yet as Ms. Heath finally stepped away and wandered off into the halls of the school, Héctor began to take stock of where he was.

There were wooden shelves stretching up to the ceiling, and they were stacked with supplies: Tile cleaner. Window spray. Toilet paper. Those bags of sawdust they used when a kid barfed in the lunchroom or the gym.

There was a bucket with a mop to one side.

A broom.

Oh.

Oh.

He was in the janitor's closet.

It was his third day at school and . . .

It started as a chuckle, then built into something bigger, and soon, Héctor had his hand over his mouth, desperately trying to hold the roaring laugh in.

He was in the closet.

Ha, ha, he thought. *The joke makes itself.*

But then he *did* go quiet. It might have been funny at first, but as the smell of cleaning agents overpowered his nostrils, he couldn't ignore the reality anymore.

He was hiding in a closet.

Because of bullies.

Because he was gay.

Maybe he really was a character in one of those terrible health class specials.

A new pain struck him: he'd forgotten to pick up his stuffed Eevee when it had flown off his backpack. There was no way it was still on the floor. This only pushed him deeper into sadness. In his silence, he noticed a web in the corner and a small black spider in the center of it. He bowed in that tiny space.

"Good evening, sire," he proclaimed in a fake British accent. "Ever so sorry to bother you in your kingdom."

The spider just sat there.

"I shan't be doing it again . . . King Ferdinand."

The spider did not reply.

Back at Alta Vista, acting out random scenes like this was an everyday occurrence with his friends and fellow theater kids. But there, in that closet, shame prickled his skin.

The first bell rang.

Héctor's heart dropped.

He couldn't be late to homeroom. That would get him sent to Ms. Heath. So he slowly inched open the door, and, as naturally as he could, he slipped into the flowing crowd, bound for homeroom. He did not look back.

If he had, he would have seen that the door to the janitor's closet was no longer there on the smooth, flat expanse of wall.

CHAPTER SEVEN

Héctor thought that changing things up a bit would steer him clear of his tormentors. On Thursday, he asked his papi to drop him off five minutes before the first bell; Friday morning, he lied and said he needed to do some reading and wanted to be dropped off an hour before class to go to the library.

And both times, Mike and the Minions found him.

Héctor *knew* that running away didn't make anything better. He still did it. He ran because it was easier.

Both times, he headed straight for the janitor's closet at the end of the hallway. He always made it there before Mike and the Minions did, it always seemed to lock behind him, and no matter what they did, those boys couldn't get inside.

So, for the few minutes he was there on Thursday, or the *hour* he was there on Friday, Héctor was safe.

Thursday, he sat at the Table of Misfits without saying anything, and he spent the whole lunch hoping no one would bring up the incident in the hallway. No one did, and he was thankful for that. On Friday, however, he wasn't so lucky. The others were already at the table when he put his lunch tray down, and Jackson looked up at him. "You doing okay?" he asked.

Héctor shrugged. "Yeah," he said, and he sat alongside Jackson. "Just mostly catching up in all my classes."

"That's good," said Jackson. There was an awkward pause. "But I meant after the other day."

Everyone at the table—even Pat, all the way down at the other end—was staring at Héctor. His heart pounded. He hated the looks on their faces. They all seemed *sorry* for him.

"I'm good," he said. "Keeping to myself."

For the moment, it satisfied them, and to Héctor's relief, the conversation continued.

When Friday afternoon arrived, Héctor dreaded all the homework he'd accumulated. But he needed *something* for himself, so as he climbed into his papi's car, he launched immediately into his plan for Saturday.

"Okay, so I'm thinking chilaquiles tomorrow morning. Only if you're up for making them."

"And hello to you, too, Héctor," Papi said. "My day was good, how was yours?"

Héctor stuck his tongue out. "Hi, Papi," he said.

"I take it you're excited for the weekend?"

"I wanna do *something*," he said. "We should get out

and explore the neighborhood tomorrow morning before I have to do homework."

"Really?" Papi turned the truck onto the main street. "Sounds like a good idea. But why?"

He did not tell Papi that he was excited to forget most of his week. Rather, he blurted out, "Because I don't *know* Orangevale!"

Which *was* the truth. All he'd really seen was a couple supermarkets and his school. There had to be more to this city, some place that would make him feel like he was home. Like, where were the good corner markets? Or the places to get boba at?

"Pues, I can ask Abuela where we should go," Papi said.

"We *could*, but . . . I kinda wanna find these places myself, you know?"

Papi nodded. "That makes sense."

"I just . . . I have to find a way to make this place mine, I guess."

Papi ruffled Héctor's hair. "Well, I'm free tomorrow. Your mami is on calls all day with the teachers' union, so it'll just be me and you. ¿Está bien?"

"Of course it's fine!" said Héctor.

And he was going to make it so.

• • •

Full of his papi's excellent chilaquiles, Héctor fastened the buckle on his shoulder bag. "Okay, we got everything?"

Papi was carrying a tote bag, and he stood near the front door. "I think so. Run it past me, mijo."

"Water?"

Papi held up his water flask. "Check."

"Sunscreen."

He tapped the tote bag. "In here."

"Cell phone?"

His papi ran his hands over his pockets. "Oh. Good lookin' out, mijo."

As he went off to go find it, Mami sidled up to him. "Sorry I can't come with you today," she said. "My to-do list only grows with each passing day."

"It's okay," he said, smiling. "Once things calm down, we can have our own day trip. Like a spa day."

She laughed at that. "Do you even *like* spas, Héctor?"

"I don't know! I *might*. Guess we'll just have to find out."

His papi returned, holding his cell phone high. "¿Listos?" he asked.

"Whenever you are," Héctor shot back. He bounded out the front door as his parents kissed goodbye, and he ran down to the end of the driveway.

There were more one-story houses like their own

in either direction on their street. None of them were in the bright, random colors he was used to, but they weren't exactly ugly. Lots of trees lined the street, and he *did* like that; he wondered what it was going to look like later in the fall. But there was so much missing: all the brightly lit storefronts. The smell of fresh tortillas from the women on the corner of 23rd and Valencia. Carson, the homeless man Héctor said hello to every day on his walk to school.

His papi caught up and grabbed Héctor's hand. "All right, mijo," he said. "You're navigating. Where to first?"

Héctor took a deep breath. He'd done research after dinner last night and had assembled a list of ten places to visit that were all in walking distance. Even though he was full from breakfast, he couldn't resist the notion of having boba on such a hot day.

"This way," he said, and he pulled Papi onto the sidewalk and toward their destination.

Four hours later, Mami rolled up in her blue sedan. They weren't exactly far from home, and Héctor wasn't even all that tired. But as he limped over to the car, he was glad he wouldn't have to try to tough it out.

"Ay, mijo, ¿que pasó?" Mami said as he laid himself across the back seat, panting.

"I was attacked," said Héctor. "I will never recover."

"Attacked?!" Her voice was alarmed. "By *who*?"

"The sidewalk," said Papi, sitting in the front passenger seat. "The *sidewalk* attacked him."

"It was *terrible*," Héctor continued, sitting up and putting on his seat belt. "It's like it opened up and ate half my leg."

"What nuestro hijo is *trying* to say is that . . . well, he tripped and scraped his knee."

"Who lets the sidewalks look like that? And there were so many places where there *wasn't* a sidewalk at *all*."

"I'm sorry, mijo," said Mami as she pulled into traffic. "Is it bad? We'll bandage it when we get you home."

"I'll be okay," he said, and then fell silent. It was barely two, and his day felt destroyed. Nothing had gone like he wanted it to. The walk down to the boba shop wasn't too bad, but when they got there, they found out that it had closed down a couple months ago. He hadn't let this discourage him; there were nine more places on his list.

Getting to them was a hassle, though. One of the routes his phone told him to take didn't have a crosswalk, and Héctor was too scared to cross the busy street—everyone drove so *fast* here. So they didn't end up checking out the bookstore or the record shop. At the antiques store, Héctor was hoping to find some cool thrifted pieces to use in an outfit, but almost everything there was camping or military gear. There wasn't *any-thing* kid-sized except for a Dora the Explorer T-shirt with some very suspicious stains.

His fish tacos at the place that claimed to make "authentic" Mexican food? Oh, they were not fish tacos. More like "soggy fish-like substance over a soggy tortilla-like substance." And there were raw carrots in them! Who put raw carrots in a taco?

His stomach was hurting by the time they made their way to a local park that was supposed to have some cool installation art. They didn't make it to their destination due to a gnarly tree root that had warped the sidewalk, causing him to fall.

Orangevale had not treated him all that kindly.

"We'll drive to places next time, mijo," said Papi. "Just so we don't waste time."

"Sure," he said, but he wasn't into it. He loved being able to walk everywhere, like he used to do . . .

Back home? Could he even say that anymore? *This* was his home now, wasn't it?

He shook the feeling away. "Mami, can we write the mayor today?" he said. "I'd like to tell him he's got a feral sidewalk issue on his hands."

She chuckled. "Of course we can."

"We can't just let these concrete monsters keep claiming lives."

"Not at all."

"I'm starting a petition, too."

Now Papi was laughing. "We support you."

They rode the rest of the way back in silence. As Héctor hobbled his way into his sky-blue house, he vowed to find some other way to make Orangevale his home.

CHAPTER EIGHT

As Héctor limped down the hallway, his black Chucks squeaking repeatedly on the tile floor, he realized he'd gotten pretty good at this.

Monday had been the same as the end of the previous week. Tuesday was . . . well, it was like his counselor had assigned him a new class that started before homeroom. It was called "Hide from Mike and the Minions."

Which is exactly what he did both days. Monday's painful run earned him a long lecture about order and discipline from Ms. Heath. Tuesday, Héctor chose something simple to wear to school that morning: a black polo shirt and blue jeans. When Mike initiated their daily chase, he didn't say anything about what Héctor wore. It was a victory! Well, a victory that immediately didn't matter that much as Mike got closer to catching Héctor.

The door came into view. Dark wood with frosted glass, black block letters spelling out JANITOR across the window.

Carlos called out: "Get him!"

But Héctor was faster.

(He had to be.)

Another voice rang out: "No running in the halls!"

Ah, Ms. Heath. *Again.*

Héctor reached the metal handle and yanked the door open. He managed to peep Mike and his red face and blond hair lunging for him. Just in time, Héctor shut the door.

The slam echoed in the tiny closet, and Héctor waited. It was all he could do. He had found this part funny before, because no matter what Mike and the Minions did, they couldn't get inside. Now, though?

The joke wasn't all that funny anymore.

The pounding eventually died out. Héctor watched the shadows of the three boys through the frosted glass. They lingered a moment more, and then they faded away.

He let out a deep breath. *I guess this is my life now*, he thought. As the Misfits said, Mike had turned on him. What came next, though? Would Mike eventually tire of chasing him every morning? Héctor leaned his head against the wall next to the door. How much longer would he have to endure this?

For the moment, he was safe here. By now, he knew every inch of the place: the dark corners, the crooked shelves, the smell of Fabuloso, and His Majesty King

Ferdinand, unmoving up in the corner. Héctor was now one of his loyal subjects.

"How's your morning, your majesty?" Héctor asked, bowing in the tight space.

Ferdinand did not move. Or speak. He *was* a spider, after all.

"It's a busy day in your kingdom, no?"

Silence.

Am I really talking to a spider? he thought.

The bell rang, clear and loud, and Héctor's heart dropped.

Okay.

He could do this.

(. . . could he?)

He sighed. Wiped the sweat from his forehead. Took a deep breath. Started humming loudly: some Prince, because that man's music could always put Héctor in a good mood.

He opened the door.

Looked left.

Looked right.

No Mike. No Minions.

He stepped into the hallway, his leg still sore from his tumble. He joined the other kids heading to homeroom. A tall kid with dark-brown skin and a close-cropped fade was dribbling a basketball, and he cast a glance back at Héctor, looking him up and down. Then he continued on his way without a word.

Well, Héctor's outfit wasn't drawing much attention. But a gnawing pain filled his stomach. He didn't feel like himself. Was Mike *changing* him? No. No, this was temporary. It had to be. Mike and the Minions couldn't chase him *forever*.

He jumped out of his skin when someone called his name. But it was just Mrs. Caroline wishing him a good morning. He waved back to her, then scurried to his homeroom.

Okay, maybe this was worse than he wanted to admit.

Héctor burned to tell someone—*anyone*, really—what was happening to him. But then he thought about how his parents would freak out. How the Misfits would get that sad look on their faces. How he'd just feel so powerless and cowardly about it all. . . .

No. Héctor would outlast Mike and the Minions. Because he didn't see any other way out.

CHAPTER NINE

When Héctor sat down at the dinner table that night, the smell of posole made his mouth water. "Abuela," he said, "it's not cold out yet. You're *already* making this?"

Abuela Sonia stood over a big metal pot, stirring it. She swatted away Papi, who tried to steal a spoonful. "Siéntate," she ordered, and Papi slunk back to the table.

"She is so mean to me," his papi whined, and then ruffled Héctor's black hair.

"Ever since I retired," Abuela said, "I need things to do. So let me serve you all some of my world-famous posole, hijo." She used a large ladle to fill a bowl with the savory soup, then brought it over to Héctor. "Only *polite* chicos get served."

"Wow," Papi said. "Forsaking your only child to manipulate your grandson."

She slapped at her son again.

Héctor blew at the posole, eager to dig in. "Gracias, abuela," he said.

Papi stretched an arm out, wrapped it around his

mother, and hugged her close. "Te quiero," he said, soft and thankful.

Mami came in then, like a burst of wind through the alleys in the Mission. She kissed Héctor on the top of his head right as he put a spoonful of posole in his mouth. It was way too hot to eat.

He didn't care. He shoveled another spoon in.

Those flavors! Savory and a little sweet, and those hominy . . . que delicioso! Héctor could eat this for every meal. He was pretty sure he'd bathe in it if he could.

"How was school today, mijo?"

Mami stood next to Abuela, and the two of them pierced him with their gazes. He swallowed down another spoonful.

"It was . . . bien. Okay. I don't know."

He focused on the bowl. On the little bits of oil he could see floating in the soup. On the—

"Héctor. Mírame."

He looked up at his mami.

Oh no.

She had her hands on her hips.

He cast a glance at his papi to try to beg for help. But he was just as intensely focused on his posole as Héctor had been.

"¿Sí, Mami?"

Her smile was gentle, but her eyes were locked with

Héctor's. "Why don't you know how school was?"

He sighed. "It's nothing," he said. "It's just . . . weird."

"Weird how, nieto?" asked Abuela.

He pushed his spoon around the bowl. When he looked up at his abuela, he could see concern on her face.

"I'm new," he told her. "I'm just trying to find a place, especially since they don't have a drama club."

Abuela nodded at him. "Pues, that stuff is hard to navigate," she said. "But you're starting to make friends."

"Sort of," he said. The Misfits were certainly friendly with him. But did that count as *actual* friends?

"I know this is a huge adjustment, mijo," said Mami. "But we're all here for you."

"Exactly," Papi said. "Any time you need something, one of the three of us can help."

He smiled. "I know."

But Mami was swamped with her new job, and his papi had gotten a new commission to help plan a building in town. They were so busy. He didn't want to add to it, to make them feel like he was a burden. So he saw this as the perfect chance to direct the conversation elsewhere. "Actually, Abuela," he said, "I was wondering if I could come over this weekend." He turned to his parents. "If it's all right with you."

"I'm free," she said, and Héctor's parents nodded at her. "What did you have in mind?"

He rubbed his hands together. "I think it's time to teach me the family recipe," he said.

She put a hand to her heart. "Am I hearing this correctly? You'd like to learn the legendary Muñoz tamale technique?" She gave Papi a pointed look. "Do you think he's ready?"

"I don't know," his papi said, shaking his head. "Twelve. That's pretty young. He might not be able to handle it."

"Come *on*, Papi!" Héctor said. "Look, exploring Orangevale by foot was *not* a vibe, and hanging with Abuela is the only good thing about this place."

Mami and Papi exchanged a look, and Héctor winced. Oh no, that was a little *too* forward. But they didn't comment on it. "Well, I'm glad you're trying your best," said Mami. "You have my blessing."

"Go," Papi said, smiling ear to ear. "Impress me."

Now Héctor had something to look forward to.

"What's good, fam?"

Tim spun in the chair in his father's music room, and Héctor admired his newly dyed hair. It was normally jet black like Héctor's, but now, half was red and the other half was blue.

"You know . . . trying my best," said Héctor. "Orangevale is a weird place."

"Please tell us," said Sophia. "Weird like how?"

Héctor told them pretty much everything: the lack of a drama club, which Tim and Sophia booed at; how everyone seemed to look at him weird; and about Mike, including Héctor's tense confrontation with him.

Tim raised his hand at that point. "Wait, hold on," he said. "Do these people seriously have a problem with you?"

"Yeah, what's that about?" said Sophia.

"Are we gonna have to take an Amtrak out there and get a little physical?" asked Tim.

"It's not that bad," said Héctor. "I promise. I just think he was uncomfortable with . . . you know."

"How can someone be like that anymore?" Tim shook his head. "Like, who actually cares about stuff like this?"

"Imagine if he met us," said Sophia. "Two bi kids, one Black and the other Mexican. His brain would probably explode."

Héctor laughed at that, but then the video chat went quiet. He watched as Sophia played with one of her knots and Tim spun around in his chair.

"Is everything okay?" Héctor asked.

"Yeah," said Sophia. "It's just . . ."

"We're worried," Tim finished. "I'll be straight with you."

"Tim," said Héctor, "you've *never* been straight."

A goofy grin spread over Tim's face. "Okay, *true*. But

neither have you! And that never mattered before."

"Are you going to be okay there?" said Sophia. "You're not in danger, are you?"

"I'll be fine," he said, fidgeting in his chair. He remembered how Jackson had warned him that Mike would eventually turn on Héctor. But why did it have to happen so quickly?

"You sure?" asked Sophia.

"He'll probably just leave me alone eventually," said Héctor.

"But what if he doesn't?" said Tim.

Héctor hadn't thought of that. Mrs. Caroline's class had gotten his mind off it. But now, as he gave it some attention, something gnawed at his stomach: fear.

"Is that why you're dressed all preppy today?" Tim asked.

Héctor stilled. "What?"

"That polo shirt thing you got on. I've never seen you wear something like that *ever*."

"It *is* a little weird for you," added Sophia.

Heat rushed to Héctor's face, but he tried to recover as best as he could. "No, no, it was just for this thing my mami had me do," he said, laughing nervously. "I just haven't changed out of it yet."

There was an odd silence after that.

"Well . . . we miss you," said Sophia.

"A lot," Tim added.

"Oooh, by the way, I got to hear a very rough rehearsal of the musical the other day," Sophia said. "We're preparing for a train wreck."

Héctor groaned. "Nick's *still* bad, isn't he?" That was one thing he wouldn't miss about Alta Vista. It didn't help that Nick's father was a history teacher, either. Everyone knew it was preferential treatment, but it wasn't like anyone could *do* anything about it.

"So he's just gonna shout his way through it all, right?" Tim said.

"He's so *loud*," Héctor whined. "Have you ever heard him try to whisper?" He then imitated one of Nick's whispers: it was like sandpaper colliding with fireworks.

Sophia began to cackle. "You wrong for that one," she said.

"But am I lying?" Héctor said.

She shook her head. "Seriously, though," she said, "we really miss you."

"I miss you guys, too," he said. "Orangevale is wack. It's just not the same."

"And it's definitely permanent?" Tim asked.

Héctor nodded. "As far as I know."

"You'll come visit, won't you?" Sophia said.

He frowned. It wasn't really up to him, but he couldn't say that.

"Yeah, of course! As soon as I can."

There was a crash, and Héctor didn't know whose video it came from. Tim disappeared off camera, then came back in a panic. "Sorry, guys, I *may* have knocked over a guitar."

"Ouch," said Héctor, wincing.

"Which knocked over another one."

"Oh no," said Sophia.

"Which knocked over like ten more."

"Say no more," said Sophia. "Go take care of it. I got too much homework anyway. Call us soon, okay, Héctor?"

They said their goodbyes. Héctor sat at the desk for a while, looking at the black screen of the computer.

They know, he thought. *They know I'm changing.*

But they didn't know *why.* He left the computer and plodded over to his room and crashed down onto his bed. His stomach felt weird as he thought about what they'd said to him. How had they noticed the change in his usual outfit? He was only doing it to avoid more negative attention. Was that a *bad* thing?

He knew then that Sophia and Tim wouldn't understand what was happening to him, and he wasn't going to tell them about it.

CHAPTER TEN

The next morning, Héctor took the long way around the halls, but it was a pointless strategy. Mike came out of the boys' room and tried to grab Héctor, and so the chase began.

His thoughts were everywhere. He was tired; he hadn't eaten a big breakfast because of his nerves, so now he was hungry.

So he wasn't paying attention when Ms. Heath stepped out of the library right in front of him.

He froze and noticed that she wore a canary-yellow tracksuit. Today, it felt intimidating rather than impressive.

"I'm sorry, Ms. Heath," he said between breaths.

"Young man, there is no running in our hallways!" Ms. Heath scolded. "Why do I *always* have to tell you this? There are rules here for a *reason*."

Shoes squeaked on the tile behind Héctor. He saw Ms. Heath's eyes go wide.

It was Mike, Frank, and Carlos, who came to a stop. She looked at them.

Then down to Héctor. Then back up.

"Were these boys chasing you?" Ms. Heath pushed her glasses up the bridge of her nose, waiting for him to answer.

Héctor had been taught long ago to find an adult he trusted if something was wrong. But did Héctor trust her?

Not really. His only interactions with Ms. Heath had shown him that she wasn't willing to listen. Yet she *had* noticed that Mike and his Minions were chasing him. Was this his only chance?

He gave it a shot.

"Yes," he said. "They always do."

Ms. Heath frowned. "Is that why you were running last week?"

Relief poured out of Héctor along with his words. "Yes! They won't leave me alone, Ms. Heath. They're always bugging me and calling me names and making fun of me for being gay. *Especially* Mike."

There. He'd *done* it. Pride swelled in his chest. This was the mature thing to do. He was basically an adult now, wasn't he?

"You're saying Mike here is responsible for all of this?"

He nodded his head, maybe a bit *too* eagerly.

"What do you have to say to that, Mr. Kimball?"

For the briefest moment, Mike's eyes were wide in

panic. Then his mouth drooped down. He tried his best to imitate innocence. Héctor could see right through the act.

"I don't know what he's talking about, Ms. Heath," he said. "Me and my friends—we were just trying to get to the library before homeroom."

"So you were running in the hall as well?" Ms. Heath crossed her arms over her chest. "You know the rules, Mr. Kimball."

"Of course I do," he said. "I'm sorry; we were just excited about getting the books we asked to check out yesterday."

Ms. Heath narrowed her eyes. "So why does Mr. Muñoz here seem to believe that you and your friends were chasing him?"

Mike ran a hand through his blond hair. "I don't really know," he said. "He's always saying weird stuff that I don't understand. Maybe they do things different where he's from."

Héctor's heart dropped. *What? Why would he say that?*

"Mr. Muñoz, where did you transfer from?"

He gulped. "Uh . . . Alta Vista Academy."

"And where is that? *I've* never heard of it."

"It's in San Francisco," he said.

Her face *changed*. Her mouth wrinkled into a frown.

"One of those *magnet* schools?" She scoffed at Héctor. "None of them know how to *properly* discipline their students."

"But I'm telling the truth!" Héctor exclaimed.

"Mr. Kimball is a *wonderful* student here," said Ms. Heath. Now her hands were on her hips. "Beloved by the teachers. And he's *never* been in trouble, this year *or* last. You're the first person to even suggest that he's not following my rules."

"But—" Héctor began.

Ms. Heath shook her head. "No, Mr. Muñoz. We don't like lying here at Orangevale Middle School, either."

His mouth fell open.

"I'll give you detention if you lie to me again," she continued. "And no hiding in classrooms, either. If you hear me call your name, I expect obedience."

Héctor watched Ms. Heath leave, her sneakers smacking against the tile. When she was out of sight, he turned around.

There was a small crowd gathered behind Mike and the Minions. Quite a few kids, actually. He saw Taylor near the back, and Carmen was beside him. Both of them looked *terrified*.

And none of them would make eye contact with Héctor.

He wanted to disappear. To be literally anywhere

else. Deep down, he hadn't expected to be believed. But to be threatened with detention for *lying*?

Deflated, he turned to leave, but Mike blocked his path. He stepped close to Héctor, until his face was maybe an inch away. "I don't know where you came from, bruh," he said. "But here? We don't snitch."

Mike yanked on one of the straps of Héctor's backpack. It tore loudly, and Héctor snatched at it to keep it from falling to the floor. The bells attached to it jingled, and suddenly he hated them.

"You know what I do to snitches?"

Mike stepped forward, pressing up against Héctor, and fear rippled over Héctor's skin. He tried to back up fast enough, but then Mike's hands slammed into his chest, and he went flying. He made to stop himself with the hand not holding his damaged backpack, but he ended up jamming his thumb against the wall.

He bit back a curse word—even though his mami wasn't here, he knew not to swear—and Mike laughed. "Come on," he said to his Minions, who followed behind him as he left.

The others? He caught a glimpse of Carmen shaking her head. Another boy from his pre-algebra class was grimacing. They all scattered quickly, leaving Héctor alone on the floor.

He stayed there for a moment, staring at the door

across the hallway from him. JANITOR, it read.

He did a double take. Was he so turned around that he'd forgotten that the closet was in this part of the school? He dismissed the thought. He *could* dart inside, take some time to gather himself.

No. It would be better for him to get to class and try to get through his day.

Héctor stood, then held his throbbing thumb against his chest. He needed a break from this, but it looked like Mike was determined to make his every day miserable.

There was a long, slow creak as Héctor turned to head to his homeroom. The bell hadn't even rung yet, but he wasn't going to hang around and see who was spying on him from one of the classrooms. He was certain that the whole school would know what had happened by the end of the day.

His head down, Héctor made his way to the other side of campus.

If he had turned around, he would have seen that the janitor's closet had opened and stood ajar, almost like a quiet invitation.

CHAPTER ELEVEN

The rest of Héctor's day passed in a blur. He sat in silence at the Table of Misfits, which had been his normal routine during lunch, but this time, *no one* spoke. Héctor wanted to ask them how Mike had stopped focusing on them. But would that ruin the already awkward mood?

Instead, no one said anything, and Héctor left lunch early to go hide in the bathroom.

Mrs. Caroline was her usual delightful self, and her mood had given him a little boost. By the time he got home, he had talked himself up. He had to show his parents and his abuela that he was trying. So he quietly borrowed some safety pins from his mami's sewing case to repair the strap on his bag. Confident that it would hold, he set it down in his room and headed for the dining room. He had to at least *try* to make the day feel normal.

But then the jingle of the bells on his bag brought him back down. He quietly removed them.

Abuela was over for dinner again, and he was thankful for the distraction. Papi was cooking, making his rolled tacos in a deep pan that spattered and spurt oil. Papi tried to dance away from the pops and crackles, and every time he got hit, he swore in Spanish under his breath, certain that Héctor couldn't hear him. (He heard Papi every time.) Soon, the smell of fried tortillas filled their home.

Héctor pulled out his notebook to get some homework done and was halfway through his history questions when Abuela sat beside him. "Dime, nieto," she said. "¿Estás bien? You are so quiet today."

He smiled. "Just trying to concentrate," he said. "I want to get my homework done so I can get some sleep. Estoy cansado."

She ran her fingertips up his arm, and bumps rose on his skin in their wake. "You can talk to me, you know," she said. "Anytime."

When he gazed up at her, there was an odd look on her face. *What is that?* he wondered.

He didn't say anything back to her. She merely smiled and walked over to Papi to talk to him.

It came suddenly: *Does she suspect something is wrong?* Héctor thought he'd been pretty good at putting on a brave front, and he wanted to maintain that. He would figure out *something* to deal with Mike eventually. He didn't want to make his family's life any harder.

Mike's voice echoed in his mind:

"You know what I do to snitches?"

Héctor gulped. Now there was *that* to worry about, too. No, he *definitely* could not tell anyone about this.

Dinner was loud, especially once Mami got home, and Héctor did his best to blend in. He helped with the dishes, gave his abuela and his parents a kiss good night, then headed to his room. Without much thought, he pulled out some gray jeans, a black T-shirt, and a long red flannel, one that was too big for him. But he liked how dramatically it flowed behind him when he walked. He laid them out on the bed, excited for the morning.

Then he thought about how many people would look at him. How he would basically be painting a target on his back.

He put away the flannel.

It'll be easier to disappear, he thought.

Before he climbed into bed, he opened up his group chat with Sophia and Tim. He wasn't sure he was going to tell them what he was feeling, but he knew they could cheer him up quickly. **What are y'all doing? Any good gossip from school?**

Moments later:

> **Sophia:** yeah. some good stuff. busy with
>   homework tho.
> **Tim:** there's always time for gossip, soph!
>   spill spill spill!

A short burst of a conversation ensued. It turned out that Nick Royce had been bad-mouthing the singing coach, so now his role was in jeopardy.

> **Héctor:** karma. it has to be.
> **Sophia:** we can only hope!
> **Héctor:** this has given me LIFE, soph. you have no idea.

He hopped into bed and flipped off the lights. Then he pulled his cobija—the one Abuela got him at the Ashby BART flea market, black with a white tiger on both sides—over his head. In the darkness and silence, his thoughts swirled. Maybe he needed to try harder with the Table of Misfits. He couldn't do another silent lunch again. All he had to do was keep his head down, get to the cafeteria, and hope that he hadn't ruined his chance at friendship.

He fell asleep with his sore thumb clutched to his chest.

CHAPTER TWELVE

But Héctor tossed and turned all night. If there were dreams, he didn't remember them. He was sluggish at breakfast. "Tú eres como un perezoso," Mami said.

A sloth. She called him a *sloth*.

Well, at least they were cute. He asked her for a cafecito, and she laughed at that. "You are not old enough for that," she replied.

"And you'd be bouncing off the walls," Papi added.

Maybe that wouldn't be such a bad thing. It had to be better than feeling like the human equivalent of a puddle. He nearly dozed off on the ride to school.

He was thankful, then, that Mike and the Minions were nowhere to be found for the first time in over a week. He trudged sleepily toward homeroom. *I just need a nap*, he thought. *Just an hour or two of sleep, and then I'll be fine.*

But it was 8:13 a.m., and the bell was bound to ring any moment. Mrs. Torres would not tolerate anyone sleeping in her English class.

Héctor thought he was imagining the long, wooden

creak when it rang out in the hallway. But then it whined out again, and he spun around slowly. There were a couple of kids getting things out of their lockers at the end of the hallway on the right side. Behind them stood an open door. No one even seemed to have noticed it.

He walked toward the door, and to his confusion, it drifted open *wider*.

He froze, watching the nearby kids. The girl slammed her locker shut, then grabbed the boy's hand. They both walked off away from Héctor. Neither looked toward the door.

Héctor approached it. It was like most of the others in this school. Dark wood, frosted glass. Except this one had a word in black block letters across the glass: JANITOR.

He shook his head. Why did this school need so many janitor's closets? There was one near his art classroom, and he'd found a second one the day before.

But when he swung the door open wider, his mouth dropped open. It had the *exact* same shelves, the *exact* same supplies . . . *no way*. He stepped inside and looked up in the corner.

Sure enough, there sat King Ferdinand, right in the middle of his web.

This didn't make any sense. He turned to leave.

The door was shut.

He didn't remember closing it. He gripped the metal handle and twisted.

It wouldn't budge.

The first thought that bloomed in him: *Mike did this.* It had to be a prank, right? Mike and the Minions must be standing on the other side of the door, holding it shut.

But . . . there were no shadows in the frosted glass. Unless they were crouching down the whole time, Héctor would have seen them. He tried the handle again.

Nothing.

"This isn't funny," he called out, but no one answered.

Exasperated, he turned back around.

The closet was *bigger*.

It was impossible. He knew it. The room could not have gotten bigger.

And yet . . . the shelves were gone. The back wall was now twenty feet or so away from him, and even in the dim light that came through the frosted glass, Héctor could see what sat in the middle of the room.

A bed.

A whole bed.

Sheets, pillows, a bed frame.

A.

Whole.

Bed.

On top, though, was the greatest impossibility of all. Héctor crept in hesitation to the bed, and then ran his hands over the soft black-and-white cobija that lay over everything. The tiger stared at him majestically.

It was the *same* cobija he had at home.

Because this was already weird enough, he let his backpack slide to the ground, and he climbed on top of the bed.

It was like sinking into a cloud. No, better than that. As Héctor stretched out, it felt like he *was* a cloud, as if the only worry he had in the world was deciding where to rain down upon the earth.

His heart was *racing*. This wasn't happening. This wasn't real.

But then he kicked his shoes off. (It would be a mortal crime to have shoes in bed, even in this definitely-fake-and-not-real bed.) He stuck his legs under the cobija and let his head fall onto the firm, yet comforting pillows. He almost laughed as he pulled the cobija up to his chin.

He just wanted to try it out. You know, see how it felt.

It felt *so* good.

He pulled one of the extra pillows to his chest and held it tight.

Oh, yeah. This was incredible.

He sank. He disappeared into darkness, into a sleep that was uneventful. Peaceful. *Necessary*. He didn't dream, either. He just . . . slept.

And then his eyes shot open.

No. *NO*.

Had he fallen asleep?!

Héctor had never felt panic rush through his body like this. He jolted upright and swung his legs over the edge. He tried to jam his feet into his shoes, but then the heel of the left one folded down, and he couldn't get it all the way on. Oh, God, how long had he been out?

His stomach rumbled in protest. He was now *starving*, and as he struggled to get his left heel in the correct position, he wished he had time to get something to eat.

Time.

Wait, what time was it?

Héctor was so wrapped up in his own fear and confusion that he didn't care who might be on the other side of the door. He burst from the closet, panting, and he looked up at the clock, which read—

That . . . that was not possible.

7:45 a.m.

He wiped at his face. No. He had gone *into* the closet

just before the homeroom bell rang!

But . . . the hallways were empty. He quickly darted down to the nearest classroom and put his face to the frosted glass.

The lights were out. No one was there.

He backed away from the door and slowly walked to the janitor's closet. When he peered inside, his stomach dropped to his feet.

"You've *got* to be kidding me."

Because as Héctor stood there, he had to accept what he saw before him.

The closet had changed. *Again.*

He couldn't even call it a closet anymore. The room before Héctor was enormous, bigger than his family's entire previous home in San Francisco. Bulbs set into the ceiling illuminated a full entertainment center. A large couch, one that looked terribly comfortable, sat on one side of the room opposite an actual refrigerator. There was a small coffee table between the television and the couch, and on it sat the controllers for . . . a Nintendo Switch?

Nope. Dreaming. He was definitely dreaming.

He pinched his skin.

It just stung a little. Which made sense, because that was what pinching did. Why was that a thing? Had

anyone ever gotten out of a dream by pinching themselves?

Héctor made his way to the fridge, and curiosity
burned in him. Why a refrigerator? He pulled it open
and there, on the top shelf, was a large plastic pitcher
with a familiar liquid inside it.

No. No *way*.

He let his backpack fall to the floor and reached inside
the fridge to grab the pitcher.

Pulled the lid off. Smelled it.

It smelled like . . .

He turned around once more. Now there was a small
table behind him, with two chairs on opposite ends, and
a single clean glass sitting in the middle of it.

It had appeared out of *nowhere*.

"Yo, what is this?" he said, his voice soft, disbelieving.

He reached out. Touched the glass. It was solid, a little chilled, and when he picked it up, it certainly *looked*
like a real glass. So . . . it *had* to be real.

So Héctor just went with it. He poured the liquid into
the glass and hesitated for only a second before he took
a sip.

Smooth. Creamy. That hint of cinnamon hit his
tongue, and he knew this was . . .

This was . . .

. . . his abuela's horchata??? It tasted exactly the same! But *how*? How could this drink be here, right now, in this room?

Scratch that, Héctor thought. *How can this room be here?*

He took another sip. It still tasted the same. There was no trick here: This was *absolutely* the horchata he had come to know and love.

Héctor shrugged and drank the whole glass down. Then he poured himself another, drank *that* down, and then his stomach rumbled again.

Ugh, I need some actual *food*. But where would he—

In the space between gulping the second glass of horchata down and realizing how hungry he was, a new item had appeared on the table: an empty bowl and a box of Cocoa Puffs. And Héctor *had* to laugh, because that meant he could act out his own personal blasphemy without anyone judging him: using horchata instead of milk in his cereal.

He poured horchata from the pitcher over the bowl of cereal, and didn't hesitate to begin shoveling those chocolaty puffs directly into his mouth. He was barely chewing—not just out of hunger, but because he knew if he stopped and thought about this, it wouldn't make sense. He was still inside a janitor's closet, and that closet could change its contents at will. Not just that, but it seemed to be able to read Héctor's mind?

Oh no.

He put the bowl back down on the table, and some badly chewed puffs fell out of his mouth and plopped on the table. He'd seen this movie! Magical room with *exactly* what you needed inside it? This was a trick. A trick set up by magical beings like fairies or wizards, and he'd just eaten a *trap*.

Except . . . that didn't *actually* happen in real life.

Neither does a room like this, his mind shot back.

His stomach rumbled again.

All right, maybe a few more bites, he thought. *If this really is a trap, then at least I won't be hungry anymore.*

It tasted *so* good. Héctor ended up finishing the bowl in a few bites. He guzzled down the delicious leftover horchata, which now had the sugary flavor of Cocoa Puffs.

The bowl clanged on the table when he set it down.

"This is really happening," he said out loud.

And then he ripped a huge belch, and it *echoed*.

"Perdóneme," he said, and then fell into a bout of laughter. Who was he apologizing to? There wasn't anyone here. He shook his head as he looked around this impossible place.

Well, he wasn't hungry anymore. He'd avoided getting caught by Mike and the Minions. Or Ms. Heath. Everything had worked out.

Maybe he wasn't going to complain about things going his way for once.

Héctor grabbed his bag and made for the door. Guilt struck him: He had left his dirty bowl on the table. His parents had raised him to always clean up after himself.

There was a sound—soft, swift, almost imperceptible—and he looked back.

Into a normal janitor's closet.

Never mind the dirty cereal bowl. All the furniture was gone. The lights, too. The TV, the Switch, the fridge, the table . . . *everything*. It was now the same closet he'd seen multiple times since coming to Orangevale Middle School. And there, up in the corner, was King Ferdinand, repairing a part of his web.

"Thanks, your majesty," said Héctor, and even if he didn't understand this, even if it was weird to thank a spider, he let the strangeness of all of this guide him to his homeroom. When he glanced up at the clock, he couldn't believe what he saw.

8:14 a.m.

In the midst of his morning English class, Héctor struggled to focus on anything that Mrs. Torres said. He wanted to text Tim and Sophia. He pulled his phone out quickly between his first and second classes. Once he glanced at his mostly ignored group chat, though, he put it back. No, he'd left too much unsaid with them lately. How would they ever believe *this*?

He had wanted to be more social with the Table of Misfits at lunch, but he fell into silence because he didn't know how to have a normal conversation. Not with the closet on his mind! He kept worrying that he'd blurt it out randomly. *Hey, y'all, do any of you have Mr. Harris for pre-algebra? Just asking, because there's a magical closet on campus, and I totally took a nap in it and traveled through time. You guys ever do that?*

Aishah nudged him as they walked to Mrs. Caroline's class. "You lost in there?"

"Huh?" he said.

"You just seem so quiet lately," she said. "My mom always says that when people get like that, it's because the world inside is more interesting than the one outside."

He couldn't help chuckling at that. "I guess you could say that," he said, and then he smiled at Aishah. "Sorry, I'm just figuring stuff out."

She smiled back. "It's okay."

Héctor entered art class with a lightness in his step

because of that. "How was your morning?" Mrs. Caroline asked him.

He grinned from ear to ear. "Unique," he said.

Mrs. Caroline twirled. "That's what I want to *hear*!" she exclaimed. "Now let's put that energy toward some new art."

As he sat down and pulled out his sketch pad, he found a small plastic bag tucked into his backpack. He examined it . . . and discovered that Mami had snuck him some alfajores. His heart swelled . . . and then beat furiously.

His parents.

There was no chance he could tell Mami or Papi. After that look they'd exchanged the other day, they definitely knew Héctor wasn't having an easy time. How would they react to him telling them . . . well, what would he even *say*? That he'd found a magical room on campus that appeared to bend to his desire?

Right. That was believable.

So Héctor began to sketch out the shapes Mrs. Caroline had drawn on the whiteboard at the front of class. He also decided that he would keep this to himself.

CHAPTER THIRTEEN

Héctor did not see the janitor's closet again for the rest of that week. He looked for it between classes, after lunch, even when he headed to the front of the school to get picked up. It wasn't *anywhere* to be found. But he also didn't need it; he never ran into Mike and his Minions.

As the weekend approached, Héctor was excited (okay, and a little bit nervous) about getting to spend Saturday with Abuela and learn more about an important family tradition. Maybe *this* was how he'd feel more at home here in Orangevale. What if he got so good at making tamales that he could start selling them at a local farmers market or swap meet? Surely Orangevale had those. He let the fantasy run wild: he imagined how they would package them; they'd have to come up with a cool logo. Maybe he could ask his parents to help him film a lo-fi commercial for it.

He was picturing his tamale takeover as his papi picked him up from school on Friday. "What you thinking about?" Papi finally said as they pulled into the driveway at home.

"Just planning my extremely popular culinary dynasty," he said.

"A dynasty?" Papi chuckled. "So you think you're gonna nail Abuela's tamales the first time?"

Héctor scoffed and got out of the car. "I am going to sit atop a tamale empire by the end of the *month*," he said. "Just you wait and see."

"We'll see," Papi said.

Héctor was sure of it. *This* would be his best plan yet.

Abuela rolled up bright and early at seven thirty a.m. on Saturday, and Héctor hopped into her car, his excitement spilling over as he immediately began to tell her all about his brand-new business model.

"Whoa, whoa, one thing at a time, nieto," she said, then laughed. "Are you sure you haven't been sneaking sips of your mami's cafecito?"

He frowned. "She won't let me. Says I'm still too young for it."

"Well, you certainly don't need the energy boost." She backed out of the driveway, then turned them onto the road. "So what's this plan you have?"

He told her as much as he could, but she put up a hand to interrupt him when he started talking about writing a theme song for their commercials.

"Héctor, let's just get you *making* them first. Okay?"

"Yes, yes, of course," he said. "I'm sure I'll be perfect at it."

"Hmm. We'll see."

He gasped dramatically, then clutched his chest. "Abuela, do you not have faith in me? Do you believe that your skills have not been passed down through your bloodline?"

She shot him an amused look. "It's not that simple. It takes practice to perfect our method. It took me weeks to master just the basic form when my own abuela taught me."

"Well, then I'll just have to do better than that, right?"

Abuela Sonia reached over and patted his leg. "You're a funny one, nieto. We gotta make one stop, and then we'll get started."

The carnicería felt familiar to Héctor, even though he'd never been to this one before. It smelled like the one he knew back in San Francisco! Even some of the decorations above the butcher station—streamers and a few oddly made piñatas—were the same. He ran his hands up and down his arms, trying to keep himself warm as Abuela waited for some pork.

Which was when he spotted Carmen at the end of one of the aisles.

He wasn't quite sure it was her, until she made eye contact with him. Yep, it *was* Carmen. Héctor waved at her and was about to call out her name when she quickly walked off.

What? he thought. *Where is she going?*

Héctor peered down another aisle, but she wasn't there. The bells over the front door rang, and he saw someone—*was* that Carmen?—quickly walking away from the carnicería.

"Héctor?"

He turned back to Abuela, and she must have seen the confusion on his face. "¿Qué te molesta, nieto?" she asked.

What bothered him? Well . . . was Carmen *avoiding* him? What could possibly explain that?

The realization was like a car crash, hitting him all at once. He'd forgotten because so many other things had happened since then.

She had witnessed his confrontation with Mike.

"Héctor?"

What if Carmen didn't want to be seen around him anymore? Mike had turned on her in the past. What if she didn't want to be associated with Héctor now that Mike was focusing on him? He didn't know how to communicate that to his abuela. He also didn't want her to worry too much, so he settled on something easier. "Abuela, what if I can't make friends here?"

Her eyebrow rose. "Why do you ask that, Héctor?"

He had a million answers. *Because I'm not like these people. Because I don't fit in. Because I think I'm the only person like me here. Because Mike. Because—*

"It's just so different here," he said, which wasn't exactly a lie. That *was* why Mike had zeroed in on him. But it was also a tiny part of the whole truth.

She pulled him closer. "Ay, nieto, I don't blame you feeling that way."

"Really?"

The butcher came back and plopped down a huge pork shoulder. "Yes, really," Abuela said, then thanked the man before putting the meat in her cart. "I've lived here ever since I came to this country. And it was hard being here after growing up in México."

He started to say something, but she ruffled his hair. "I know, I know. San Francisco is not the same as México. But what I mean is that this was a very different place for me. The language. The clothing. The food. Ay, nieto, sometimes I went a whole day without eating because I couldn't stand the tortillas they use up here."

Héctor laughed at that but fell back into silence as they got in line at the checkout. There was more he wanted to ask about. He kept thinking of how Carmen darted off. Why would she avoid him *outside* of school?

He had just wanted to say hello. What if Héctor went to school on Monday, and *all* of the Misfits refused to be near him?

Shame rippled through him. This was supposed to be a magical weekend, the start of his tamale enterprise, and here he was, worrying about Mike and the magical closet and the Misfits.

He glanced up at Abuela just before it was their turn to put their items on the moving belt.

Eyebrows creased. Lips pursed.

What wasn't Abuela saying?

He helped her take the items out of the cart, and she suddenly put her hand on top of his when he grabbed a bag of masa.

"Tiempo, Héctor," she said. "It will just take time. I think you will find what you need."

In the car ride home, only one thought ran through his mind:

Exactly how much time would this take?

Héctor put all his thoughts aside once he was sitting at Abuela's dining room table. It was time to *focus*.

There was a giant bowl of masa in front of her, and a smaller one sat in front of Héctor. Empty corn husks— las hojas de elote—were stacked next to that, and then the filling. The savory pork wasn't hot anymore, and he watched his abuela scoop out some of the shredded, seasoned meat with one hand.

It was time for him to finally learn how to make Abuela's tamales.

"I'm ready, Abuela," he told her. "Time to fulfill my destiny."

"You want to make sure that there aren't any spaces in the masa," she explained, "so that when the tamale is rolled up tightly, it covers the whole thing."

She used a wooden spoon to flatten masa across the husk, and the movement was so *smooth*. A few flicks of her wrist and it perfectly covered la hoja.

"After that, we add the pork," she said, and she reached into the bowl and grabbed some of the meat with her fingers, then plopped it on top of the masa. She spread it out a bit. "Then comes the rolling! My favorite part."

It was like watching a magician. One second, la hoja was flat on the wooden board, and then, three quick movements, and she was folding the excess husk up and tucking it under the tamale. Into the empty pot it went.

Héctor watched her make a few more, his heart racing. It looked *effortless*. He bet she could assemble a perfect tamale with her eyes closed.

His nerves gnawed at his stomach. What if he *wasn't* good at this? What if he let down his abuela? His family? His whole PEOPLE?

You gotta do this yourself, he thought.

Héctor grabbed an empty husk from the pile in front of him, then scooped some masa with a wooden spoon. His hand shook as he spread it over la hoja. It didn't seem to cover it all that well. He looked up at his abuela.

"Un poco más," she said, then pointed at a spot he'd missed.

"Ugh," he groaned.

"It's okay, papito," Abuela said. "I don't always get it right either. It takes practice."

He used too little puerco the first time, but she gently corrected him. He tried rolling it up all neat and tight like she did, but he couldn't manage that well either. His first tamale? Kind of a huge mistake.

Yet Abuela was still smiling at him. "Not bad," she said. "For a first-timer. And it'll still taste good in the end anyway!"

Héctor winced. "But who is gonna eat a tamale that looks like it was run over by a truck?"

"Héctor, it wasn't that bad. I promise."

He scowled at the lumpy, uneven tamale in the big pot.

"Nieto, why do you make that face?"

Héctor looked up. Abuela held a husk covered in masa in her hand, one of her eyebrows raised.

"It's nothing," he said, grabbing for some more masa.

It wasn't even the tamale making that was frustrating him. Well, it *was* that, since he had talked a big game to Papi, and this had turned out to be a lot harder than he had assumed it would be. But he still couldn't get the image of Carmen fleeing the carnicería out of his head.

"I just want to make them right," he finally said.

Then he smiled.

But it wasn't that good of a smile, either.

He tried focusing on making more tamales, but before long, he could tell Abuela was staring at him. He glanced over at her, and sure enough, she had *that* look on her face again.

Eyebrow up.

Lips pursed.

"You know you can tell me anything, Héctor," she said. She wasn't assembling tamales anymore.

"Yo sé eso," he answered.

Then her hand was on his, stopping him from making one more tamale.

"*Anything,*" she said.

He sighed and put the husk down. Her words rang in his head: time. That's what he needed. But what had Abuela actually *done*? Did she just wait around?

"How did you figure out where you belonged, Abuela?"

She was silent for a moment. She placed a finished

tamale in the pot, then fixed Héctor with her gaze.

"I had to take some risks," she said. "In order to make friends. And it was very, very uncomfortable sometimes. But you also don't know who might be able to be your friend unless you try."

He thought of the Table of Misfits. He *had* made some progress in the last couple weeks, but then things had gotten super awkward again because of Mike. Maybe Carmen had only run off because she didn't want to talk about that.

Or maybe Héctor needed to stop hoping friendships would just *happen*.

Abuela Sonia smiled again. She opened her mouth as if to say more. But then she waved it away. "Vámonos," she said. "We got so many more of these to make."

Hours later, Héctor did not feel that he had improved his tamale-making technique. "These all look sick," he said, defeated. "Seriously, can we call 911 on my tamales? They need a doctor."

"Don't be so critical of yourself, nieto," said Abuela. "I know you can't see your progress, but you're getting better. And you'll keep getting better if you practice."

He sighed dramatically. "I just thought maybe I'd be so good at this that it could be my *thing* here in Orange-vale."

"Maybe you need a hobby," she suggested, fixing one

of Héctor's sad tamales. "We can revisit your tamale empire as you get better!"

"Yeah, you're probably right," he said. "But what kind of hobby could I start?"

She stood up and squeezed his shoulder. "That's for you to decide, nieto. You've got to do these things for yourself."

Right, he told himself. *Do it alone. Don't rely on other people.* That was exactly what he'd thought! And now he was much more certain about it. Do it yourself.

It seemed like solid advice. Yet why did it all feel so difficult?

CHAPTER FOURTEEN

Mami had the morning off from teaching, so she drove him to school on Monday. It wasn't a long drive, but he liked to pump himself up with some good music in the morning. However, halfway to school, she turned down his playlist.

"¿Qué pasó, Mami? What you do that for? I was just getting in the groove!"

She smiled. "I have some questions."

"Oh no," he said, grinning. "I didn't do anything. It was Papi."

She laughed at him. "No, not like that, mijo. I just want to check in with you."

He narrowed his eyes at her. "Check in?"

"I know these past two weekends have been super busy for me," she explained. "It's not always going to be like this. I promise it'll settle down."

"It's okay," he said. "We're all adjusting, right?"

"We are. And I'm proud of what you're doing."

He narrowed his eyes again. "You're trying to trick

me into doing something, aren't you? You didn't have questions to ask me at all!"

Mami rolled her eyes, but there was still a smile on her face. "Héctor, I am not tricking you into anything."

"I'm onto you," he said.

"Okay, then: worst teacher," she said. "Go."

"Worst?" He laughed. "Mami, that is *definitely* a trap. All my teachers try to be good."

"I raised you well, mijo," she said, nodding and stopping at a red light. She pulled her long black hair back and used a band to secure it into a ponytail.

"But if I had to pick . . . ," he began.

She shot him a glare.

"They're all fine!"

"That's my boy," she said.

He giggled. "I really like my art teacher, Mrs. Caroline. She's weird."

"And you like weird. 'Cause you *are* weird."

"Don't forget it, Mami," he said.

"So why haven't you worn that shiny camisa you had me get you this summer?"

And just like that, his reality slammed back down on him. Was he *that* obvious? Tim and Sophia had picked up on his change, and now, his mami had noticed.

He couldn't let her suspect the truth. "Well, I don't

think the kids at Orangevale Middle School are ready for it," he said. "It's just not the right time for its debut."

As she rolled through the intersection, he caught her casting a quick glance his way. "I've never heard you turn down the chance to wear something over-the-top. What gives?"

Ah, Mami was more direct than Papi and Abuela.

"It's just different here," he said, then turned his face away to hide his grimace. How many times had he used this same excuse? He recovered quickly. "Some of the kids here aren't used to high fashion, so I'm taking it easy."

"Are they picking on you, Héctor?"

Panic ripped through him. *She's a teacher, Héctor!* he thought, scolding himself. *Of course she is gonna pick up on something like that!*

"No, no, not really," he said, but it came out too fast, too certain. "Not anything that bad. I promise."

"Because I'll walk into the principal's office right now and—"

"Mami, *no*," he said forcefully. "Don't do that! I will *definitely* get bullied if you do that."

She took a deep breath. "Right, right. Get yourself together, Lilliam."

"Mami, it *really* isn't that bad," he said, and his heart sank a bit. Maybe that wasn't a lie. Maybe it was wishful thinking. "I'm just trying to do my best."

She reached over and grabbed his hand. "That's all we ask of you, me and your papi. You know that, right?"

Héctor squeezed back. "I know."

It's not the right time, he thought. He wondered, though, if she would get it. Maybe she *was* the best person to be honest with.

Nah. He *would* tell someone, though.

Eventually.

After he figured it all out on his own.

That morning, Héctor did not have to wait for Mike to reveal himself. He and his Minions were standing next to the concrete steps that rose up into Orangevale Middle School. Héctor hadn't even noticed them because he'd been so distracted by almost spilling the beans to his mami. Frank—who had his greasy hair shaved into a really, *really* bad fade—waved at Héctor.

Just ignore them, he thought. *There's no winning otherwise.* He had tried to be friendly with them; he had faked confidence; he'd told Ms. Heath the truth. Had *any* of it worked? No. *Never.* So what option was left?

He ascended the steps.

Heard the footfalls behind him.

Knew they were following.

So he ran. Because what else could he do? It was what he knew.

He heard Mike call out to him from the bottom of the stairs: "Hey, Flower Boy! Where you going?"

Héctor rather liked flowers and floral prints, so did that *really* hurt him? No. So ignore, ignore, ignore . . . and run. He flung open the front doors. Ms. Heath was thankfully not at her post just inside the school, which was a small victory for Héctor.

He paused for a moment. Was the closet nearby today? Would it show up where he needed it? Where was he supposed to go? Not wanting to waste time, he fled to the left.

In those few seconds of hesitation, though, Héctor's hope for escape was destroyed. Ms. Heath came around the nearest corner, and her voice boomed down the hallway, the echo of it crashing into Héctor's ears.

"NO RUNNING IN THE HALLS!"

Héctor froze. *No!* Where was the closet? Had he gone the wrong way? In less than ten seconds, Ms. Heath would be at his side, and there was no way he could avoid getting in trouble this time.

"Mr. Muñoz, not another step!"

Should he run? Would that only make things *worse*?

He grimaced as Ms. Heath strolled up to him, this time wearing her all-red tracksuit. He glanced back, and sure enough, Mike and the Minions had slowed and were now creeping up to watch this confrontation.

Héctor wished that he was anywhere else.

Ms. Heath sighed, exasperated. "Why can't you just follow the rules, Mr. Muñoz?"

"I'm trying," he said, but he knew he sounded defeated. Pathetic.

"Well, I saw you running," she continued. "And you weren't trying *not* to."

"But—"

"No, I don't want to hear it."

"They started it!"

He bellowed the words at her, much louder than he intended to.

"It doesn't matter who started what," she said, her voice soft. "What matters is what I *see*. And I saw *you* breaking the rules again."

Héctor could sense his heart sinking down lower into his body. Héctor had been kind. He'd been *himself*. Wasn't that what all those goofy after-school specials told you to do? Be yourself and tell adults when something bad happens to you?

These boys had targeted him. They made him feel like there was a part of him that was *wrong*. But here he was, doing what he was supposed to, and Ms. Heath wouldn't listen to him. The only thing that mattered was her stupid rules, and even then, she obviously didn't care when *other* people broke them.

Héctor burned with the unfairness of it all.

His heart flopped when he saw the entire Table of Misfits—Pat included—huddled behind Ms. Heath.

"I am afraid I'm going to have to put this incident on your permanent record," said Ms. Heath.

Some of the kids gasped. Héctor merely frowned. *Is that even a real thing?* he wondered. But he didn't feel like challenging Ms. Heath on the spot. There was nothing he could do to change her mind, was there? This would repeat, over and over.

So he gave up.

"I'm sorry, Ms. Heath," he said, his head drooping. He had to sell the performance to get her to believe it. "I'm not doing my best. I promise . . . this is the last time." He looked up at her. "You won't have to tell me again."

There was a moment there, so terribly brief, where Héctor saw pity on her face. Did she believe him? Maybe. She probably thought he was a troubled kid who didn't know how to follow the rules. It was like she was making up a story about him in her head, and he couldn't do anything to change it.

Ms. Heath didn't say anything more. She nodded and walked away, and soon, she was chirping at another student for having their shoes untied.

The crowd departed, and Mike slammed his shoulder into Héctor's as he passed, nearly knocking his backpack onto the ground. Héctor wondered if the Table of Misfits were going to say anything to him, but they were already gone.

Was his worst fear coming true? Was he going to be abandoned by everyone here at Orangevale Middle School?

Creak!

To Héctor's left, a door sat ajar. Was he imagining that he'd heard it open? He grabbed the edge of the wood, ran his fingers up and down the smooth surface, then looked at the frosted glass.

JANITOR.

The door?

It *absolutely* had not been there five minutes ago. He would have seen it! Yet here it was. He peeked inside and saw the pitcher of horchata on the table next to a bowl of cereal. It was waiting for him.

It was tempting. And he hadn't been late last week when he'd taken the nap or had breakfast. But the uncertainty was a little terrifying. How was it possible that this room defied the passage of time?

Héctor's stomach growled.

I could use a glass of horchata, he thought.

But if he did end up late, Ms. Heath would definitely give him detention.

Héctor pulled open the door wider and slipped inside

quickly, ignoring the dread that begged him to go to class. But relief washed over him immediately when he walked in. It was exactly as it had been that last time. He turned and closed the door, then rested his head against it, taking in one breath after another, trying to slow down his racing heart. His backpack slipped off his shoulder and came to rest on the floor.

He heard footsteps in the hallway. They passed.

No one knew he was here. He could have a moment of peace. And somehow, this room seemed to know exactly what would calm him down.

Crash!

A shattering sound rang out behind him, and Héctor's soul nearly leaped out of his body. He spun around.

His mouth dropped open.

NO!

There was a girl there—her skin dark, her hair black, separated down the middle and tied off in two puffs, her face twisted up in shock and horror—sitting on the couch.

His couch.

Eating *his* Cocoa Puffs.

No.

How?

How had someone else found *his* room?

CHAPTER FIFTEEN

Héctor screamed.

She screamed.

He backed up until he hit the door behind him.

She backed up until her shoulders smacked against the wall behind her.

"Who are you?" Héctor shouted.

"Who are *you*?" she shot back.

"How did you get in here?"

She came toward him. "No, how did *you* get in here?"

"Through the *door*?" He gestured at it behind him.

"You just walked through that door?"

"It *is* how doors work," he said, laying on the sarcasm.

"But how did you *find* the door?" she demanded. "You can't just *find* it."

"What are you talking about?" Héctor was out of breath, and his hands were in his hair. "I just . . . walked through it?"

She sneered at him. "Clearly! But I've never even seen you at my school." Her dark-brown eyes went wide. "Were you *following* me?"

"What?! Ew, *no.* I would never."

"Well . . . that's the only way you could have found this place."

This made no sense. Why was she talking about the janitor's closet like she knew what it was?

"How do I know you haven't been following *me?*" Héctor finally said, once he was able to make his mouth work again. "Maybe that's how *you* found this place. You followed me, you watched me go in here, and you just . . . beat me to it today."

She was already shaking her head. "Nah. Not possible, bruh."

"And why not?" He took another step toward her.

She took one toward him. "Because only *I* know about this place."

He took a step closer. "Well, that's clearly impossible, because here I am."

Another step closer. "I was here first."

"But were you?" Héctor asked. "When was the first time you went inside the janitor's closet?"

Her face crinkled up at that. "Inside the *what?*"

"The janitor's closet," he said again. Now, they were maybe a foot from one another. She was taller than him by a few inches. Her hair was gorgeous, and he loved the way that she matched her red Jordans with the two red barrettes that held her puffs in place. *She's got style*, he thought.

"It's not a *closet*," she insisted, crossing her arms. "It's a bathroom."

He threw his hands up in the air. "No, it's not! The door *literally* says JANITOR on it! In all caps!"

"It's the teachers' bathroom right next to the drama room!" Now her own hands were up in the air in frustration.

He froze.

Took a few steps away from her.

"Next to the *what*?"

She frowned at Héctor. "The . . . the drama room?" Her voice was finally uncertain. "You know, where the *drama* club meets?"

Bumps rose on his skin.

No. No, he hadn't heard that.

"Pinch me," he muttered.

"What?" She grimaced. "Why would I do that?"

"Something is wrong," Héctor said, and his head spun. His center of balance seemed to disappear, and he pitched toward the couch on his right. He caught himself on the back of it, then lowered himself into a seat.

She came around to stand in front of him. "Yeah, just like I said! You're in *my* room."

"No, that's not what I meant," he said, shaking his head. "What you said is impossible."

"There you go using that word again," she said, her hands on her hips.

Héctor tried not to scream. "Because *we don't have a drama club*."

He watched confusion spread over her face.

"Yes . . . yes, we do," she said, her voice so terribly quiet.

It was happening to her, too, the same thing that was going on in *his* head.

"What's your name?" he asked. "Mine is Héctor."

She sat down next to him. "Juliana," she said, her brow still furrowed in confusion.

"I have to ask you something," he said.

"I know," said Juliana.

"What school do you go to?"

She turned to him, her eyes wide. "Swifton Middle School."

Héctor pointed at himself. "Orangevale Middle School."

Juliana swallowed and turned away. "I don't know where that is."

"California," he said. "Just outside Sacramento."

"I've never even heard of Sacramento," she admitted. "Wait! Isn't that the capital?"

He nodded. "Yeah. I'm kinda close to that." He paused, his heart flopping in his chest. "And you?"

"I'm in Charleston."

His mouth dropped open for what felt like the hundredth time that morning. "In *South Carolina*?"

"At least you know what state it's in," she grumbled. "One of my cousins swears I'm in Georgia."

"This is not happening," Héctor announced.

Then he stood up.

"Nah, this is *not* real."

He stormed over to the door of the room.

Flung it open.

And looked upon the hallways of Orangevale Middle School.

"See?" He gestured out of the room. "That's my school. Not . . . whatever you said." Then it hit him, so completely he could not believe he had not considered it before. "Is this a prank? Did Mike put you up to this?"

Juliana scoffed at him, then rose from the couch to join him in the doorway. "I have no idea who you're referring to," she said. "But you're wrong."

She closed the door.

She opened it.

Héctor had not expected the day to get weirder, but here he was.

Staring into the halls of *a different school*.

The walls at Juliana's school were shiny and gray, and rows and rows of lockers spilled out in either direction. Students rushed by to make it to their next classroom, talking to one another, and apparently completely oblivious to the presence of Héctor and Juliana.

This was . . . a hologram. Something out of a science fiction book. It couldn't be real. He fully expected that if he left the room now, this would all be revealed to be a computer simulation. That would make more sense to him than . . . than *this*.

But he watched Juliana enter the hallway and then do a little spin with her arms out. "Welcome to Swifton Middle School," she announced. "It's a lovely fall morning here. Class is about to start."

And then Héctor finally stepped out, his gaze pulled up by the skylights in the ceiling. There was so much more natural light here. He'd gotten used to the lifeless fluorescent bulbs that lined the hallways of Orangevale Middle School.

"How am I here?" Héctor said. "I'm in another *state*."

Juliana bounded back into the room, and he followed. She shut the door, and the two of them just stared at one another.

"So," he said.

"So," she said.

"When *did* you find the room?" Héctor asked.

It seemed like the most sensible thing to ask. But for a few seconds, Juliana didn't say anything, like she was struggling to remember how to speak again.

"Maybe a couple weeks ago," she finally said. "I almost got in a fight. Found this place just after it."

"What kinda fight? With who?"

This time, she didn't answer his questions. "I needed a place to calm down. Sometimes . . ." She paused, and it looked like she was trying to find the precise words. "Sometimes, I get so angry I feel like I'm going to explode."

"And so you found *this*." Héctor waved around him. "This place."

She nodded at first, then shook her head. "Actually, *no*. It's never looked like this until today."

"What?"

Juliana returned to the couch. "It was . . . different. Really dark. Only a few lights. And there was this *huge* beanbag in the middle of the room, and it was like . . . three times the size of my whole body!"

She seemed so excited when she spoke about it. But then she looked at Héctor. "Wait, how did *you* find the room?"

He took a deep breath. Could he tell Juliana the truth? Could he trust her? This was not something he'd had to think about a whole lot when he lived in the Mission, but now? Héctor recalled how quickly Mike had turned on him when he had said he was gay.

Juliana seemed nice. She also went to a school thousands of miles away from him. What could it hurt to tell her at least a little of the truth? She wasn't going to affect his life.

"I was having trouble with some kids at my school," he said. "And I needed a place to hide."

"And this is what your room looked like?" Juliana smiled. "Not bad. This is pretty comfy."

Héctor sat down next to her. "I know. And it has all my favorite games and my favorite food in the fridge and . . . well, it's nice. I keep wanting to spend more time in here."

Time.

Oh *no*.

He shot up from the couch. "Juliana, I'm sorry, but I'm going to be late if I don't leave right now."

"I don't know if this is the case for you," she said, "but I've actually *never* been late when I spent time here."

"Wow," he said, his eyes wide. "I thought I imagined that. I took a nap and had breakfast here once. Somehow, time *reversed* so I wouldn't be late."

"No way!" she said. "How is that even *possible*?"

"It's not! It's imposs—"

He didn't finish saying the word; a grin spread over Juliana's face.

"You were gonna say it. That word. *Again*."

"I *was*. But . . . how do we explain this?"

"Maybe we don't," she said. "I don't really care to. I'm just glad it's here."

He hadn't thought about it that way. That was when the idea popped into his mind.

"Juliana!"

She looked up at him from the couch. "What?"

"Can we try this again?"

"Try *what* again?"

Héctor gestured to the room around them. "This. This room. Whatever it is. We should try to be in it at the same time again."

She furrowed her brow. "I don't know. . . ."

"It's too weird *not* to try, right?"

Maybe he was coming on too strong. Maybe he was too excited. Juliana studied his face, and she didn't seem all that convinced.

"Just . . ." He sighed. "I don't know what this is. And if I come back, and you're not here, then I'll never bother you again. It's worth a shot, right?"

She shrugged. "Okay."

He tried not to let his excitement pour out of him.

"How does two forty-five p.m. sound?"

"Sure, I guess." She paused. "If this is real, then wouldn't we be in different time zones?"

It was a good point.

"Maybe," Héctor said. "But when we just stepped out into your school, you said class was about to start, right?"

She tilted her head to the side. "Yeah. It is."

"Same with my school!"

Juliana's mouth dropped open. "So . . . maybe this place will let us be here at the same time. Is that what you mean?"

"I think so. It can make us not be late for things, right?"

She nodded. "Okay. That makes a weird kind of sense." She smiled and it lit up her whole face. "I'm down. Let's do this. Two forty-five p.m., I'll be here."

"Perfect," he said. "I guess I'll see you then?"

"I guess so."

She raised a hand up awkwardly. "See ya."

He waved back at Juliana, then turned and opened the door. There were the halls of Orangevale Middle School.

He pulled the door shut behind him, but then, just to satisfy his curiosity, he opened it again.

Same old janitor's closet. He glanced up—there was His Royal Highness, King Ferdinand. Héctor sent up a silent greeting, then closed the door once more.

He settled into his seat seconds later, and the bell for homeroom rang right after that. The timing was *exact*.

Héctor's theory was correct! And now, he couldn't wait to see if he would be right again.

CHAPTER SIXTEEN

Héctor had never been so distracted in his entire life.

He just couldn't concentrate. At *all*. Every time a teacher's voice droned on, his mind drifted. He thought of the Room, which he now capitalized in his head because it felt right. He thought of Juliana. He thought of how easily the Room was able to change. To move. To camouflage itself. To adapt. Why couldn't *he* change himself like the Room could? That would make things so much easier.

This couldn't be real.

But it *was*.

When lunch rolled around, even the sad-looking chicken sandwich, discolored broccoli, and plastic-wrapped cookie did not faze Héctor. He joined the Misfits, his lunch tray clattering on their table. "Do they *ever* serve real food here?"

Carmen locked eyes with him. He almost said something, but she looked away quickly.

"Oh, never," said Jackson, who had not seemed to notice the interaction. "You can count on that."

"You doing okay?" asked Aishah.

He felt the eyes of all the Misfits on him at once. He shrugged. "It's whatever," he said. "I just have to adjust to Mike and his Minions picking on me every day."

"Yeah, we saw," said Taylor. "I'm sorry, man. He really is the worst."

"We've all been through it at one time or another," said Aishah. She took a bite of her sandwich and then grimaced. "Nasty," she said through the food.

"The food here *always* is," said Jackson. "Soggy and flavorless. Like Mike."

Aishah put a hand over her mouth. "Stop!" she said, holding back laughter. "You're gonna make me choke."

Héctor glanced back at Carmen, who continued to examine her food. He shook his head.

"What is it, man?" said Jackson.

Héctor's day had already been completely unbelievable, and so it gave him a well of courage. A question he had wanted to ask the week before bubbled up to the surface:

"What did you all do to get him to leave you alone?" Héctor asked.

No one said anything at first, and Héctor thought he'd ruined the moment. But then Jackson shrugged. "To be honest?" he said. "Nothing. He just moved on from me to Aishah."

"Which is how we became friends," she said. "Jackson saw it happening and he helped me out when he could."

They exchanged fist bumps.

"So he just . . . stopped one day?" Héctor asked.

Aishah nodded. "Yeah. I mean, it helped that I switched into Mrs. Caroline's art class. I used to be in Shop with Mike, but after I swapped, I just wasn't around him anymore. So, less opportunity for him to zero in on me."

"But then he moved on from Aishah to me," said Taylor. "And it was bad, bro. I think he followed me for like half a year."

"Half a *year?*" Héctor's mouth fell open. "That's so long!"

He looked to Carmen, who now struggled to keep his gaze. She fidgeted on the bench. "And then it was me," she said. Then she sighed. "Up until last month."

Oh. So that meant . . .

"He went from you to me," said Héctor.

She winced. "And I'm still afraid," she said. "That he's gonna come back."

That's why she avoided you on Saturday, he thought. *She doesn't want to risk it.*

"Well, aren't you all putting yourself on the spot by letting me sit here?" Héctor asked.

"He doesn't ever seem to go back to someone," said

Jackson. "Like, once he's bored with picking on you, he always moves on to someone else."

Then why did Carmen avoid me the other day? Héctor wondered.

Aishah sighed. "It's not like we can sit anywhere else."

"Yeah, and we don't care," said Jackson. "He can't make things worse than they already are."

Héctor smiled at that. He was glad that these people weren't going to ditch him. Maybe they *could* become his friends.

But he also hoped Jackson was right. Because he *really* didn't want things to get worse.

CHAPTER SEVENTEEN

It figured that on this of all days, Mr. Holiday, the gym teacher, had to keep everyone past class. "Extra laps are good for your health!" he yelled, holding up his stopwatch. "Two more before we're done!"

Héctor took the quickest shower of his life in the locker room. His black hair was still wet as he made his way to the other side of the building.

Because of this disastrous delay, Héctor only had a few minutes to make this work before his papi arrived to pick him up. Thankfully, Papi had a tendency to be late. He worked at home, and it made him forget how the concept of time worked most days.

So Héctor sped through the hallways, but immediately crashed into his own overwhelming sense of doubt. He froze as other kids poured around him, like he was a stone in a river. Could he *summon* the Room? How was he supposed to find it? There wasn't any pattern to when or where it showed up. It appeared in random hallways almost every time.

But he needed the proof. He wasn't sure *why* that

was the case, but the idea that he had just imagined all of this felt devastating. No, Juliana had to be real. The Room had to be real.

It just *had* to be.

Héctor turned the corner, his breath caught in his throat. *Please*, he thought. *It has to be there. I need this.*

The hallway was lined with doors on either side, all of them the same.

Except *one*.

He rushed forward, relief flooding his body, and something like a spark flew up his arm when he touched the handle to the door that read JANITOR.

I am more excited to see a door than most people, Héctor thought. Maybe it was weird, but these past couple weeks had been strange enough as it was.

He swung the door open.

Juliana stood up from the couch.

And Héctor knew then that this was real.

It was *real*.

"Yo," said Juliana. "Sorry, I thought I was late."

"No, *I* am the late one," he said, huffing as he closed the door behind him. He made for the fridge and was immensely pleased to see there was a full pitcher of horchata. "Excuse me," he said. "My parents would literally murder me if they saw me do this, but I'm so thirsty."

He removed the lid and drank straight from the

pitcher. He regretted absolutely nothing, not even when he drained half the horchata in one go and felt bloated.

"Wow," she said. "That was . . . impressive. But also kinda gross?"

He bowed. "Welcome to my life."

"I mean, who just chugs *milk* like that? Not my lactose-intolerant self."

His eyes went wide. "Oh, Juliana, I am going to change your life!" The idea came to him, and he just went with it. He put the pitcher back in the fridge and closed it. Upon opening it, he found a brand-new pitcher, completely full.

"Perfect!" Héctor exclaimed. He looked to the table behind him.

There was now an empty glass.

Exactly what he needed.

He poured only a quarter cup of horchata and handed it to Juliana. "This is mi abuela's recipe," he explained. "Don't ask me how it shows up here."

Juliana hesitated as she took the glass. "So . . . it's *not* milk? Then what is it?"

"Definitely not. Some people make it with milk, but Abuela only uses five ingredients: arroz, water, cinnamon, sugar, and vanilla."

She tentatively took a sip. He watched her roll the flavor around her tongue, and then she tipped her head to the side. "Whoa," she said. "That's *good* good."

Juliana downed the rest, then held out the glass. "Okay, I'm sold. This is *incredible.*"

As he poured her another glass of the liquid of the gods, a warmth spread in his chest. Juliana drank most of it down, and she looked to him, a huge smile on her face. *I guess that's all it takes to make people happy to see me*, he thought, then smiled himself. He was being dramatic, he knew that, but it still felt nice that she was pleased.

So he quietly thanked his abuela for the horchata.

Juliana was the first to start talking. She asked about Orangevale: What the weather was like. How long he and his family had lived there. What his life was like back in San Francisco. He asked about living in Charleston, and she told him that one of her favorite things about the city was the food. "Even our cafeteria meals are bomb," she said. "Every. Day."

"Can't say the same of my school," he said. "I don't even think what we eat qualifies as 'food.'"

She grimaced. "That sounds awful."

"That word isn't strong enough to describe it."

Juliana's phone buzzed and she took it out. "Guess we still get service in here," she said. After a moment, she sighed. "It's my big sister. She's here to pick me up."

Then she tucked her phone away in her jeans. "Do you

want to do this again, Héctor? Like . . . maybe tomorrow morning?"

He smiled at her. "Yeah, I would like that," he said.

"Okay, then I gotta go." She grabbed her backpack from the couch. When she opened the door, it was still a shock. The hallways of Swifton Middle stood beyond the doorway. *That's never going to get old*, he thought.

This time, when Juliana turned to look at him from the doorway, she waved at him.

Then she was gone.

He approached the door slowly, then ran his hands over the wood. It felt solid under his fingers. When he opened it, Orangevale Middle School beckoned to him.

Just like that. Without a sound, without any effort, this Room had taken him back home.

"I don't understand you," he said aloud, shaking his head. "But . . . you're real."

Héctor's mind was in a whirl as he ran to get picked up.

CHAPTER EIGHTEEN

This was not how Héctor thought he would be spending his Saturday.

His week had passed in a blur, and it seemed that every waking moment, all Héctor could think about was the Room. He had no theories about how it worked or where it came from. It was just . . . there.

Unfortunately, Héctor found that it was hard to focus on literally anything else. Schoolwork was a challenge, and at home, his head was in the clouds. His abuela noticed it on Wednesday evening at dinner, which meant she got to deploy her favorite Spanish saying:

"Héctor," she said, and she was already grinning. "Estás comiendo moscas."

Ugh. It literally meant "eating flies" in English, but sometimes things didn't translate directly. It was her way of saying that his mind was wandering.

It wasn't like she was wrong, though.

When he had gotten home from school on Friday, his mami was standing in the driveway. "Tengo una sorpresa para ti," she said, and he could tell she was trying her hardest not to be *too* excited.

He loved his mother's surprises. Usually it was a trip to the thrift store, or some piece of clothing that she knew he would love. Once, it was his favorite pan from the panadería. She always gave it a lot of thought, so this was finally enough to pull Héctor back to the present.

"I know you didn't have a great time walking around the neighborhood," she said, coming up to him as he got out of Papi's car. She grabbed his hand and led him toward the front door. "So I thought maybe it wasn't the exploring, but the *method* of exploration that needed to change."

"Okaaaaaayyyy," he said, hesitant. "I don't know what that means." His eyes went wide. "Did you get me my own helicopter?"

"Close," she said, and then she let loose a peal of laughter. "Look!"

She pointed to the stoop, where a purple bicycle sat upright on its kickstand.

"No. WAY!" Héctor screamed.

He dashed over to it, then ran his hands over the steel frame. Héctor's last bike had been stolen the previous summer, and his parents had promised to get him a new one. But summer had turned to fall, which was when Mami got her busiest, and it just never happened.

Until now. He loved how the paint job sparkled in the sunlight. Draped over one of the handlebars was a sleek black helmet. When he picked it up, Mami helped him put it on his head and secure it tightly.

"I got a plain helmet so you can dazzle it up to your liking," she explained. "And as long as you stick to this neighborhood, your papi and I agreed you can do unsupervised rides."

After the day he'd had, Héctor wasn't sure he could have felt any more happiness, but he bowled into Mami to give her a hug. Papi came over to join them. "I'm glad you like it," he said. "And that you're willing to keep trying here."

This is it, he thought. *This is what I was missing.* And they had given him freedom to explore the neighborhood *by himself.* Alone! He was basically all grown up now, and he went to bed Friday night eager to get on the road the next morning.

Héctor's parents basically had to force him to eat breakfast. He was fitting his new helmet onto his head while Papi stood at the front door. "Stay within the neighborhood," he said. "Remember, once you get to the far end of Pecan Park, don't go any farther."

"Deal," said Héctor.

"Be safe, papito," said Mami. She stood in the kitchen, beaming. "I'm glad you're so excited."

"Thank you," he said, breathless. "This is the best gift *ever.*"

Moments later, as he pedaled down the driveway, he let out a whoop of joy. The cool morning air glided over his skin as he headed down the street, sticking as close to the right side as was safe.

His bike was fast and smooth, and it was like he was floating over the asphalt. He pedaled faster as he passed through a clear intersection, then turned right on the next block to head up to Pecan Park. How quickly could he do a lap? Maybe he'd time himself. He picked up the pace, then used his right thumb to flick the tiny bell on the handlebars.

Everything felt perfect.

Pecan Park wasn't very big, and most of it was taken up by a dog run, but Héctor was still excited to race around it. He biked up to the south entrance and was greeted by dogs barking at one another. He pulled out his phone to open up the stopwatch when he thought he heard someone call out his name.

Which was impossible. Still, he looked around the park, but couldn't see anyone who might know him. There were three kids on bikes riding down the path toward him, but they were too far away.

Believing he'd imagined it, he looked back down at his phone.

"Is that *Heck-tor?*"

No.

NO.

Héctor glanced up, quietly seething at his luck.

And looked straight into the face of Mike astride a black mountain bike.

Oh, the Minions were there too, both of them on bikes. Héctor was aware of them in his peripheral vision, but the look of utter, evil *joy* on Mike's face had all his attention.

Great. *Does he live in this neighborhood, too?* he wondered, distraught. *Why does he have to be in every part of my life?*

"Is that your bike, HECK-tor?" said Mike.

He wanted to say: *No, I just stand over random bikes in the street. I am the Bike God! This is my child.*

He did not opt for the *weirdest* possible answer. Instead:

"Yeah, it is."

Mike cackled, and the others joined him. "Who rides a purple bicycle?" he said. "A *girl?*"

"I do."

Mike's laughter stopped abruptly, and he glared at Héctor. "You should have a bike like this," he said, gesturing to the one he sat on.

Héctor wanted to say: *That's a mountain bike. It's not meant for riding on the street. Also, you're riding the wrong size and your seat is too low.*

Instead, what came out of his mouth was:

"No, thank you."

It was certainly one of Héctor's worst comebacks, and he knew it. He wasn't even sure it *counted* as a comeback. Why was he talking to Mike like he was Ms. Heath?

"Where are all your little friends?" Mike said, rolling his bike closer. "They know what a *loser* you are?"

"I don't know," said Héctor, and he could feel himself shrinking, folding in on himself. "They're . . . somewhere. Not here."

Mike laughed while looking to his Minions, but Frank and Carlos weren't joining in. Frank seemed bored, and Carlos had a strange expression on his face, one that made Héctor feel even more uncomfortable.

"Well?" said Mike to Carlos. "Aren't you going to say anything?"

Carlos just shook his head.

"Come on," said Mike. "This is too gay for me."

As he and the Minions pedaled off, Héctor said to himself, "Well, *obviously*."

That was only slightly better than before, but still . . . not great.

Héctor stood over his bike for a while, long after they had turned a corner. By the time he started slowly making his way back to the house, his heart was still racing. He looked over his shoulder constantly: Would Mike be back? Would he find out where Héctor *lived*?

He wanted to push the thought out of his mind. But when he got to his block, he began to pedal faster and faster. He stopped abruptly two doors down from home and scoped out the block in both directions.

No Mike. No Carlos. No Frank.

Héctor wheeled his bike up to the open garage. He let it fall to the side against the wall, and when he looked at the purple frame, it seemed a little bit duller. Why did Mike have to say anything about it? He was ruining *everything* that Héctor had.

He pressed the button to close the garage, and soon, he was shrouded in darkness. The plain door that led into his home was nothing like the wooden door to the janitor's closet, yet he imagined what it would be like if he opened it to the Room. It would have made him feel better, if only for a moment.

Héctor opened it, and there was no Room through the doorway. The hallway that led down to both his and his parents' bedrooms now had some family portraits.

Papi was cooking something savory in the kitchen. Mami hadn't heard him come in; she was poring over some papers at the table, her back to him.

He kicked off his shoes and left them near the door, then made for his bedroom, hoping to bury himself under his cobija and forget his whole morning.

CHAPTER NINETEEN

By the time Héctor arrived at school on Monday morning, he had a new technique in hand: he would *bore* Mike away.

He had to do something. All day Sunday, Héctor kept expecting Mike to show up outside his house. Did he even know where Héctor lived? Probably not, but Mike was slowly creeping into every part of his life, and literally *nothing* had worked before.

Until Héctor had bored Mike at Pecan Park.

Abuela dropped him off near the front steps, where Mike was waiting with his Minions.

He gripped the handle in the car door, and took a deep breath. This would be the first time to test his theory.

And it *had* to work. He didn't have anything else.

Abuela must have seen his hesitation. "¿Estás bien, nieto?"

She rested her hand on his leg. He reached down to put his on top of hers.

Tell her.

The voice was so clear, so certain. But it was immediately swallowed by doubt.

"Yeah, I'm fine," he said, and he smiled ear to ear. "I just spaced out, that's all."

She bought it and wished him a good day. He got out of her car as confidently as he could, imagining he was back on the stage. This was all just a performance, right?

He waved to Abuela, who lingered for a moment, her lips in a straight line. She smiled—a small, reluctant thing—and then she pulled away.

Breathe, Héctor.

He could do this.

Just . . . be as boring as possible.

Mike wasted no time. "What's up, Heck-tor?" he crooned, wagging his head from side to side as Héctor approached. "Why didn't you ride your girly bike to school today?"

Bore him, Héctor told himself.

"Just didn't feel like it," he said.

And he kept walking.

"I bet you wear girl clothes sometimes, too!" Mike shouted, and Frank laughed at that.

"Maybe," said Héctor. "Not today, though."

Mike's face fell.

Because it was working.

"Well . . . I bet you look good in a dress," said Mike, hesitation creeping in his voice.

"Probably," said Héctor, nodding. "See ya around."

He climbed the steps at the front of school, and Mike didn't say anything to that. A burst of hope raced through Héctor. This had worked better than he expected! No one was chasing him; no one was calling him names. It was a success!

Unfortunately, he didn't make it more than ten feet past Mike before the pudding cup hit him square in the back.

He didn't know it was pudding at first. He knew the object was solid, but then something cool and wet splattered over the back of his left arm.

Two students in front of Héctor froze, their jaws on the floor, their eyes wide. A girl from Mr. Holiday's class whispered, "Ewwww," and then covered her mouth.

And Mike cackled loudly.

Héctor ran his fingers over the wet spot on his left arm. Ah. He figured out it was pudding once he looked at it. Not just any old pudding, either!

Tapioca.

Héctor couldn't even remember the last time he'd seen tapioca pudding. Wasn't that something everyone stopped eating in second grade? Perhaps the people of

Orangevale had much different taste. (Bad, bad taste.)

He stood there motionless for a moment as Mike's laughter rose in volume. Héctor had on a black Henley shirt; he'd chosen it last night to wear today because it was simple but still stylish.

Now, it was just a mess.

Like him.

He did his best not to react. He wiped away what he could reach and flicked the goop on the ground. There was a high-pitched giggle next to him, and he stared at Kelly Fordham, the president of the student government, as she turned away from him in disgust. "That's *so* gross," she said to the girl with her, someone Héctor had never met.

The girl laughed too. "*Totally* gross," she agreed.

Mike and the Minions were howling, and there was no way Héctor could bore them if he was now going to be used for target practice.

So much for his new strategy.

He passed through the double doors and ignored the noise behind him: The laughing. The whispering. All the gossip and pity. His face burned, his stomach hurt, and a rage swirled in his chest. He passed Ms. Heath, who said nothing to him, even though there was clearly some sort of white substance on his shirt. She barely registered that he was there. He didn't necessarily *want* her attention, yet it still stung. The evidence was *right there*, and she just . . . didn't see it.

Héctor slyly pulled his phone out to use the camera to see the damage, and there was a text.

Sophia: hey boo, miss you. sorry I been so busy.
   talk soon?

A pang of sadness hit his chest. He missed her—and Tim—so much. But then he thought of replying to her, thought about telling her what had happened, and that sadness became an ugly shame. How could he tell them about his life here?

So Héctor stuffed his phone back in his pocket. He had intended to go to the boys' room, but there, on his right, sat the door. JANITOR.

And for the first time since he'd come to this school, the sight of the janitor's closet brought him dread.

This was not how he wanted to see Juliana again, but there it was: the Room. Beckoning to him. Maybe . . . maybe it *knew*. Somehow, it *knew* what had happened.

He had to clean himself off regardless. And he *did* feel comfortable around Juliana. He wasn't sure why, but he knew that she wouldn't judge him.

So Héctor swallowed his fear and stepped inside the Room.

Juliana rose from the couch, an expectant smile on her face. "There you are!" she said. "There's been a— what happened to you?"

She was *definitely* looking at the pudding on his hands and his clothes. Fantastic.

"It's nothing," he said. "Just dropped some food on myself on the way to school."

Juliana frowned at that, and her colorful skirt twirled around her when she spun and walked to her backpack. She came back with some wipes and began to help Héctor.

"You don't have to do that," he said.

"Please," she said. "Lemme guess: Someone threw this at you?"

His mouth dropped open. "How did you know?"

She pointed a yellow-painted nail at his shoulder. "It's on the back of your shirt, bruh," she said. "How would you spill something back here?" Then she was silent for a second. "And kids used to do that to me."

The words were out of him before he could think twice. "How did you get them to stop?"

"They caught these hands," she said, plain as day. "Never thought twice about picking on me again."

He laughed. "I wish I could do that, but . . . I'm not really a fighter."

"That's fair," she said. "But you have to do something."

Then he heard it, just to his left: a scuffling sound,

like a shoe being scraped against the ground. He looked in that direction.

And *screamed*.

The Room was ENORMOUS.

It stretched off into the distance. There were rows and rows of bookshelves as far as he could see, and perhaps even farther. All of it was shrouded in a dim light, like an old library that wasn't visited very often. It all looked so *theatrical* to him, as if some sort of dark noir play would unfold in the shadows.

But that wasn't really the reason Héctor screamed. Yes, he was *very* dramatic. He knew this.

No, he screamed because *someone else was there*: tall, their skin a light brown, standing at the end of one of the shelves, a book clutched to their chest, short black hair atop their head.

"Who are *you*?" they asked.

CHAPTER TWENTY

"I was about to tell you," said Juliana. "That there's been a complication."

"I'm sorry," said Héctor, "but who are *you*?"

They lowered their book. "Sal," they said. "Sal Ocampo."

"Okay, so we're on a formal-name basis," said Juliana. "Well, I'm Juliana Chin."

"Héctor Muñoz," said Héctor. "How did you—?"

"Did you say Chin?" Sal took a few tentative steps forward. "Adopted?"

"No," said Juliana. "Most people can't tell, but my dad is Chinese, and my mom is Black."

"No way!" Sal beamed. "My dad is Filipino, and my mom is white."

"Whoa, I don't meet too many biracial people who are also Asian," said Juliana.

"Me neither!" Sal said.

And then the two of them just started *gabbing* at one another. Héctor had a hard time following it at first. They yelled about how complicated it was to be mixed race, and then Sal was telling some sort of joke about how everyone thought their family only made "fusion" food, and then Juliana launched into a whole line of questioning about whether Sal's hometown was like Charleston and—

"Um, hello?" interrupted Héctor. "Hi? Can the train come back to the station and pick me up?"

Juliana turned to Héctor and smirked. "Sorry, got a little carried away. Anyway, I've decided to be friends with them already, so hurry up and get on the same page."

Héctor sat down on the couch, which now looked out on the bookshelves. "I'm so confused," he said.

"By the whole 'them' thing?" Sal said, frowning. "It's okay, it's—"

"No, not that!" Héctor put a hand to his heart to add a flair of drama. "I would *never*." Then he nodded at Sal. "So what are your pronouns?"

"Uh . . . yeah," said Sal, and Héctor could see the relief soften their body. They had tensed up so visibly before. "Don't think I'm a guy or a girl at all, so if you could use 'them,' I would be happy."

Héctor raised a thumbs-up in response, and then saw how delighted Juliana was. "You're enjoying this," he said.

"I might be," said Juliana, and then turned to Sal.

"What I think Héctor meant is that he is confused by . . . well, all of *this*." She waved her hands at the Room.

"Exactly," he confirmed. "So . . . what happened?"

Juliana sat next to him. "I think our little Room just got bigger."

"Yeah!" Héctor gestured in front of him. "A whole lot bigger!" He walked over to the bookshelves, ran his hand along the wood, pulled out a book. A *real* book. With *pages*.

"Every time I think this can't get weirder," said Héctor, "it gets *weirder*."

"Sal, tell him what you told me," said Juliana.

They smiled at Héctor when he looked at them. "Well . . . I found this place a week ago. The library at my school got closed down, and that was my favorite place to be. I used to go there as much as I could."

Héctor raised a hand. "Hold on," he said. "Where exactly is *your* school?"

Sal looked at Juliana, who nodded. Then they continued. "Ummm . . . I think I'm pretty far away from you two. Juliana is in Charleston, and you're in . . ."

"Orangevale." When Sal narrowed their eyes at Héctor, he sighed. "Northern California."

Sal paused, and their mouth dropped open.

"I'm at Saguaro Academy. Just outside . . . Phoenix. Arizona."

"Phoenix," said Héctor.

"Uh-huh."

"Arizona."

"Yep."

"You're in *Arizona*."

"I am," said Sal, looking a little self-conscious.

"You're really not joking," said Héctor, shaking his head. "You know, I wish I knew how to, like . . . faint on cue. That would be a great skill to have right now so I could do it."

"Wow, you really *are* dramatic," said Juliana, smiling.

"Wait, you do theater?" Sal asked.

Héctor nodded. "Unfortunately, I can't do it here, since they don't have a drama club."

"Was it shut down like my library?"

"Years ago," said Héctor. "Before I moved here."

"That sucks," said Sal. "Anyway, I found a door I had never seen next to the entrance to the library, which had been locked up. It led to this place." They spun around, waving their hand at it all. "I've just been calling it the Library because . . . well, that's what it looks like."

"I've started calling it 'the Room' in my head," said Héctor.

"Well, I guess it *is* just a room," they said. "So it *never* looked like a library for you two?"

Héctor and Juliana both shook their heads. "It was

like a chill-out room for me," said Juliana. "Whenever I got too angry."

"And it was more like a second home at school for me," said Héctor. "A fridge, a couch, video games . . . at one point, there was a super-comfy bed in here."

"A *bed*?" Juliana scoffed at him. "You never told me about that."

Sal was running their hand over their short-cropped hair. "Wow. This is . . . this is a lot to take in. How can this place just *do* that?"

"Do what?" asked Juliana.

"Change."

When Sal said it, it seemed so simple. That was really what this Room did: it changed. *All* the time. Not just the contents, either! It changed locations. It changed what it looked like on the outside, too.

It had given Héctor a place to hide when he needed to get away from his bullies. It had given Juliana a place to calm down when she needed some peace and quiet. It had given Sal a sanctuary full of books when they needed one.

Needed.

Need.

"You okay, Héctor?"

Héctor sat next to Juliana on the couch, and she

scooted closer to him. His eyes snapped up to her. "Sorry, yeah," he said. "Just thinking about something."

"You went quiet on us," she said.

"Is something wrong?" Sal asked, and they inched closer.

Héctor gestured to the empty space on the couch. "Come sit down," he said. "It's okay. I think I'm finally wrapping my mind around this place."

Sal finally moved close to Héctor and Juliana. They sat down, pulled their legs up to their chest, and got comfortable.

"Lay it on us," said Juliana. "What are you thinking?"

Héctor smiled. "Okay," he said. "What if this Room isn't just *randomly* doing things?"

"What do you mean?" asked Sal. "Do you think someone is controlling it?"

"No," Héctor said. "I think . . . I think *we're* doing it."

Juliana huffed. "I don't know about that," she said. "I'd spend every day here if I could, but sometimes, the Room doesn't even show up!"

"Yeah," said Sal. "If I had the choice, I'd just stay in this library all day and not even go to classes." Their voice lowered. "*There are so many books to read.*"

"Now I kinda wish I'd asked for a library, too," said Juliana. "I got a lot of catching up to do."

"But do you *need* to do all that?"

After he dropped the question, Sal and Juliana went quiet. It was like wheels and gears were turning in their minds, and he watched them put the pieces together.

"I needed a place to calm down," Juliana said slowly.

"And I needed my library back," said Sal, their face lighting up with the epiphany.

Both of them looked to Héctor.

Oh. They wanted him to share, too.

Say something, he thought. *Anything.*

"I moved away from the only home I'd ever known last month," he said. "I'm originally from San Francisco. Orangevale is . . . well, it's certainly not the Mission. And I feel left out most days." He paused, took another breath. "I don't think I belong here."

Juliana reached out and took his left hand. "I'm sorry," she said. "That's gotta suck."

"Yeah," he said, trying so very hard to get past the terrible awkwardness blooming in his stomach. "So I needed . . . I don't know. A place to be alone. To hide. To think about everything."

"So . . . is it bad that we're here?" Sal's face crinkled up. "Should we *leave*?"

Héctor bolted upright. "No!" He shouted the words. "Please, don't leave. This is . . . this is the *longest* conversation I've had with someone who wasn't a teacher since I got to this school."

He didn't speak the thought that ran through his head:

And I need you.

"Well, we're not going anywhere," said Juliana. "Except school. I can't miss school, or my mama will be *real* mad. But . . . I want to be here, too."

"So do I," said Sal, smiling.

Héctor's heart warmed at that, but his stomach twisted up in doubt at the feeling, too. He resisted the urge to shoot the kindness down. "So . . . now what?"

The three of them exchanged looks with one another.

Juliana broke the silence by clearing her throat. "Just a question for y'all," she said. "I have a friend at my school, and she is worried. About a secret she has possibly getting out."

"What kind of secret?" Sal asked.

"Well, that's not important," Juliana said quickly. *Too* quickly, Héctor thought, but he didn't call her on it. "My friend doesn't think there's a way to stop the secret from coming out. Not that it's a bad secret!"

"I'm a little lost," said Sal, scratching their head. "So the secret isn't bad but it's still going to get out?"

"Well, my friend—who is *definitely* not me—is just

worried about what might happen after."

"Are people going to be mad at this friend?" Héctor asked.

"I don't think so," said Juliana, twisting up her face as she thought about it. "I think they'll be supportive of her. It's just scary."

"But once it's over, it won't be so scary, right?" Sal said.

She sighed. "Yeah, I guess you're right. I'll tell her what you said."

Héctor was now certain that Juliana was talking about herself, and he wondered what she was *actually* talking about. Why did it make her so *nervous*? Was it really that bad?

But he didn't press her. He had secrets of his own, and he wasn't exactly forthcoming about them. He could hear his abuela's voice in his head, telling him that things take time.

So he would give Juliana time. And maybe she'd actually tell him and Sal what was going on.

As the three of them gathered their stuff up to head to the start of classes, Héctor let hope bloom. He could see himself becoming friends with Sal and Juliana. Just maybe! It wouldn't be easy if they could only meet through the Room, but this was definitely much better than what *had* been happening to him.

"So . . . after school today?" Héctor suggested. "Should we meet up again?"

"I'm down," said Sal. "My tita Juana doesn't pick me up until four."

Juliana nodded. "Yeah," she said. "I wanna come back. Let's do it."

"Perfect," said Héctor.

Because it *was*.

He was the first to leave. He told Juliana to offer Sal some horchata, and she jumped up and down, clapping her hands. "Oh, Sal, you are *not* ready," she said.

Héctor smiled at that. He waved to them both and said he hoped to see them soon, then left. He nearly collided with Ms. Heath seconds later. Thankfully, she just looked down at him. "Have a good morning, Mr. Muñoz," she said, then went on her way.

Well, he'd already had the best morning he'd ever had at Orangevale Middle School.

CHAPTER TWENTY-ONE

The joy didn't last long.

Héctor floated through his classes. By the time lunch rolled around, he was *still* thinking about Juliana, Sal, and that strange place that seemed impossible but was very much real. He joined the line in the cafeteria at lunch, filled his tray up, and then found his usual table in the back, but the Misfits hadn't arrived yet. Today's food—some sort of pasta dish, steamed veggies, and a chocolate-chip walnut cookie—didn't even look that bad. Maybe all it took was a change in fortune to see things differently.

Not long after he sat down, Aishah sat across from him, and Jackson followed her, setting his trumpet case down underneath the table. "'Sup," he said to Héctor, nudging him with his shoulder.

Héctor smiled at him and, riding the wave of energy his morning had given him, decided to be bold.

"So," he began, pushing noodles across his tray, "I gotta know more."

"More about what?" said Aishah.

Taylor sat down next to her and nodded his head at Héctor. "What's happenin'?"

"Apparently Héctor needs to *know*," said Jackson, smirking.

"Do you wonder how they get all that juice inside the Capri Sun packets, too?" Taylor said, excitement spreading over his face.

"Wha-what?" said Héctor. "I—I guess I never thought about it?"

"That little bag is just so funky and *perfect*. How do they fill it up? It's magic, right?"

Aishah was shaking her head. "Taylor, the package is sealed *after* they put the juice in," she said. "It's not that big of a mystery."

"But how do you *know*?" he said, his mouth slightly open, his face confused.

"So, were you confused by Capri Suns, too, Héctor?" asked Jackson, trying to stifle a laugh.

"I don't even know anymore," he said.

"So what *were* you going to ask about?" said Aishah.

"This place," said Héctor. "I know about the Table of Misfits, obviously."

"The best table," said Taylor. "Never forget."

"And obviously, I know about the *worst* table," said Héctor.

The four of them slowly glanced over to where Mike's

table was, and Héctor scowled at them.

He quickly scanned the cafeteria. Where was Carmen? Would she join them? When he couldn't find her, he turned back to the Misfits.

"What else is there?" he asked. "What should I know about Orangevale Middle School that I don't? Any teachers to avoid, or maybe . . ." He paused, then threw caution to the wind. "Maybe like cool spots or secret rooms or something?"

"I don't know about that last one," said Jackson. "The building is pretty boring. Though there are some rooms I've never explored behind the auditorium."

"Wait, what?" Héctor said. "There's an *auditorium*?"

"Yeah," said Aishah, peeling an orange. "It's pretty big. It's through those weird double doors over by the gym."

"How is there an auditorium but no *theater* class?"

Jackson shrugged. "Beats me."

"The only art stuff they seem to have is band and Mrs. Caroline's classes," said Aishah. "And you lucked out because she's the *best* teacher here."

"I really like her," said Héctor. "She's kinda weird, which is always a good thing."

"No teacher compares to her," said Taylor, who . . . no. Héctor did a double take. Taylor had part of a Capri Sun pouch in his mouth, and he was . . .

"What are you *doing*, man?" asked Héctor. "Where did you even get that?" He hadn't seen them in the cafeteria line.

Taylor removed the pouch from his mouth. Sure enough, he had *bitten* into it and sucked the juice out of the holes his teeth had made.

"I always keep some with me," said Taylor.

Taylor lifted his backpack above the table, and more Capri Suns than Héctor could count spilled over the table.

"Dope, right?" said Taylor, smiling ear to ear.

Héctor grabbed one. "Taylor, every new thing I learn about you makes you more and more of a mystery."

Taylor bit into another Capri Sun, which immediately sprayed in his face. Everyone started laughing until Taylor froze, his eyes wide.

"What's up, HECK-tor?"

Oh no. *Mike.*

"Enjoying your lunch?" Mike sat down and squeezed in between Héctor and Jackson. "Maybe you're missing a special ingredient."

He grabbed Héctor's lunch tray, and someone laughed behind Héctor. He was pretty sure it was Frank. He tensed up again, and braced himself for whatever was about to happen.

And what did happen . . . well, it was not what Héctor expected.

"Do it, Mike," Carlos said, egging him on.

"Heck-tor, do you *want* the special ingredient?" Mike smiled, all teeth and no humor, and he leaned in closer. "Not everyone gets it."

Héctor gulped. He just wanted this to be over.

But it wasn't. And he also noticed something new: the entire lunchroom had fallen silent.

Héctor looked slowly behind him. Saw students at multiple tables—the sports kids, the cheerleaders, the band geeks—staring his way, all waiting for the inevitable.

His heart sank. Not just because of what was happening, but because of who he saw sitting with the meme kids:

Carmen.

She immediately twisted away when he spotted her.

"I asked you a question, man," said Mike, and Héctor turned back around.

What else was there to do but play along at this point? So he shook his head. "Nah, I'm good," he said.

"Are you sure about that?" Mike gestured to the tray. "One of a kind. I promise."

"No thanks," said Héctor. "It's fine like it is."

Héctor hated the words coming out of his mouth.

Improvisation was his *thing*. So why was that the best he could come up with?

"That's too bad." Mike looked back on his two Minions. "Isn't that too bad?"

"I guess Hector doesn't want that special flavor," said Frank, grinning ear to ear.

"You know what?" Mike stood up, then placed his hand on Héctor's shoulder, as if he was a friend, as if he was about to impart some sort of wisdom. "You should get a sample. Free of charge."

Please don't, Héctor thought.

"Since I know you like that sort of thing."

I'm sure I don't.

"We're friends, and this is what friends do, right?"

Most definitely not.

And then Mike spat up the biggest loogie Héctor had ever seen, and let it hang from his mouth as it dripped down. It came to rest all over Héctor's pasta. Carlos and Frank were laughing so hard they were practically screaming, and it echoed even louder in the cafeteria because no one else was talking.

Héctor didn't know why he gave into this impulse, but he turned sharply to look at Carmen.

Who was *laughing*.

"Enjoy, *Hector*," Mike said, and Héctor's name was nothing but a curse in his mouth.

The three of them walked off, snickering to one another, and the cafeteria came back alive. Well, all of it except for Héctor, whose appetite was gone. Whose meal was ruined. Whose eyes were filling with tears.

He didn't deserve this.

. . . did he?

"I'm sorry, Héctor," said Aishah. "I hate him so much."

He looked up at her, his view blurred by the tears. Taylor was gathering up the scattered Capri Sun pouches.

"You don't deserve—" Jackson began, but it was too much. Héctor couldn't listen to it anymore.

He bolted up from his seat, leaving his tray behind, and he made for the exit on the other side of the room. Unfortunately, he would have to pass the table Carmen sat at, where there was nothing but riotous laughter. He didn't want to see her, but if he went the other way, he'd pass by Mike and the Minions.

So Héctor made his choice. Carmen's table couldn't be worse than interacting with Mike. He kept his gaze down as much as he could. He pushed through the double doors and out into the cool hallway, and he was finally alone.

The tears streamed down his face; he couldn't hold them back anymore. But he kept walking, past empty classrooms and quiet corridors. He coughed out, once, twice, and then the fit took him over, pushed him into sobbing, and he leaned up against a locker to steady himself.

Héctor finally wiped the tears off his face and looked up at a soft creak to his right.

A door slowly opened. A head popped out.

"Héctor?"

Mrs. Caroline.

If there was anyone here at school he could have talked to, it was probably her. But right then, Héctor couldn't speak to her. He didn't need this. He spun himself in the other direction and started running, ignoring her calling after him, until he saw the boys' bathroom in the next hallway, and he pushed his way through the door, certain he could hide out in a stall. Like a cliché. But wasn't that what his life was? The gay kid, bullied at school, hiding in the bathroom and crying.

But that thought died a second later when the bathroom door closed behind him.

Because he wasn't in the boys' bathroom.

There was no refrigerator, no bed, no television. Instead, a dim but cozy library stretched out in front of him. There were candles flickering in sconces on the wall, and multiple armchairs, all lined with something that looked like velvet, were tucked into nooks and spaces between the shelves.

And in one of them, directly across from Héctor, was Sal.

"Héctor?" Sal put a bookmark between the pages, then closed the book. They now wore a big, dark sweater that fell nearly to their knees. "Everything okay?"

Héctor wiped at his face again. He had not expected to be seen in the middle of this.

Sal rose suddenly and crossed the Room to him. "Héctor . . . what happened?"

Sal looked concerned.

They looked like they *cared* what had happened.

And it broke him.

It was like Sal was a key to a lock Héctor did not know he had. The tears were like a waterfall, and he was crying so hard that none of his words came out like words. They were just sounds, blubberings, coughs with vague consonants in them.

Sal ran their hand over Héctor's back. "Slow down, slow down," they said. "One thing at a time."

"It's just—" He fought for breath. "I wish that—"

His anxiety rose from his gut up into his throat, and he cut through it, refused to let it hold power over him anymore.

So Héctor blurted out the truth. "Do you know what it's like not to fit in?"

Sal froze. For a moment, they didn't say anything at all, and Héctor worried he had said something terrible.

But then: "Every day."

Héctor breathed in deep, trying to slow down his heart. "Really?"

"Some days, it's not so bad," they explained. "Usually, those were the days I spent in the library."

"Which is why you're here," said Héctor. "Did something happen today?"

They shook their head. "No, not like . . . well, whatever happened to you. Some days are just harder than others."

"What do you mean?"

"Can we sit?" Sal asked, and the two of them plopped down in comfy armchairs that faced one another. Héctor looked to his left . . . and there was a tall glass of his abuela's horchata.

Sal sighed. "Tell me what happened with you first."

And for the first time since this had all started, Héctor told someone *everything*. His story was full of starts and stops, as he kept finding that he had to explain little things about his old school, his family, or Orangevale to Sal. Héctor had never been to Phoenix, but it sounded like a much, much bigger city than Orangevale. And then there was Ms. Heath, and Mike and the Minions, and—

"And that's how I got in here," he said. "I just . . . I don't know. I was so overwhelmed, and I *thought* this was going to be the bathroom."

"But the Room knew you needed it," said Sal, smiling.

"Whoa." Héctor sat back into his chair. "I think you're right."

"I'm sorry that happened," they said. "People can be so . . . so cruel."

"Is that what it's like at your school?"

Sal frowned. "Sort of. I think it's a little different for me. I confuse people. Some days, the kids have fun just trying to guess what I am, like it's some sort of game." They sighed. "I started dressing different, too. Just to protect myself."

"I did, too!" Héctor said. "I mean, not for the same reason. I just didn't want to draw attention to myself." He gestured at himself, at the plain T-shirt and jeans he had on. "I don't normally wear stuff like this."

Sal lit up. "Exactly! I wanna wear different things, but I get . . . worried. Worried what people are gonna do if they see me wearing a blouse or a dress one day. . . ."

"Because they don't know what to think of you," said Héctor, nodding his head. "And they take it *out* on you."

"Yeah, that!" said Sal. "And some people just call me names. They use 'it' a lot to describe me, which feels . . . bad. Like I'm a *thing*."

"That's so gross," said Héctor. "Why do people try to make us fit their labels?"

Sal shrugged. "At least my parents support me. They're really good about pronouns, and my dad is always ready to fight someone on my behalf."

"But at school?"

"It's hard because . . . well, no one knows what to do with me." They stood up. "That's why I keep finding myself here. Where I don't feel judged. Or trapped."

"I'm sorry you're going through this alone," said Héctor. "I know it's not the same as my situation, but it's got to suck."

"Well, I'm not really alone anymore."

A fondness spread in Héctor's chest. He was having the same epiphany.

"I just wish there was something we could do," they said. They helped Héctor to his feet. "Something to change the places we live in."

"Let me know if you figure that out," he said.

Then Sal pulled him into a hug.

The two of them stood there for a moment, and Héctor felt . . .

Safe.

When Héctor left the Room, he turned back to see that it had once again disguised itself as the boys' bathroom. The bell announcing the end of lunch must have recently rung, as students were pouring through the hallways. Héctor watched as a kid rushed into the bathroom, and inside, he could see the sinks and stalls.

Back to normal.

He walked the few feet to Mrs. Caroline's classroom, and it was only once he entered it that he remembered that his art teacher had seen him crying.

Mrs. Caroline rushed up to him. "Héctor, is everything okay?"

Heat rose to his cheeks. "Sorry, Mrs. Caroline," he said. "Just having a bad day."

He shuffled to his seat, but she followed right behind him. "Well, if you ever need anything, don't hesitate to ask." She tapped on his desk after he sat down. "I did want you to know that I was very pleased with your recent project."

He scratched his head. "My what?"

She raised a finger to the wall in the rear of the classroom. "I really liked your last pastel piece," she explained. "There's something so touching about it. And *mysterious*. You're showing such growth in a *very* short span of time, Héctor. Good job."

There, prominently mounted near pieces from other

students, was a drawing he had done.

It was a door. A door opening on a secret, colorful world.

Héctor looked back to Mrs. Caroline, but she had returned to her desk, shuffling papers as more kids streamed into the room. Did she say something nice about his art so she could cheer him up? Maybe. He had to admit it felt nice that she noticed that he was trying so hard.

Héctor smiled at Mrs. Caroline, even though she wasn't looking. Today had felt like he was on a roller coaster, his emotions reaching new highs and lows. But as class started, Héctor let the tension of Mike out of his body.

You can beat this, he told himself.

And he was starting to believe it.

CHAPTER TWENTY-TWO

After an unnecessarily sweaty gym class—How was it *still* hot in October? How did *anyone* in Orangevale survive this utter tragedy?—Héctor wasn't sure where to go. He knew his destination was the Room, but he lingered outside of the gym, his eyes locked on the double doors that led to the auditorium. Part of him wanted to dart inside and explore it. Did it have a stage? Full curtains? If so, who would let something like that go to waste?

Another time, maybe. But where was the Room this afternoon? Was he just supposed to wander the halls until it showed up? That seemed a little unfair.

Unfair? he thought. *Bruh, you're talking about a magical ROOM. How can it be* fair?

But there had to be a logic to it, some guiding force that allowed it to change as it had for Héctor, Juliana, and Sal. There was no way it would let him wander aimlessly without making itself known.

The halls were emptying out quickly at the end of

the school day. He headed toward the main entrance on campus, near where he'd seen it before, and—

There it was: JANITOR. The door was tucked in between two others, and if Héctor hadn't known better, he would have thought that it *belonged* there. How was it able to do that, to blend in so effortlessly?

Héctor looked both ways, worried someone might see him go inside, but the coast was clear. He opened the door to the Room and was greeted immediately by Juliana, Sal, and the most unbelievable sight he'd ever seen.

The Room had changed, yet again. Juliana and Sal sat at a large booth in what looked like a diner, shrunk down to be just the right size for the three of them. Next to the table was a large glass case with various slices of pie, cake, and other desserts slowly rotating inside it.

"What *is* this?" said Héctor, letting the door close behind him.

"I was hungry," said Juliana. "And I kinda have a sweet tooth, sooooo . . ." She shrugged. "This was what was here."

"But why a *diner*?" he asked. "Why not just have food show up magically like it does for me?"

"It just . . . shows up for you?" said Sal as they scooted over to make room for Héctor. "What do you mean?"

"Well, whenever I'm not looking, the things I want

appear," he explained. "Like . . . okay, let me try this." He sat up straight and took a deep breath. "I'm really thirsty. I need a glass of water."

It happened just out of sight, before Héctor could look at the table: a glass of cold water, condensation running down the side, sat before him. As if it had always been there.

"That is *wild*," said Juliana as Héctor took a drink. "Everything I ever used or needed was always in the Room. I guess I never thought to *ask* for anything specific. It was like . . . like it always *knew*."

"But *how*?" asked Héctor. "How can it *know*?"

Sal shrugged. "You got me stumped. I have no idea how any of this is possible."

Héctor stood up. "We need to figure this out. Like, how does this all work? Are there rules?"

"There have to be," said Sal, after swallowing down a bite of apple pie. "I mean, it hasn't given me *everything* I've ever wanted."

"Well, what if your theory is still right, Héctor?" said Juliana.

"You mean that it has to be what we *need*?" he said.

She nodded. "You needed water. I needed a place to calm down and to have some food. Sal needed a quiet room to read. It makes sense."

Sal scratched their head. "But how would we test this?"

"Well," said Héctor. "What do we need?"

The three of them were silent for a moment. Juliana twisted up her face while she thought. "I guess I really need a nap," she said, rubbing at her eyes. "Today has been really hard, and I could use—"

"Oh my *God*," said Sal, interrupting Juliana. "Look!"

When Héctor turned to look at what they were pointing at, he saw that the diner motif was gone, just like that. Had he seen it change? Nope. On the other side of the Room, tucked up against the wall, was the cloudlike bed he had used in one of his early visits. He felt a pull then, like the bed was beckoning him, and he yawned. Which was followed by Juliana yawning, which caused Sal to yawn, too.

The chain reaction nearly looped back to Héctor before he shook his head. "I didn't realize how tired I was," he said.

"Me either," said Sal, who then pointed to the bed again. "So . . . there's a bed here. A *whole* bed."

"There wasn't even a sound!" exclaimed Juliana. "Isn't that, like . . . not even scientific?"

"I have a feeling this place cares nothing about science," said Héctor, and he walked over to the bed and touched it tentatively. "Please stop me from taking a nap *right now*."

"Okay, I got one!" announced Juliana. "I need a pony."

There was silence. A lot of it.

"I really do!" she continued. "It would make me happy, so cough it up, Room. A pony."

She held her hand out, as if a pony could fit in her palm.

Nothing happened.

Juliana crossed her arms in front of her. "I guess the Room thinks I don't need a pony. I disagree!"

"Lemme try," said Sal. They closed their eyes and took a deep breath. "I need . . . a thousand dollars."

"Okay!" said Héctor. "Go big!"

But much to their collective dismay, no money appeared in the Room.

"Maybe we're not taking this seriously enough," said Héctor. "It's easy to think of things I *want*, but *need*?"

"I do need rooms to be cooler," said Sal. "I always run kinda hot. So . . . could the temperature go lower?"

Within seconds, Héctor felt a noticeable chill in the air. "Oh my *God*," he said. "That worked."

"It's so weird!" said Sal. "Like, who are we even talking to? Is someone listening to us?"

Héctor ran his hands up and down his arms. "Well, now I need a sweater," he said.

The booth the trio had been sitting in minutes before was gone. Of course, Héctor never *saw* it disappear. In its place was a standing coatrack, one that had multiple sweaters—pullovers, a few hoodies, and a thick cardigan—hanging off it.

"You're kidding me," he said, and he heard Sal and Juliana gasp once they spotted it, too.

"This is amazing!" said Juliana, who dashed over to the rack and ran her fingers down one of the sleeves. "You basically summoned it."

Héctor grabbed the black cardigan and slipped his arms into it. It was *so* soft!

"I can't believe this," said Sal, reaching out to touch one of the hoodies. "Except it's really happening."

"We've got to get more creative," said Héctor. "There has to be a way for us to use this Room to our advantage."

"I read a lot of science fiction," said Sal. "And I wonder if maybe we need to think . . . bigger? More theoretical?"

"What does that mean?" said Juliana.

Sal took a deep breath. "I need to feel like I belong," they said.

Héctor froze. "Whoa," he said.

"That's deep," said Juliana.

Sal's eyes went glassy. "Well, it's true," they said. "I know that's why I found this Room in the first place."

Maybe that's why I found it, too, Héctor thought, but he didn't share that with the others. But how did it *know?* How could that possibly be true?

"Well, I think you belong right here," said Juliana. "With us."

"Really?" said Sal, their glassy eyes lighting up.

"Yeah," she said, then turned to Héctor. "*Both* of you. It seems that we all feel safe here, so . . . maybe that's a sign. Maybe this place already gave you what you needed, Sal."

They smiled. "I like the sound of that."

And as the three of them tried (and mostly failed) to get the Room to grant them every absurd thing they could wish for, Héctor realized that he liked the sound of that, too.

CHAPTER TWENTY-THREE

Héctor's abuela had plans for him that weekend, and they filled him with anxiety:

A Muñoz family day of making tamales.

Héctor hoped his second attempt would be better than his first, but as Papi pulled his car into Abuela's driveway, doubt crept back under Héctor's skin. He'd already abandoned the idea of becoming the famous twelve-year-old tamale vendor of Orangevale. All he wanted to do was just make his papi y abuela proud.

The three of them sat around the dinner table in Abuela's brightly decorated home. There was art all over the walls. Colors and patterns clashed, like every item had its own personality. Héctor's favorite were the matching sugar skulls on a shelf on the wall in the living room, each of them intricately painted.

He tried to let the creativity in the room seep into his bones, as if the walls let out a magic he could absorb. *If only*, he thought, as his abuela set out all the ingredients on the table: Chicken, seasoned and cooked until it fell apart in Héctor's hands. Masa. Las hojas.

You can do this, he told himself.

Héctor watched his papi and abuela make a few tamales, their hands moving quickly and delicately as they assembled them. Again, it seemed so effortless! How were they able to do that so fast?

Unfortunately, Héctor found that he was nervous every time he grabbed some masa or tried to spread the pollo evenly inside. His abuela had to reroll some of them because too much of the insides squeezed out at the end.

"You'll get it, mijo," said Papi. "Do you need me to show you how again?"

Héctor grimaced, but before he could say anything, Abuela raised her hand. "Ay, Félix, leave him be," she said. "He needs to concentrate. He'll do it on his own."

But *would* he? He couldn't concentrate. His hands shook, and any confidence he gained from the energy in Abuela's home had disappeared. Where had it gone? Why was this so frustrating? It was like there was a swarm of bees in his stomach, stinging him over and over again.

Then he remembered: Mike, leaning over Héctor's lunch tray, spit trailing down to the food.

Even this far from school, he still couldn't get Mike out of his head.

He tried to assemble another tamale as Papi and

Abuela chatted, and even their words felt wrong, like they were banging around inside his head. He watched as Papi grabbed some masa, spread it inside the husk, put chicken on top of it, and rolled the tamale up . . . all without even *looking* at it.

And of course it came out perfectly.

Héctor tried his hardest to imitate them both. But after he spread some masa out, his abuela raised a hand and pointed. "Más," she said. "Missed a spot there."

He looked at the pot in front of her. She'd made *six* of them in the time he'd failed to make a single one correctly.

He let the husk fall to his plate, and gave up. When he shoved his chair away from the table, it screeched against the floor.

"Héctor?" his papi said. "You okay?"

Héctor couldn't even make eye contact with Papi. Tears stung his eyes, and soon, he found his feet taking him out of the kitchen, through the front door, and he plopped down on Abuela's lawn so that the afternoon sun hit his face.

Why was he like this? He had been feeling so good after the time he spent with Sal and Juliana, and now, it was like his own brain had turned on him. Shouldn't he be able to control it, like everyone else in his life did? No one else ever seemed as messed up as he felt.

He choked back another sob. What was he *doing*? Crying on his abuela's front lawn? He pushed himself up with his elbows and stared out at the quiet neighborhood. It was *still* all wrong. He couldn't walk to a panadería. Where were the people with the carts selling helados and ringing their bells? The smell of roasted coffee or carne asada or the flowers in the shop on 22nd Street? The duplexes and row houses that looked like they had their own vivid personalities?

He was in the wrong place. Most definitely.

Héctor didn't even hear Abuela Sonia approach. "Nieto," she cooed, her voice soft. "You need anything?"

He looked up at her, and her face was etched with concern.

"No," he said. "Well, not anything you could give me."

She crouched down next to him. "I know something is . . . off," she said. "And I can't force you to talk about it."

He didn't say anything to that, but nodded.

"I'm not gonna bother you again," she continued, "but I want you to know that the day you're ready, you can always come to me. ¿Me entiendes?"

He gave a weak smile in return. "It's just that . . ."

Her eyes lit up then, in anticipation of what he was about to reveal. Until he chickened out. How? How could he tell her about Mike, about the Minions, about Ms. Heath, about the *Room*? He thought about

· 172 ·

his conversation with Sal:

"Do you know what it's like not to fit in?"

"Every day."

He didn't know how to communicate all that. So, he went for a simpler approach, something that was close enough to the truth.

"Some days," he said, "it is really hard to be myself."

Because it was. He was glad to finally be getting closer to the Misfits; he was thrilled about the Room, Juliana, and Sal. But what about the moments in between, especially those where his new friends or the Room weren't there? How was he supposed to make it through *that*?

Abuela reached out and ran her fingers through his hair, her fingertips brushing against his scalp. "I know what you mean," she said.

"Really?"

She opened her mouth.

Closed it.

And she kept whatever she was about to say to herself. What did she mean by that? He didn't have a guess, but perhaps she would tell him one day when he was older.

She stood up, smiled down at Héctor. "I'm proud of you, Héctor. I'm so happy you are my nieto."

She walked back to the house, and Héctor saw that his papi was standing in the doorway. He knew his papi wanted to rush forward and say something; he started to move toward Héctor. But Abuela put a hand on his chest and shook her head.

"When you want to come back inside, we'll be here," Papi said. "We'll . . . we'll give you your space."

Héctor smiled to try to show Papi he appreciated that.

The two of them disappeared into Abuela's house, and Héctor looked back on the neighborhood. He watched as a couple of older kids biked by. Would that be Héctor in a few years? Would he have friends he'd be able to explore with? Maybe. But years . . . that seemed *so* far away. What was Héctor supposed to do in the meantime? Hope a bizarre, magical janitor's closet solved his problems?

Truthfully, Héctor just felt tired of waiting.

The weekend seemed to stretch out around Héctor, so when Monday morning rolled around, it was like he hadn't been to school in a whole year. He felt torn between anxiety over the next inevitable confrontation with Mike and excitement over the possibility of being in the Room again. Why couldn't his heart just choose one emotion to feel?

He pulled out his phone as his mami drove him to school and scrolled to his group chat with Tim and Sophia. In the past week, they'd only exchanged ten messages. *Total.* He knew it wasn't entirely their fault, though. It had taken him days to respond to Sophia's last message.

"Have a good day at school," said Mami, kissing him on the forehead. "I'll see you at dinner tonight, okay?"

He nodded. "Love you, Mami."

Mike was nowhere to be found in the halls of Orangevale Middle School that morning. It wasn't that comforting; it just meant Mike would attack at some other point during the day. He shivered at the thought. This was his new normal, wasn't it?

Seconds later, it was there, tucked into the wall near one of the science classrooms:

JANITOR.

It has to be there for a reason, Héctor thought. He looked around in the hallway. Two kids were checking stuff into their lockers, and the group at the far end were deep in conversation. None of them were even aware he existed. So he slipped into the Room, and was met with his new friends, Juliana and Sal.

The couch was back. The library was gone.

And Juliana was crying.

Héctor dropped his backpack on the ground near the door, and he rushed over to the couch. "Juliana, what is it? Is everything okay?"

She looked up at Héctor. "I have to tell you something."

Héctor cast a glance at Sal, who shrugged. "I don't know," they said. "I just got here, right before you."

He sat down on the other side of Juliana. "We're here," he said. "Talk to us."

"I didn't tell you the truth earlier," she sobbed, then wiped at her nose. "When I told you about my friend who needed help."

"Oh," said Héctor. "Don't worry about that. I knew you were talking about yourself."

Juliana's mouth dropped open while Sal covered their laugh with a hand. "What?" she said. "How did you know that?"

"It was obvious," said Sal. "We *both* knew."

"And it's okay," said Héctor. "We all just met. I didn't expect you to tell me your entire life story in the first hour."

Juliana sniffled again. "Still. I feel bad. And I don't know what to do."

Héctor furrowed his brow. "About lying? I promise you, it's fine."

"No," she said, shaking her head. "About my problem."

He watched as Juliana's shoulders sagged, as she let out a long breath. And just like that, as Sal had done the day he and Juliana met them, Juliana let go. "Something happened," she began. "And I don't know how to stop it."

Héctor didn't get what she meant by that, but figured she was about to explain herself. "Okay," he said. "Maybe we can help."

So Juliana told them both. She told them about Sascha, the girl that she'd met at the beginning of the school year. They had bonded over protective hairstyles like braids and twists, over their loud and loving Southern families, over a million different things that they had in common. Juliana explained how Sascha made her feel something she hadn't before. It was a funny sensation, deep in her heart.

"Oh, so you *like* like her," Héctor quipped.

"Don't make fun!" she said, playfully hitting him on the arm. Then she pressed her lips together. "But yeah. I do."

She told him that she had asked Sascha to the fall dance, where Juliana was going to DJ.

And she told him that when the principal had found out about it, he took the DJ job away from her.

"It happened a few weeks ago," she said, wiping away the tears that were falling down her cheeks. "He called me into his office and told me that the school had hired an outside DJ for the dance."

"That's *horrible*," he said. "When is the dance?"

"In a couple weeks," said Juliana.

"And that's what you're scared about? People finding

out that you aren't going to be the DJ?"

She shook her head, and when she looked to Héctor, the tears came back again. "He's going to tell my mom today. Like . . . I need to go to the office after this."

It took a moment for Héctor to understand.

"Oh no," he said. "She doesn't know, does she?"

Juliana put her face in her hands. "No," she said. "This is how she's going to find out that I like girls."

"That's what made you so angry," said Héctor, realization dawning on him. "And why you found this place."

"Héctor, what do I *do*?" she said, and there was a desperation in her voice. "I kept putting it off because I was afraid, and now I won't have time to do it myself."

"Your principal is taking this moment away from you," said Sal. "And forcing you to come out." They shook their head in frustration. "That's *really* messed up. I haven't figured out who I like or even if I like anyone at all. But it should still be my decision about when to tell someone!"

Héctor's heart started racing. He knew something he could tell her that might make her feel better. But it would require him to be vulnerable to someone he barely knew. Still, as he saw how distraught Juliana was, he thought it would mean something to her if she knew she wasn't alone.

Héctor took a deep breath.

"I'm gay," he said to Juliana. "And I told my parents a couple years ago."

Her eyes went wide. "Wait. *Really?*"

He laughed. "Did you think I was dramatic because I like theater?"

She chuckled at that. "I don't know! I try not to assume I know anything about other people." Then she went quiet. "Was it okay? Are your parents okay with it?"

"It was terrifying," he said. "I knew I was gay for *years*. I mean . . . I didn't think there was anything wrong with it. It's just who I've always been. Still, I took *so* long to say anything to my parents. So I might know what you're going through."

"How did they take it?" she asked.

"Juliana, I don't know what your parents are like," said Héctor, "but I hope they are like mine. My mom and dad just wanted me to know that they loved me." Then he smiled. "My abuela said she always knew."

Juliana let out another long breath. "I think my mom will be fine with it. And I'm not worried about my dad either. It's the situation that freaks me out."

"Will you be safe if you tell her?" asked Sal. "Or will it be safe if it gets out at your school?"

"What do you mean?" asked Juliana. "Safe?"

"I dunno," said Sal. "Do you, like . . . go to one of those ghetto schools?"

It was like all the air was sucked out of the Room, and Héctor's heart jumped at that. *Ghetto?* he thought. *Who says that anymore?*

Juliana's face was scrunched up, her mouth slightly open. It was clear she didn't know what to say to that.

Sal sensed the change in both Héctor and Juliana, and they stood up.

They opened their mouth to say something.

Then . . .

Nothing.

Because Sal was gone.

There was no sound. No warning. No fading from sight. One second, they were there, and then . . . poof. Gone.

Héctor heard a voice, far away, like it was in a distant room at the end of a hallway. "Juliana? Héctor? Where are—?"

It cut off, and the two of them were met with silence.

"Sal!" Héctor called out, and he ran to the other side of the Room, toward where he had heard their voice. "Where are you?"

There was no response.

He turned back to Juliana. "What just happened?"

Juliana gulped. "Héctor," she said. "I think *I* happened."

CHAPTER TWENTY-FOUR

"I'm sorry," said Héctor. "*What?*"

Juliana began to pace back and forth across the Room. "Remember your theory?" she said. "About this place?"

"Yeah. What about it?"

"I think it's more complicated than that," she continued. "Not just what we *need*. I think this place also keeps us *safe*."

"Safe?" Héctor shook his head. "I don't get it."

She stopped pacing. "Okay," she said after a short pause. "Like this!"

Juliana walked to the door of the Room and flung it open. Beyond it were the bright and shiny halls of Swifton Middle School. Juliana stepped out into the hallway. "You ever notice that the Room doesn't open up into a spot in the hallway where people can see us leave it?"

He thought about that for a moment. She wasn't wrong, was she?

She came back in and closed the door behind her. "There were times when I wasn't paying attention when

I went back into the world, and I only realized after the fact that no one ever noticed me."

"Really?" he said.

"*Ever,*" she said. She crossed her arms in front of her. "I think it protects us, too."

"But I feel like we should be a little worried, because . . . *where is Sal?* Did they, like . . . get zapped into another dimension? Do they even *exist* anymore?"

Juliana's mouth dropped open. "I don't think this place would do something like *that,*" she said. "They must still be here. Maybe we just can't see one another?"

"Maybe," said Héctor. "But you were saying . . . you think the Room was protecting you? And that's why this happened?"

"It's gotta be that," said Juliana, and then she went quiet and pressed her lips together. "I think it happened to me before."

"Whoa, *what*? When?"

"The day I found the Room," she said. "I was so furious after what Mr. Stafford did to me that I couldn't see straight. I felt light-headed, like I was in a tunnel that was getting smaller and smaller. And I almost did something *bad.*"

"Bad?" said Héctor. "Bad like what?"

She winced. "I turned around and went straight to Mr. Stafford's office. I didn't really know what I was gonna do, but I was so furious that I just wanted to say mean things to him."

"I'm assuming you didn't, though?"

She nodded. "Yeah. Because when I opened his office, I was *here*."

Héctor gasped. "No!" he said. "No way!" "Yep," she said. "I'm pretty sure the Room protected me."

Héctor sat back down on the couch. "Because what Sal just said was super messed up. Which would mean that you felt unsafe."

"Exactly!"

"I get it," he said. "But also . . . who says something like that?"

"Right?" Juliana sat next to him. "People always assume the worst because I'm Black. I even get it from other Asian people, too. It's not fair!"

"I remember the first time I heard someone say that word like that," said Héctor. He told her about an older white man on the Muni train who was mad that Tim, Sophia, and Héctor were being "too loud" in the afternoon. He had looked directly at Sophia when he said it, too.

Juliana scoffed at him. "Isn't it super bougie there?"

Héctor sighed. "Yeah. It's changed a lot lately." He allowed a silence to grow between them. "I still miss living there, Juliana. Every day."

"I can tell," she said. "I guess I don't really know what that's like. I've *always* been in Charleston."

"I don't think it would be so bad if we had moved somewhere cool," he said. "Orangevale feels like I'm living on another planet. I guess it's not that bad, but I don't understand anything here." He sighed. "And my old friends . . . I don't know. I think they aren't that interested in me anymore."

"Why do you say that?" Juliana asked, and then she smiled. "You're a *very* interesting person, Héctor."

"It just seems like I can't really talk to them anymore. Not about the important stuff."

"I'm sorry," she said. "Well, at least you have this place." A pause. "And us."

But his thoughts from the past weekend crept back in his head. He had the Room, sure, but only when he was at school. Only when he was in the hallways. Only when it decided that he needed it. He couldn't spend his whole life inside a magical janitor's closet.

Juliana finally stood up and sighed. "Well, I have to go deal with the principal," she said. "So, by the next time you see me, I'll have come out to my mom." She took a deep breath. "I'll be fine, I'm sure."

"I wish we could help you," said Héctor.

"I know," she said. "And I wish I had gotten the courage

· 184 ·

to tell you sooner."

"No, don't feel bad!" he said, and he quickly stood. "I'm just glad you trusted us enough."

Juliana closed the space between them and gripped Héctor in a tight hug. "Thank you," she said. "Really."

She made for the door, then stopped and turned around. "If you see Sal, tell them we can talk later. Right now, I'm too hurt, and I'll probably say something mean." She paused. "If it was possible, though . . . I wish you two could come with me."

"Good luck, Juliana," Héctor said. "You got this."

And with that, she left the Room to meet her fate.

Héctor only had time to sit down on the couch before Sal popped back into the Room right in front of him. He yelped and pulled his legs up on the couch.

"Héctor!" Sal cried out, their face twisted with regret. "I messed up so bad. Is Juliana still here?"

"You just missed her," he said. "She has to meet with her mom and the principal now."

Sal groaned. "I wanted to apologize to her before she left. I think . . . I think the Room did this on purpose."

"That was Juliana's theory, too," said Héctor. He grimaced. "You . . . you shouldn't have said that, Sal. You judged her just because she's Black."

"I didn't even really think about it," said Sal, and they

put their head in their hands. "I just . . . assumed."

"She said you two can talk later," said Héctor, "but I would give her some space. She needs to feel comfortable with you again."

"Yeah, you're right," said Sal, and they wrung their hands together repeatedly. "I don't have a whole lot of friends back home. I don't want to lose either of you, too."

Héctor patted Sal on the shoulder. "Apologize when you get the chance. And . . . I don't know. Do better?"

They nodded. "Yeah, of course. You heading to class?"

"Yeah," he said. "Wish we were with Juliana, though."

They said their goodbyes, and Héctor opened the door to the Room, preparing himself for another day at Orangeville Middle School.

So he was surprised when, instead, he found himself staring out into the halls of Swifton Middle School.

Okay, he thought. *So the Room has a sense of humor. Ha ha.* He chuckled and closed the door.

Opened it again.

Same shiny hallways. Same bright skylights in the ceiling.

"Um," said Héctor. "Hey, Sal, can you come try this?"

Sal joined Héctor at his side and looked out into the hallway. "Where is this?"

"It's Juliana's school," he answered.

"This is a *school*?" Their mouth dropped open. "But it looks so fancy!" Then they grimaced. "Wow, I really was messed up to call this place ghetto, wasn't I?"

That wasn't quite the point, but Héctor ignored it because there were much more urgent things to deal with. "Sal, can you close the door and open it?"

"Sure," they said. Sal did as Héctor asked, closing the door and opening it.

"Um . . . that's not right," they said, and did it again.

Both Héctor and Sal stared at the same hallway as before.

At Swifton Middle School.

"What's happening?" said Héctor.

"I don't get it," said Sal, and they shut the door once more. Opened it *again*.

Nothing had changed.

"Sal . . . ," Héctor said.

"Dude . . ." Sal couldn't even finish the sentence.

Héctor turned to face Sal. "I don't think the Room is letting us go home."

CHAPTER TWENTY-FIVE

"This doesn't make any sense!" said Sal. "Is the Room trying to make us late for our classes?"

But the Room had *never* done something like that. They'd always been perfectly on time. Why would it start making them late?

"This isn't happening," said Héctor. "It's gotta be a mistake or something." He flung the door open after closing it, but nothing was working. That didn't stop him from repeating himself: Close the door. Open it. Close the door. Open it. Close the door. Open it.

Every time, the halls of Swifton Middle School were on the other side.

Suddenly, Héctor *got* it.

"Sal," he said. "I think we're *supposed* to be here."

They threw their hands up. "What? *How?*"

Héctor's mind was swirling. "What if this is what Juliana *needs*? Before she left for her meeting with the principal, she told me that she wished both of us could be with her."

"Both of us?" said Sal. "She wanted me there?"

Héctor nodded. "She doesn't *hate* you, Sal. She just needs you to get why you can't say something like that."

"Oh, good point," they said. "This stuff is hard, but I don't want to hurt her again." Sal looked up and down the hallway. "So . . . what exactly are we supposed to do *now*?"

Héctor did not have the answer to that, but his heart thumped in his chest. He was *excited*. This was like one of those improvisation exercises he had to do in theater, except this one was real life.

"Sal, we should go find her," he said. "We can do this!"

And he took a step forward, out into the hallways of Juliana's school, and he beckoned for Sal to follow him. Sal looked to Héctor, fear in their eyes.

"We'll be fine," said Héctor. "I promise."

He put his hand out for Sal, who finally took it and joined him in Juliana's school. As soon as they did, the door shut behind the two of them.

And immediately, it *disappeared*.

Héctor couldn't deny the bolt of panic that shocked his system, and he saw it reflected on Sal's face. Both of them ran their hands along the wall, trying to maybe find a gap or a frame or *any* evidence that the door was still there.

They found nothing.

Héctor turned around, breathing heavily, and leaned

against the wall. Sal just laughed.

"Well, I guess we *have* to go now," they said. "But which way, Héctor?"

To the left was the bulk of the hallway. There was a set of silver double doors at the end.

To the right was a shorter hallway and a large glass cabinet full of awards and trophies.

"I don't know," he said. "I've never been here."

"Well, neither have I!" said Sal. "We can . . . guess?"

Héctor had to laugh at that. None of this made any *actual* sense. "To the right, then," he said, grinning. "We probably won't get lost. How hard could it be to find the main office?"

Minutes later, after making multiple turns and getting caught peeking in on a math class, Héctor and Sal had still not found anything resembling the principal's office. Héctor had started to sweat. The *idea* of coming to Juliana's aid had been a whole lot more attractive than the execution of it.

"I don't understand the shape of this school," Sal whined. "Is it a square? A circle?"

"Why can't the Room just download maps to our brain?" Héctor said. "Ugh, it figures that we'd get lost in another state because of a magical closet."

Sal froze, but Héctor didn't notice until he was twenty feet ahead of them. "Sal?" he called back. "You okay?"

Their eyes went wide. "Dude," they said. "We're in another *state*."

"I know," said Héctor, walking back over to Sal. "You ever been to South Carolina?"

Héctor felt another rush of adrenaline, but Sal's eyes were only getting wider. "Héctor, what if we can't get *back*?"

Héctor's blood chilled. "Oh," he said. "I . . . I hadn't thought of that."

"We're so far from home," they said. "I'm scared."

Héctor grabbed Sal by the shoulders. "Breathe, Sal," he ordered. "I don't think the Room will abandon us here."

Sal took a few deep breaths, but the color had not returned to their face. "Okay, you're probably right," they said. "But we still don't know how to find Juliana!"

"We'll probably find her eventually?" said Héctor, and it came out more like a question.

Sal's features twisted up again. "What have we done?"

"What are you two doing out of class?"

The voice echoed down the hall, and both Héctor and Sal turned slowly to come face-to-face with a very tall, *very* angry white woman. Her hair was cut in a rather stunning bob (Héctor *had* to appreciate that), and it waved side to side as she spoke. "Do you have hall passes? And does your destination require that you be out and about during first period?"

Sal said nothing, but Héctor was okay with that. It was *his* time to shine.

So he put on a face, one of confusion and discomfort. "I'm sorry," he said in his best apology voice, and he put an arm around Sal. "Sal here isn't feeling well, and I didn't have time to get them a pass. They just . . . well, they just left a *horrible* mess in the bathroom back that way."

Héctor vaguely gestured behind him. Was there even a bathroom that way? He sure hoped so!

"A *mess*?" The woman sighed and looked at Sal, who didn't have to perform being sick at all. Héctor could tell that Sal was probably going to throw up if this didn't work. "I'm sorry you're not feeling well. Get them to the nurse's office, okay?"

She started to leave, but Héctor called out to her. "Sorry, I got turned around. Which way am I going?"

The woman pointed behind Héctor, in the opposite direction from where they'd been headed. "Around the next corner." Then, more to herself: "I don't get paid enough for this."

Once she was gone, Sal busted up. "Héctor! How did you do that?"

He bowed once for them. "Well, some thanks must go to you for your convincing performance!"

"I was so nervous," they said. "Trust me, it was *real* easy."

Héctor led the way as the two of them rushed down the hallway. Moments later, it was clear they were in the right part of the campus. They passed the nurse's office, then a set of counselors' rooms, and then . . .

Juliana, sitting on a bench outside of one of the offices. She heard the pounding of their shoes on the tile and looked up.

"What are you *doing* here?" she said, probably a bit *too* loudly, and bolted off the bench. Her gaze jumped from Héctor to Sal. "How did you even get here?"

"Juliana," Sal said, "I just wanted to—"

She raised a hand. "Later. This isn't the time. *How* are you *here*?"

Héctor wanted to tell her, but he didn't get the chance. The door next to them opened, and a short white man with a shiny bald head stepped out. "Juliana Chin?" he said, then cast his gaze on the three of them. "Have you been socializing with your friends while waiting? Do either of you have a hall pass?"

Héctor sputtered for a moment. He hadn't antici- pated this.

The man's phone rang loudly behind him, and he held up a finger. "Don't go anywhere," he said, and dis- appeared back into his office.

Juliana wasted no time. "You *have* to leave," she said, her arms crossed, a scowl on her face. "Y'all can't be here!"

"We don't really have a choice," said Héctor. "Trust me."

"What does *that* mean?"

Sal gulped. "The Room won't let us go home."

Juliana closed her eyes. "This isn't happening. It's just *not*."

"They're telling the truth," Héctor said. "Every time we tried to open the door back to our own schools, it kept sending us *here*."

"But you don't go here! What are you supposed to do?"

Héctor smiled. "I think we're supposed to come with *you*," he said. "Just like you wished for."

Her face warmed at that. "Wait," she said. "You really want to do that? For me?"

"Yes," said Sal. "Absolutely."

There was a burst of awkwardness as Juliana and Sal looked at one another.

"Look," Sal began. "I said something—"

Juliana held up a hand. "I know. But . . . not now. We have to figure *this* out. My mom is gonna be here any minute."

Héctor's heart flopped. He had never done anything

like this before. Was this what the Room intended?

"Juliana," Héctor said, "we're here for you. Do you want us in that office with you?"

She stared at the two of them for a brief moment. "You're really here."

"We are," said Sal.

"Am I actually doing this?" she asked.

"You are," said Héctor, and he reached out, taking her hand. "We'll be there."

"Every step of the way," added Sal, grabbing her other hand.

Juliana looked as if she was going to cry. "Then let's do it," she said. "I can't thank you enough," she said.

She didn't even get to try. The office door opened again, and the principal grunted. "Miss Chin?" he said.

It was now or never.

CHAPTER TWENTY-SIX

"Please, sit down."

The principal gestured at the two empty chairs across from him. Héctor glanced at Sal, who shook their head and gave a knowing look. *Right*, he thought. *This isn't about us.* So Héctor then said, "If it's okay, we'll stand."

"Excuse me," the principal said, "but why are you two here?"

Héctor glanced at the nameplate on the edge of the desk. *Principal Edward Stafford.* Ah, yes! He'd heard Juliana say his name before.

"We're here to support Juliana," replied Héctor.

Principal Stafford grunted. "I don't recall asking you to bring guests, Miss Chin."

"You also didn't tell me *not* to," she said. Almost *too* quickly, and Héctor, who now stood behind her, watched her shoulders go up right after the words came out of her mouth. "I mean . . . I needed my friends with me."

At that, Héctor grabbed Sal's hand and squeezed it, hard.

"Do the two of you have passes from your first-period teachers, then?"

Héctor's eyes went wide.

"Um . . . ," said Sal.

"They're in Mr. Franz's class with me," said Juliana quickly. "You could call him right now, if you like. He said they could come with me." She crossed her arms.

The principal sighed. "No, I just want to get this over with." He looked at his watch. "Does your mother have a habit of being late, Miss Chin? It's five minutes past—"

There was a gentle knock at the door, and then it opened. "Sorry," said a woman, tall, her skin dark like Juliana's, her hair in a braided crown. "I couldn't find this place. This school has such a confusing design!"

Héctor tried to muffle a laugh, and Mrs. Chin glanced down at him. She smiled—Héctor *really* liked how her smile made him feel—but then it was gone in an instant as she took in the room. Her gaze turned to the principal, then to Juliana, and then to the two random kids standing awkwardly behind her daughter.

"Well, this is a crowd," she said, then stuck her hand out to the principal. "Angie Chin. I'm Juliana's mother."

Principal Stafford shook her hand, then gestured to the empty chair next to Juliana. "It seems your daughter wanted some sort of audience today, though I can't imagine why."

Héctor shuffled from one foot to the other, trying to get a good look at Juliana. But his friend had her head bowed, almost like she was afraid to look up.

"Juliana?" Mrs. Chin ran her hand down her daughter's back. "Is something wrong?" She glared at the principal. "Is my daughter in trouble?"

Principal Stafford pressed his lips tight, then looked up at Héctor and Sal. "Well . . ."

"No, I want to hear it from her." Mrs. Chin turned her chair so that it directly faced Juliana. "Honey, you can tell me *anything*. You know that, right?"

She reached out. Put her fingers gingerly under Juliana's chin. Tilted her head up.

"Literally *anything*, okay?"

Juliana didn't speak at first. She looked to Héctor— who recognized that look. He'd worn it the same morning he stood in front of the mirror in the bathroom, practicing the words over and over again, trying to muster up the courage to say them to his parents.

Mami, Papi . . . I'm gay.

So Héctor smiled at Juliana, sending his words in that expression: *We got you.* And when he looked to Sal, he saw that they were leaning forward just a bit, nodding.

They both had her back.

"I don't know that that's necessary," said the principal. "I can summarize the issue quickly and—"

"No."

Juliana had spoken. She shook her head at Principal Stafford. "No, I *have* to do this."

She turned to her mother. "I have something to tell you."

Mrs. Chin took a deep breath. "Okay, baby," she said, and she leaned back in her chair. "I'm listening."

Now it was Juliana's turn to take a deep breath. She cast one last look at Sal and Héctor.

Then she exhaled.

"Mom, I like girls."

Héctor held his breath as Juliana went still as a statue, her eyes glassy and frightened. A moment passed in silence, and it was agony, because right then, Héctor *needed* to hear something, *anything*. He knew exactly what it was like to reveal your true self to someone and wait for the words to come. He had been there, too, and now, Juliana was all anticipation.

"I know, baby," said Mrs. Chin, and a huge smile spread across her face as her eyes filled with tears. "I've known for a while."

Juliana's mouth dropped open. "Wait—what?" she said. "You *knew?*"

"Honey," said Mrs. Chin, wiping at her eyes, "you

told me last summer that you wanted to marry Janelle Monáe."

"Well . . . yes, that is true," said Juliana, a little embarrassed. "I didn't think you'd think I was *serious*!"

And then Mrs. Chin's arms stretched out, and she beckoned for her daughter. Mrs. Chin's eyes met Héctor's over Juliana's shoulders, and he saw that she was crying.

His parents had cried, too. Papi way more than Mami, actually, and he had said that he would immediately go to war with anyone who hurt his son. "Full warfare," he said. "No holds barred, mijo."

Looking at Juliana and her mom right then, Héctor knew that Mrs. Chin would go to war for her daughter, too.

Mrs. Chin pulled back and wiped at her eyes. "Oh, Juliana, *this* is what Mr. Stafford brought me here for? We could have done this at home!" She sighed, and the tears came back. "Your father will be so thrilled to hear your truth, baby."

Principal Stafford cleared his throat. "Actually, ma'am," he said, "I think your daughter just wanted to be the one to impart that information to you. It's not why you're here."

Mrs. Chin frowned, and her eyebrows rose dramatically. "I don't understand. Then why am I here?"

Here we go, thought Héctor, and then: *I shouldn't be here*. This was too personal, and as the awkward silence filled the room, he wanted to escape. To run out into the hallway and—

But then Sal grabbed his hand and squeezed, and Héctor thought, *No, this is where I* need *to be.*

"Mrs. Chin, your daughter was set to be the DJ for our upcoming fall dance."

"I know," said Mrs. Chin. "She told me all about it. Was all excited to pick out a good playlist. You know she's really good at her transitions, right?"

"I . . . did not know that," he said. "And I'm sorry to have to inform you of this, but Juliana will no longer be the DJ at the upcoming dance."

That frown returned again. "Okay," she said. "Why is that?"

Principal Stafford fidgeted in his seat, and Héctor dreaded what was about to come next. "We have a family environment here we're very proud of," he began.

"Oh, I'm aware," said Mrs. Chin, and she took Juliana's hand in hers. "This school has a wonderful reputation in the community."

"It's just that . . ." Principal Stafford fidgeted in his seat more, and there were now beads of sweat on his shiny bald spot. "Your daughter wanted to bring someone to the dance."

"As I am sure she is allowed to do," shot back Mrs. Chin. "The other students can bring their peers to the dance. Correct?"

"Well, yes, of course," said Principal Stafford. "It's just that your daughter wants to bring someone who . . . who might be . . . well, it's the way that it might *look*, Mrs. Chin."

"Do tell me how it might look, Mr. Stafford." She let go of Juliana's hand, leaned back, and crossed her arms over her chest. "Because it sounds like you're singling out my daughter here."

"No, no, of course we're not," he said, his hands up. "I think we—"

"Is she breaking the rules?"

"No, there's no explicit rule about—"

"So you'll be reinstating her as the DJ and letting her go to the dance with whomever she desires, correct?"

The principal's mouth dropped open, and Héctor's heart felt like it was going to burst out of his chest. No, he was *very* glad that he'd gotten to see this.

"It wasn't fair that you took this away from me," said Juliana, her voice soft at first. But then she looked up at Principal Stafford, and she didn't hold back. Her words were certain and powerful. "You made me feel like I don't belong here."

The principal's face twisted up. "That is not the aim of what we—"

Mrs. Chin stood up. "Come, baby. I think this is resolved, and I'm signing you out of school for the day. Maybe we'll go see a movie. Get some ice cream. And Mr. Stafford won't have a problem with any of that, will he?"

Principal Stafford stood, almost tripping over his own feet while trying to do so. Sal and Héctor did their best to hide their giggling, but when Principal Stafford shot them a glare, he knew they had failed.

"No, not at all," the principal said, and he continued glaring at Héctor and Sal as he shook Mrs. Chin's hand. "I'll keep you updated about any future developments."

"I hope you will," she continued. "And please don't waste my time like this again."

Héctor and Sal darted out of the room first. Personally, Héctor did not want to spend one more moment in that office. Juliana came out holding her mother's hand, and the door shut behind them quickly. Héctor wasn't sure, but he thought he heard Mr. Stafford swearing softly on the other side.

"Do you want to invite your friends to come along?" Mrs. Chin asked Juliana. "As long as we call their parents first and see if they can be signed out."

Panic spread through Héctor. While Mrs. Chin wasn't looking, he shook his head at Juliana.

"Oh, I don't think that's a good idea," she said. "Just not today."

Héctor's eyes went wide.

"Or ever."

He heard Sal suck a breath in quickly.

"Ever?" Mrs. Chin turned to Héctor and Sal, a perplexed look on her face. "Well, I appreciate the two of you sticking up for my daughter. It seems she trusts you both if she wanted you there for that. You *are* welcome over to our house any time you want."

"Thank you, Mrs. Chin," said Héctor, all smiles. (Inside, he was all terror.)

"Give me a moment, Mama?" Juliana said. "Just to say goodbye to them."

Mrs. Chin waved joyously at them all. "Meet me out front," she said, and then she was gone.

The second she was out of sight, Héctor loudly let out a breath. "'Ever'?" he said. "What was that?"

"I don't know!" she said. "It was the only thing I could think of!"

"It's okay," said Sal. "We're safe. And you did it!"

Juliana burst into joyous laughter. "Oh, that was *too* good! Did you see Principal Stafford's face?"

"I honestly thought he was gonna fill the room with his sweat," said Sal.

That sent the three of them into a round of laughter. "Could you imagine?" said Héctor. "We'd have to put floaties on our arms just to survive Principal Stafford's sweat."

"You're so gross!" said Juliana. "Though, to be honest? I kinda thought he was gonna let out a little fart because he was so nervous."

Héctor laughed so hard that he thought his lungs were going to explode.

"Thank you," said Juliana after she recovered. "For being there for me."

"Of course!" said Héctor.

"We wouldn't let you down," said Sal.

Juliana raised an eyebrow, and a terrible silence fell between the two of them.

Sal hung their head. "Juliana, I'm so sorry for what I said." They looked up. "I didn't even think about how bad it sounded. I thought I was actually being caring, but the truth is that I hurt you really bad. I never should have used that word, especially not like that. I'm sorry."

"I know you are," she said, sighing. "And for what it's worth, I appreciate you *actually* apologizing. And not only that, but showing up for me when I really needed it, even though you didn't have to."

"I always will," they said.

"It's just . . . you know, why did you go to 'ghetto' first? That's what hurt the most."

"I assumed," said Sal, hanging their head. "And that's the problem. I should know better, too. People make assumptions based on my appearance all the time."

Juliana nodded her head. "As long as it doesn't happen again."

"I'll do better," Sal promised. "Okay?"

They shook on it, and Héctor had hope that this bump in the road could be repaired. "So . . . what now?" he asked. "Because Sal and I are still thousands of miles from home."

Sal's eyes went as big as plates. "Oh. Right."

"I don't know," said Juliana. "I assume the Room will let you go home?"

As if on cue, Sal pointed behind Héctor. "Is *that* what it looks like to either of you?"

There, between the staff bathroom and another office, was a door.

JANITOR.

"That's *my* door," said Héctor, and a swell of pride rose in his chest. "I guess it's time to go home."

He waved to Juliana and Sal, then opened the door

and stepped through. The Room was a janitor's closet. He greeted King Ferdinand, closed the door, took a breath, then opened it again.

The clock in the hallway of Orangevale Middle School read 8:14 a.m.

Héctor ran. It didn't matter if Ms. Heath called his name at that moment, because *nothing* could stop him.

CHAPTER TWENTY-SEVEN

Somehow, Héctor was supposed to have a normal school day after that.

His classes happened. That was the best way he could think about it. He may have learned something in them, but who could tell? All he could think about was the Room. Juliana. Sal. The unbelievable absurdity of it all.

Except it wasn't unbelievable because *it really happened*.

At lunch, he did his best not to think *too* much about the Room. It wasn't that hard, since as soon as he sat down, Taylor offered up his theory that all fruit on the planet wasn't really fruit. "I think aliens planted them here."

"That makes no sense," said Jackson, aggressively taking a bite of his apple. "This thing is *delicious*."

"That's what they *want* you to think," said Taylor.

"Why is that?" Héctor asked.

"So that you'll eat more."

Aishah shook her head. "Okay . . . and then what?"

"And then have lots of their alien babies."

At first, they all burst out laughing, but Taylor stopped. "You don't think I'm right?"

"No!" said Héctor. "If you think fruit is nothing but alien eggs, why haven't we seen any aliens yet? Fruit has been around for like . . . a million years or something."

Taylor narrowed his eyes. "Maybe they already *are* among us."

"Sometimes, I don't think *you* are from planet Earth," said Aishah, pointing a colored pencil at Taylor. "How do you think of these things?"

"Maybe you should write them down," said Héctor. He cleared his throat. "I have a . . . a friend. Who really likes science fiction stories. Maybe they would read them."

"Well, my stories wouldn't be *science fiction*," said Taylor, hesitant. "They would be history books."

"Sure," said Héctor, nodding sympathetically. "They'd still read them, though."

Taylor smiled and pulled out a notebook from his backpack, then furiously began to scribble things down on the page.

"Who's your friend?" asked Aishah, as she continued to work on her drawing. "Someone we know?"

When Jackson locked eyes with Héctor, Héctor felt a flash of panic jolt through him. "Oh, someone from my old school," he lied.

Jackson nodded. "Dope."

Héctor quickly changed the subject. "Are you working on the project that's due today, Aishah? Can I see?"

"The artist is not ready to display her work," she said dramatically. "The artist thinks she needs more time."

Héctor laughed. "So we're referring to ourselves in the third person now?"

Aishah raised her chin up. "The artist shall not respond to such rude questions."

Jackson cackled. "Well, then we *must* respect the artist."

She smiled, then passed her sketchbook over to Héctor.

He was not ashamed of the gasp that escaped from him. Aishah was . . . whoa, she was *really* good. She'd drawn a river scene that looked almost like a photo. There were two kids in the center of it, clearly frolicking in the water, and he could even see tiny droplets on their skin.

"Aishah!" he said. "This is . . . *this* is what you think needs more time?"

She shrugged. "I dunno. I don't think my shading techniques are that good." She pointed to some pine trees on the far side of the river. "See how these look too bright? It makes it seem like the sun is shining from the wrong direction."

Both Jackson and Taylor were now huddled around the drawing, and all three of them slowly looked up at Aishah.

"Yo, this is . . . ," Héctor said, then shook his head. "I don't even know what to say."

"Seriously," said Taylor. "Can I hire you to illustrate my alien invasion history book? I can pay you in Capri Sun."

Aishah couldn't help but laugh at that. "We'll talk, Taylor," she said. "Y'all really think this is good?"

"Yes!" Héctor cried out. "You're *amazing.*"

The bell that signaled the end of lunch rang, and everyone gathered up their trays. Aishah's food sat uneaten, though. "Not hungry?" he asked.

"Nah," she said. "I'm too nervous. What if Mrs. Caroline doesn't think this is good enough?"

"Oh, I *really* don't think you have to worry about that," he said. "Trust me. You're fine."

The two said goodbye to Taylor and Jackson, and as they walked to Mrs. Caroline's class, Aishah told Héctor what she wanted to do with her art: draw comics.

"But not like superhero stuff," she explained. "I have this idea of this older hijabi who lives in the forest and has for a long, long time, and she's made friends with all the creatures who live there. And I just wanna draw, like . . . stories. Of how she survives."

"Wow," he said. "I would read that."

"Really?" she said, raising a brow at him. "I never thought anyone else would find it interesting."

"Well, I disagree—"

He didn't get to finish. The door swung open so fast in front of them that Héctor actually yelped in fright.

There stood Mike, thankfully by himself, and the first thing he did was twist his face and imitate the sound Héctor had made.

Ugh, Héctor thought. *I can't even escape him in Mrs. Caroline's class?*

"What are *you* two doing here?" Mike sneered.

Aishah rolled her eyes. "Going to class."

Suddenly, Mrs. Caroline appeared behind Mike. "Ah, welcome, Aishah, Héctor!" she said, and she seemed genuinely thrilled. "So lovely to see you, and I am so excited for what you will share with me today."

Then she looked from Héctor to Mike. "Oh, Héctor! Have you met Mike? Mike is in my second period, but sometimes, he joins me at lunch to work on his technique."

Héctor did his best not to let his face betray how he felt.

"He's really turning out to be a talented artist," she continued, oblivious to the rage pulsing through

Héctor. "Maybe you two could learn something from one another?"

A mean, petty thought filled his head: *Who CARES if Mike does art?*

But he was smart enough not to say that aloud. He smiled at Mrs. Caroline and nodded. "Yeah, we've met."

Mike brushed by Héctor, barely grazing his shoulder. "See you around, Heck-tor," he said, and Héctor swore he could hear the tiniest bit of malice in Mike's voice.

His heart was still thumping as he and Aishah took their seats. She tapped him on the shoulder while other kids came into the room. "You okay?" she asked.

"I'll be fine," he said. "He's gone."

"I can't believe she asked you that!" Aishah whispered. "Like, she has no idea, but *still.*"

Maybe he should have told her the truth. But *when?* Certainly not in front of Mike, when Mrs. Caroline had asked if they knew each other. Oh, they *more* than knew each other. Practically best friends!

Héctor wanted back in the Room. It seemed to be the only place in the whole world where he had no problems at all.

CHAPTER TWENTY-EIGHT

The events of that day followed Héctor home. He was thinking about them when his mami picked him up, and he was sure she noticed that he wasn't really listening to her, that all his answers were one-word responses. He was thinking about them while he struggled with his math and history homework at the dinner table, all while Abuela Sonia and Mami chopped vegetables and cilantro, throwing them in a steaming pot that smelled better and better each minute. And they were still swirling around in his head when Papi joined them at the table and they began dinner.

Everyone was so chipper and eager to talk that night, and Héctor just pushed his spoon around in his caldo de res, listening to his family gossip about their relatives in Mexico. His thoughts pulled him from one direction to another.

Did someone make *the Room? Or has it always existed?*

Is it possible that someone is watching us? That one creeped Héctor out a lot, so he tossed it aside.

Why now? And why is all of this happening to me?

He had no idea. Was there some lesson he was supposed to learn from all of this? If so, he'd prefer it if someone just *told* him the lesson.

Why is everything so complicated? It was never this bad back in San Francisco.

He sat with that thought for a while. He didn't think he was being overdramatic. His life in San Francisco hadn't been perfect, but he had close friends. He loved school, loved being in theater, loved singing random songs in the hallways.

He thought he'd found his people here in Aishah, Jackson, and Taylor, but they weren't *best* friends. Juliana and Sal, on the other hand . . . well, Héctor could see that happening. But *how*? Juliana and Sal lived thousands of miles away from him. How did you become best friends with someone you could only see through a magical room?

And . . . what would happen if he *lost* it?

"Nieto, are you even hungry?" said Abuela.

"Lo siento," he said, and he spooned some of the soup into his mouth. It was perfect as usual.

"Él estaba en el otro mundo," said Mami. "Always in that head of his."

"Not always!" he said, and now, he was devouring his

· 215 ·

food. "It's just been a long day."

"You don't have to tell me," said Mami. "We had to suspend a kid today."

That got Héctor's interest. He loved hearing about awful kids at other schools. It was like a free lesson in what *not* to do. "Tell me!"

"It's . . . silly," she said, dismissing Héctor with a wave. "It wasn't that bad."

"Oh, come *on*!" Héctor pouted over his bowl. "Please?"

"Okay, just this once," said Mami, and Héctor nearly leaped out of his chair. "But you better not get any ideas."

"Ideas?" Now he was confused, and he wrinkled up his forehead. "What does that mean?"

She sighed deeply and closed her eyes. "I cannot stress this enough: Please don't do this at school, Héctor."

He put a hand to his heart and raised the other up. "I swear, Mami."

"We had a student today who was . . . disruptive."

"And?" said Héctor.

"Well, he brought one of those red-and-white things to school. It's like a sphere? A ball? You know, it's from that game where you catch cute little animals?"

Héctor's mouth dropped open. "A *Pokéball*?"

"Yes, *that* thing. And he kept throwing it at students. Trying to catch them."

Héctor was lost in another fit of laughter, and he

nearly choked. Abuela kept patting him on the back. "Ay, no lo entiendo," she said. "What does that mean?"

"Trust me," said Héctor, once he recovered. "It's the best thing I've ever heard."

Just like that, Héctor's foul mood was gone. They all finished dinner and Héctor helped clean up. Afterward, he thought about texting his old San Francisco friends. But he wrote a text. Erased it. Wrote another. It had been days since the group chat was active. How could he just pop back up with *this* story? Would they even find it funny? He frowned at his phone. Why was this so hard?

Maybe that's okay, he thought, and he plopped down on his bed. *Maybe it's fine if I focus on making friends here.*

That was his final thought as he fell into sleep with a full belly and a full heart.

He drifted into a dream.

He was in a hallway. It looked a little like Swifton Middle School, but the walls were just . . . wrong. He couldn't figure it out. They seemed *too* shiny. Too high. Too far apart. But he sped down the halls, turning here and there, trying to find the door. But each time he flung himself around a corner, a longer corridor awaited him. All the classroom doors were open, but no one was inside them. He called out Juliana's name. Sal's name. Héctor's high-pitched voice echoed back at him.

No one was there.

He rushed down another hallway, and there, at the end of it, was the door: JANITOR. He ran faster, his feet pounding against the tile. Was the Room moving *farther* away with each step? No, that couldn't be. The Room would *never* do that to him.

He stopped. Turned to his left. And there it was, the same frosted glass as always, and Héctor yanked it open, so desperate for the relief that place always gave him, and—

No.

Not the Room.

There was Mrs. Caroline, hunched over a desk, deep in conversation with another student.

It was Mike.

And when Mike saw Héctor, he raised a finger and pointed it right at him.

"I can't work with *him* here!" he cried out, and then Mrs. Caroline was advancing toward Héctor, moving closer and closer, but there was no joy on her face, no kind greeting on her tongue. She was *scowling* at him. Héctor tripped over his feet as he tried to back up and leave. He landed hard on the tile, and his heart was in his throat.

"You're ruining the creative energy in here," said Mrs.

Caroline, and she pointed her finger in his face. "I can't have that."

"But . . . but I—" Héctor stuttered the words out. How could she do this to him? Didn't she enjoy having him in class?

He scrambled backward, unable to stand up, and so he rolled over and out into the hallway and pushed himself up. Then he was running, running toward the cafeteria, and her voice echoed all around him.

"No running in the hallways, Mr. Muñoz!"

Héctor glanced behind him, and Ms. Heath was *sprinting*, moving way faster than a human should. He screamed and flung himself around the corner, shoved his way through the double doors into the cafeteria and—

All the tables were gone but one: the Table of Misfits. There, surrounding Mike, were Taylor, Aishah, Jackson, and Carmen.

"Ocupado," said Carmen, moving her tray over to the empty space to her left.

"Find another table," said Jackson. "We don't *like* theater kids here."

But there were no other tables. Héctor approached the Table of Misfits in a panic. "Please, guys, I'm being chased by—"

He looked down.

Aishah was *drawing* him.

It was a stunning likeness, but . . .

She had completely blacked out his eyes.

"You're not from this world, are you?" asked Taylor. *"Are you?"*

Héctor ran. It was all he knew.

Mike's cackling rang out in the cafeteria, and it seemed to follow him into the hallway. "Stop it!" Héctor cried out. "Leave me alone!"

Silence.

Héctor froze. He was completely alone in the hallway.

He spun around, and the janitor's closet was right there, so close that he could touch it.

Finally, he thought. *Some relief.*

He twisted the handle, pushed the door open, and—

No. This was *wrong*.

There were people there. Sitting on *his* couch. Playing *his* games. Drinking *his* horchata.

No!

Mike.

Frank.

Carlos.

They laughed. They roughhoused with one another while playing *Smash Bros*. Héctor screamed at them, but they didn't react, didn't look back at him.

They couldn't hear him at all.

He rushed forward, stood right in front of the television, waved his arms back and forth.

They kept playing. Kept laughing. Kept ignoring him.

Héctor held his hand up in front of his face, or at least what he *thought* was his hand.

There was nothing there.

Because Héctor was invisible.

Until Mike looked at him. *Directly* at him. Smiled.

"This isn't yours," he said, his grin spreading. "It never *has* been."

Héctor woke up then, covered in sweat, his heart racing. He flipped over and screamed into his pillow, long and fierce. When he couldn't scream anymore, he lay there, his breath heaving his chest up and down. He wished this all wasn't so hard. No one ever told you how *tiring* it was not to fit in.

He passed out again, and this time, he slept without dreaming.

CHAPTER TWENTY-NINE

Héctor hesitantly stepped through the double doors at school the next morning. The images from his dream flashed in his mind, and he gulped down his anxiety. *That didn't actually happen,* he told himself. *Mike isn't going to be in the Room. EVER.*

But he needed to duck inside and see his friends, to make sure that the place was still theirs.

Apparently, Héctor didn't actually *need* the Room, because he never found it. Who judged that? Who decided that what he was feeling that morning wasn't strong enough?

He went to class full of a quiet bitterness. He moved from one class to another, and he took notes, and he listened, but was any of it sticking? Was any of it important?

His foul mood carried over to lunch. He tried to participate in the Misfits' conversation, but they were arguing over which video game console was best, and Héctor owned none of them. He mostly stayed quiet, at least until just before lunch ended. Jackson put his hand on top of Héctor's. "Hey, man," Jackson said, loud enough so only Héctor could hear. "You okay?"

Héctor shook his head, comfortable enough telling Jackson that much of the truth.

"I'm sorry," said Jackson, squeezing Héctor's hand.

The moment passed, but Héctor still felt like a robot, like someone else had programmed him and he was running on auto. Without a word, he stood up and left Aishah behind. He needed time to think.

Alone.

He wanted the Room back. He wanted to get out of this slow-moving nightmare. Not even a particularly cheerful Mrs. Caroline could rip him from his sadness, especially with that image from his nightmare: his art teacher angrily lunging at him. He worked on a new pastel for a while, but the image he was trying to capture—a photo of Stow Lake in Golden Gate Park—felt wrong. Warped. The colors were off, and in the last couple minutes, he scratched over all of it with black. You could only see the outlines of what used to be there.

Mrs. Caroline said she loved it, that it was a *very* emotional piece. He wasn't exactly sure that it was worth any praise, but he thanked her.

He moved through the hallways after his last class was over, his mind a mess. He couldn't stop the rush of thoughts, either. He had done a good thing the day before, so why was it so hard for him to just be *happy*?

Creeeeaaaaaak.

Héctor looked up suddenly, and there, just to the left, was *the* door. His heart flared in anticipation as he raced toward it, unsure why the Room had shown up *now*.

He tore it open.

And looked upon a janitor's closet.

Not even *his* janitor's closet. He looked up into the corner—no King Ferdinand.

What?

"Yo, Hector!"

His stomach dropped.

"That's where you belong, isn't it?"

The others—Carlos and Frank—laughed at that as Mike strolled up to Héctor, a black garbage bag in his hand. The bag looked full. Héctor gave an educated guess: *I bet it's full of garbage.*

"Not today, Mike," said Héctor, his shoulders sagging. "Please."

"Aw, Mike, you're making him *sad*," Frank teased. "You don't want that, do you?"

Mike narrowed his eyes at Héctor, and for the briefest moment, Héctor believed that this boy wouldn't go ahead with whatever he had planned.

But then his lips curled up at the edges. "Well, it's a good thing we found you here, Hector," he said. "You know your people are good at cleaning things up!"

Two things happened then. The first was obvious: Mike lifted the bag up and dumped a pile of smelly, moist garbage all over Héctor, laughing all the while.

But then Carlos socked Mike on the arm immediately afterward.

"Bruh, what was *that* for?!" Mike shouted.

Héctor couldn't believe what he was seeing. He also couldn't ignore the sensation of the remains of today's pasta and meatballs dripping down his back.

"Why'd you go and say that?" said Carlos, his eyebrows smashed together in anger. "What did you mean by 'your people'?"

The sound of Carlos and Mike yelling had grabbed the attention of other kids, who were drifting closer. Frank stood off to the side, his mouth open in surprise. It was obvious to Héctor that Frank didn't know what to do if Mike wasn't ordering him around.

"Who cares?" said Mike, stepping closer to Carlos. "You got a problem?"

More kids arrived, and Jackson and Aishah pushed through the gathering crowd to stand next to Héctor. No one seemed to mind them trying to get closer to the action, but then he noticed that none of the other kids were even paying attention to him anymore. They were all watching Mike and Carlos.

"You shouldn't have said that, Mike," said Carlos, and then *he* took a step closer.

"Man," said Mike, "it's just a joke. Chill."

"Yeah, he didn't mean anything by it," added Frank. "Why you gotta be such a loser about this?"

Carlos cast a quick glance at Héctor, locking eyes with him. Was Carlos trying to find someone to back him up? Héctor and Carlos had never really spoken to one another, but the unstated truth was hanging between them: *He meant Mexicans*, thought Héctor.

Despite having no reason to help Carlos, Héctor gave Carlos the tiniest nod.

"I'm not a loser," said Carlos, glaring at Frank, and then he turned back to Mike. "Don't say something like that again."

"Or *what*?" said Mike, scoffing at him. "What are you gonna do?"

Héctor held his breath, unsure if this was about to get physical.

Carlos shook his head. "Man, y'all are wack," he said.

Just as Héctor was about to let out his breath, Carlos turned and walked straight up to him. Héctor's heart fluttered and he backed up a few steps. He flinched as Carlos raised a hand.

But all Carlos did was remove a banana peel from

Héctor's shoulder and let it fall to the floor.

Then he was gone.

Uncertainty bloomed in the silence. Héctor looked around at the gathered crowd, and no one said anything. When he made eye contact with Aishah, she shrugged, as if to say, *I don't get it either.*

Then Mike shook his head. "You better clean up your mess, *Hector*," he said, hissing his name.

No one else said anything, and the crowd dispersed. Héctor brushed more of the trash off himself, still reeling. Had he *actually* just seen Carlos stand up to Mike?

"Come on, Héctor," said Jackson, putting a hand on his one clean shoulder. "I'll help you get cleaned up in the bathroom."

"Wait, really?" said Héctor.

Jackson nodded. "I walk home from here. It's okay if I'm late."

"You got this?" Aishah asked Jackson.

"Yeah, most def," he said.

"I'll see you both tomorrow," she said. "My mom is waiting for me outside." Then, after a pause: "I'm sorry he won't leave you alone."

Then she ran off.

Héctor picked at something slimy on his arm. "I really thought it couldn't get worse," he said. "And now look."

Jackson didn't respond to that. He guided Héctor to the boys' room, but they only made it a few steps before *her* voice stopped them.

"Mr. Muñoz!"

This day truly cannot get worse, Héctor thought. *But apparently it's about to!*

He and Jackson turned, and Ms. Heath strode up to them. Today's tracksuit: the all-yellow one. Kinda resembled the banana peel that Carlos had picked off him.

Ms. Heath examined the pile of garbage at his feet and the stains over his clothing.

"Mr. Jackson, why are you not leaving campus?"

Jackson's eyes went wide. "Well, I have to help Héctor with—"

"There is no loitering after the final bell rings," she interrupted. "You know the rules."

"But Ms. Heath, it's not fair that—"

"Would you like to debate fairness with me in detention tomorrow afternoon?"

Jackson sighed. "No, ma'am."

She pointed down the hallway. Didn't say *anything*.

"Sorry," said Jackson, and with a small wave, he left Héctor behind.

Ms. Heath then focused on Héctor, who was doing

his best not to let his anger show. "I hesitate to ask why, but . . . *why* are you standing in a pile of trash?"

He sighed. He could give Ms. Heath the truth, but would she even care?

"If you're thinking of concocting some bizarre story again, save it."

Well, that answered that.

"I just had an accident, that's all," he said, and even as the words left his mouth, he knew how *terrible* that lie sounded.

Ms. Heath clicked her tongue against her teeth. "Please clean up after yourself and the floor before you leave."

And she walked away.

Clean up after himself? He wanted to punch the wall. He had *never* had an urge like that, but Ms. Heath . . . ugh, why was she like this? Did she think he'd dumped garbage on himself? Who would do something like that?

It felt so painfully obvious to Héctor that he was being bullied. Trash! There was trash all over him!

A creak echoed in the now-empty hallway.

The door to the janitor's closet inched open.

Wiping his filthy hand on his jeans, Héctor then gently pulled on the handle. Would he have to face his friends in this state?

It was the Room, all right. But this time, it had fashioned itself into . . . well, it looked like a fancy dressing room. To the left was a rack with clothing hanging on it, and Héctor did a double take. The black T-shirts and jeans were the *exact* ones he was wearing, as were the solid black Chucks.

And to the right was . . . a shower. Tall and shining, with one of those showerheads that hung directly above and let water fall on you like rainfall.

"Really?!" Héctor yelled. "*Now* you show up?"

The Room did not reply.

He let the door close behind him and began to peel off his ruined clothes, thankful that he wasn't going to have to explain this mess to anyone else.

Mess.

Oh *no*.

He quickly pulled down his dirty T-shirt and opened the door, certain he would see Ms. Heath standing over the garbage that Mike had dumped on him, ready to send him to detention.

There was no garbage on the ground anymore.

He didn't question it. He shut the door, and soon, the warm water was pouring over his head, calming his nerves. He toweled himself dry, got dressed in an identical set of clothing, and headed out of the Room. As soon as the door closed, he realized that he'd been deposited directly across from the exit to the school.

Perfect location, he supposed.

But not perfect enough to stop this nightmare from unfolding.

He rode home in Papi's car in a terrible, bitter silence.

CHAPTER THIRTY

The next morning, Héctor realized that he had yelled at the Room. Like it could speak back. Out of context, it seemed ridiculous.

But Héctor's frustration wasn't. No, he was definitely tired: tired of running away from his bullies, tired of hiding, tired of *feeling* tired. And for once, the Room *didn't* seem to be helping him, not when he needed it most.

So when he stood outside the door before homeroom, his anger boiled over.

Why? he asked the Room silently. *Why do you show up when you do?!*

He actually wanted to scream those words out loud, but then he thought how that would look. He was already unpopular at school. Why add "Yells at doors" to the list of uncool things about Héctor Muñoz?

Yet as soon as he got inside, all his frustration washed away. Sal stood up quickly from the couch, wiping at their face. "Sorry," they said. "I didn't think anyone would be here today."

Héctor rushed over to them. "What's wrong, Sal?" he said. "You okay?"

"Nothing, nothing," they said. "Don't worry about it."

Héctor sat on the couch and patted the spot next to him. "Oh no, boo," he said. "We are *not* doing that again."

"Doing what?" said Sal.

"This whole song and dance! Remember when Juliana tried it? You can talk to me, I *promise*. About anything."

Sal sat down next to Héctor, but didn't talk at first. Héctor waited patiently; he didn't want to push Sal to say anything. Soon, though, their lip curled and quivered, and then the tears came, spilling down Sal's face.

"Do you want a hug?" Héctor asked.

Sal mostly coughed out an affirmation, and Héctor held them. "I'm sorry you're going through something," he said. "If there's anything I can do, I'm here."

"That's the worst part," sobbed Sal. "You literally *can't* do anything."

"Why is that?"

Sal leaned away and took a few deep breaths to calm down. "I didn't think they'd actually do it," they said. "But I got to school this morning, and the trucks were already there."

Héctor scratched at his head. "I don't get it."

"They didn't close down my library," said Sal, and the tears came back again. "They *tore* it down."

"What? Like . . . *literally* tore it down?"

Sal nodded. "No one could save it. They boxed up all the books, stuck them in some ugly metal container out behind the gym, and then . . . I don't know. The building is just *gone*."

Héctor shook his head. "Why destroy the whole building?"

Sal sniffled. "To make more room for the athletic fields. Or at least, that's what they told us."

"I'm so sorry," he said.

Sal wiped at their face again. "You know, some of us tried to save it. My parents are great; they got a bunch of other parents to sign a petition, and there was this big meeting with the school board or something last month. I even threw a bake sale last week, but . . ." Sal sighed. "None of it was enough."

None of it was enough.

That was too relatable for Héctor, though for entirely different reasons. Everything he tried to do to resolve his own problem—tell Ms. Heath the truth, stand up to Mike and his Minions, make new friends—wasn't solving anything. The same nightmare remained.

None of it was enough.

"Well," said Héctor, "why don't you just use the Room when you need the library?"

"It's not the same," said Sal. "Plus, I can't control when

it shows up. What happens if I need the library but can't find the Room?"

"Oh, that's a good point," said Héctor.

"So I need something else." Sal sighed. "I just don't know what that is."

Sal leaned their head until it rested on Héctor's shoulder. Why didn't he have any answers? He felt so helpless.

"Sometimes, the world stinks," said Héctor. "And I wish I could fix everything for you."

"I know," said Sal. "And I know things haven't been easy for you, either. I hope I'm not being weird about all of this."

"Not at all! Why would you think that?"

"After yesterday," Sal said, "I just want to be more careful. That's all."

"I appreciate that," said Héctor. "You want some horchata? It always makes me feel a *little* better."

Sal nodded, and then Héctor was up and at the fridge, pouring a glass. Sal took it and downed half the drink in a few gulps. "At least I have this Room," they said. "I can still come here to read."

As Héctor watched Sal drink his abuela's horchata down, he wondered if Sal had told anyone else about what they were going through. Maybe this had been as hard for them to talk about as it had been for Héctor.

Héctor's curiosity pushed him forward. "I hope I'm

not being pushy or anything, but . . ." He stopped, then sighed. He refilled Sal's glass. "Do you not really have friends at your school? Or someone you hang out with?"

Sal shook their head. "Not really," they said. "I mean, I'm not getting picked on like you are. It's mostly that people just ignore me. I'm not very popular. It's like . . ." Sal went quiet for a moment. "It's like what I said before. I confuse people so much that they treat me like I'm not there. Because I guess that's easier for them."

Héctor nodded. "So it's like . . . like, no one has to worry about getting your pronouns right or anything because they're just not talking to you at *all*."

Sal's eyes went wide in recognition. "Yeah. Yeah! That's exactly it."

But then they smiled. "Except Ms. Pérez. She was the librarian. She's really great. Lets me read anything I want, and sometimes, she'll order books that we don't have."

Their smile evaporated, though, and Sal fell into silence. Oh, Héctor *hated* this! Why did things have to be so challenging for Sal? For Juliana? For Héctor?

But, once again, there wasn't really anything to do, right? They'd definitely helped Juliana, but this . . . this felt too big, too complicated. Héctor remembered something he'd overheard his mom say on the phone once:

"This sounds above my pay grade." *That* is what this seemed like.

The two sat in an awkward silence before Héctor nudged Sal with his shoulder. "Come here whenever you want," he said. "I think you deserve to have your own space."

Sal stood and told Héctor that they had to head to class, but before they left, they put their arms around him. "Thank you," they said. "For listening. And being nice. It's good to know I have you as a friend."

He watched Sal leave, and he knew for certain that Sal was his friend.

That was a nice thing to know.

Héctor had a lot on his mind as he wrenched open the Room's door, wishing he could just stay here all day and skip school completely. But that thought vanished instantly.

It was dark beyond the doorway.

Real dark.

He shut the door, opened it again.

Nothing changed.

He took a tentative step forward into the darkness and saw faint lines of light coming through a broken set of window blinds to the right side of the room. There were a few desks, upturned and resting on the ground, and one larger desk on the opposite side. *Must be where the teacher sits*, he thought. Because this sure *looked* like a classroom. There was some sort of homework tacked up to one wall, but the edges of it had peeled up, as if it had been there a long, long time.

He took another step forward, then another, then ran a finger over one of the student desks. It was gritty, and even in the dim light, he could see that his finger was covered in a thick layer of dust.

Where *was* he?

Héctor coughed again. There was a bookshelf back behind the larger desk, though one of its shelves had collapsed.

Why had the Room sent Héctor *here*?

He got close enough to see in the dim light that the shelf was stacked with copies of a mathematics textbook. Okay, so this definitely *was* a school. He picked up a copy, which sent another wave of dust into the air. Once Héctor stopped coughing, he flipped open the cover.

There was a stamp on the inside of the cover used to keep track of who had borrowed a book. What it said didn't make sense.

He turned around and rushed over to one of the windows, searching for the long cord that would open the blinds. He found it and tugged on it, and searing light spilled into the room, so bright and hot that Héctor had to close his eyes.

When he opened them and his sight adjusted, he saw two tractors on a field, about thirty feet or so from the window, right next to an enormous pile of rubble and debris. Was that—?

It had to be. He looked back down at the stamp inside the book:

SAGUARO ACADEMY

This was *Sal's* school.

Okay, okay, he could deal with this! This had happened before. The Room had made him and Sal go to Swifton to help Juliana. So, here he was! At Sal's school! Maybe the Room had an idea about how he could help them.

But . . . in a long-abandoned classroom? What was he supposed to do here?

He spun back around. There was an old wastebasket sitting on its side. A pile of crumpled-up papers spilled out of it. Two of the desks had broken legs, and under them, he found another stack of old crusty textbooks.

And then Héctor knew exactly what he needed to do.

He dropped the book and ran back to the Room,

shutting the door for one moment before opening it again.

No!

The halls of Orangevale Middle School greeted him.

"No, this isn't what I need!" he said, and this time, he didn't care that he was saying it aloud. "I need Sal, *now*!"

He tried opening and closing the door a few times, but he was always back at his own school.

Héctor hit his forehead with an open hand. Why hadn't he gotten Sal's phone number? Then at least he could have texted them!

The bell for homeroom rang out, and Héctor groaned. *Later*, he told himself. *I'll come back to the Room and hopefully Juliana will be there. She'll want to help. I have to do this!*

Héctor rushed off to class, his heart alight with possibility. He was going to make this work.

CHAPTER THIRTY-ONE

Unfortunately, Héctor's plan was delayed.

When Héctor went looking for it again, the Room was nowhere to be found. Thankfully, Mike and the Minions (was it *Minion*, now that Carlos had told Mike off?) left him alone, too; perhaps that was why the Room never bothered to show up. It wasn't there when he tried to find it after Mrs. Caroline's class on Thursday, nor did it appear when he asked Mr. Holiday if he could leave a few minutes before the end of gym on Friday.

And since it was Friday, he wouldn't be able to look for it again until Monday. That weekend, he was restless and nervous. He was mostly stuck at home, too, jumping from one assignment to another. But his attention kept drifting, and it sometimes felt impossible for him to concentrate on anything.

He could barely stay still at dinner Sunday night, and he stuffed himself with four tamales in under fifteen minutes. "Nieto, I see your hunger waits for no one tonight," Abuela said. "I know you like my tamales, pero . . ."

"Just . . . feeling better," he said.

And it wasn't a lie.

"Well, you know what I always say." Abuela smiled from ear to ear.

"Oh, I do," said Papi. "Barriga llena—"

"—corazón contento," Abuela finished.

Okay, yes, he did have a full stomach. But was his heart *content*?

No. Not yet. By that evening, Héctor was certain the Room wouldn't keep him from his friends. His idea to help Sal was too good, and they *needed* it!

When Monday morning finally rolled around, he was all nerves as he arrived at school. Unfortunately, he didn't find the Room before the first bell. After English was over, he knew he had a few minutes before his pre-algebra class started at nine forty-five. Rushing past Mike, who called something out that Héctor did not hear, he sent a silent request into the school:

I need Sal and Juliana.

He turned round the nearest corner.

And there it was.

Just where he needed it.

Héctor gleefully burst into the Room to find Juliana and Sal there, playing *Smash Bros.* on the couch. "Yo, Héctor," said Juliana, her hand over her heart. "You scared me. You okay?"

Héctor didn't answer—he went straight to Sal and knelt before them.

"I know what we can do."

Sal looked to Juliana. "Do *you* know what he's talking about?"

She shook her head. "Why all the dramatics, Héctor?"

He fell backward, his hand palm out and over his forehead. "You haven't *seen* drama yet," he said, and he grinned wide as his friends laughed. "Because I came up with the most dramatic solution to *your* problem, Sal."

Sal raised an eyebrow. "I don't know," they said. "It's okay. I appreciate you thinking about me, but it's pointless. The library is already gone."

"Which is precisely where you're wrong," said Héctor, rising up from the floor. "This whole time, you've been worried about saving your library when instead, you could just *move* it."

"Move it?" Now Sal was scowling at Héctor. "I can't *move* a library."

"Not by yourself, no, but with some help from your wonderful friends and a magical room"—he spread his arms out to gesture at himself, Juliana, and the Room—"it's *totally* possible."

"Where do you move a library to, Héctor?" asked Juliana. "It's . . . well, a library! They're *huge*!"

He took a deep breath. This *had better work*, he thought.

A moment later, he was at the door. "You put it *here*," he said, and he really, really hoped that he had not screwed this up. He yanked the door open.

Juliana and Sal rose from the couch and walked over to him. "Héctor, what *is* this place?" said Juliana. She let Sal go first, and then Héctor heard them gasp.

"No way," they said.

"Sal, you know what this place is?" asked Juliana.

"The abandoned math classroom," they said, their eyes wide. "Oh, why didn't I think of this? Ms. Pérez will be so *happy*!"

"Who is that?" said Juliana.

"My English teacher, who was also the librarian," said Sal, and their face lit up while they talked about her. "Oh, you'd both love her. She's so funny and she always recommends the best books. She's been running a mini library out of her class, but it's just not the same."

"Perfect," said Héctor. "I bet she'll love it. You can tell her after we're done."

"We?" Juliana put her hands on her hips. "You want us to move all the books into this dirty classroom ourselves?"

"Well, why wait for someone else to say no?" said Héctor. "Isn't it a better idea to just do it ourselves?"

"I don't know," said Sal. "*How*? It's really, really far from that storage container to this room. We can't carry all those books *and* do it during school. We'll get caught."

Here it was: the moment where Héctor's plan *had* to come together, or this would all fall apart.

"So we *don't*," he said, relishing in the drama of this next reveal. He closed the door to the Room.

Opened it again.

Warm air rushed in.

Juliana and Sal gasped.

And it was oh so satisfying.

"Remember my theory about what we need?" Héctor asked. "Well, I've been thinking about it a lot, and I think Sal *needs* this."

His friends stepped out into the balmy night air of Phoenix, Arizona. Héctor watched them look upward, and he did it too, gazing up at the stars that twinkled in the dark sky. And there, sitting on the field in front of them, was a metal storage container, illuminated by moonlight.

"Is it the middle of the night?" Juliana said. "Héctor, you might need to pinch me."

"You are not imagining this," said Héctor, silently relieved that this had worked.

Sal pointed at the container. "That's where they're keeping the books. Which means . . ."

They turned around to gaze at Héctor. He stood triumphantly in the doorway of the Room, which had appeared on the *outside* of a building.

"Which means my plan worked," Héctor said. "And we're gonna get your library back."

CHAPTER THIRTY-TWO

"Pinch me, please," said Juliana.

Héctor stepped toward her.

"Actually, never mind," she said, immediately stepping back. "I forgot I don't like pinching." She looked back up at the night sky.

"I told you," said Héctor. "I had a plan."

"But . . . did we travel in time?" Juliana paced back and forth. "Are we in the past or the future?"

"Uhhhh . . . I guess I didn't think about that," said Héctor. "Does it really matter? The Room always seems to put us back when we—I mean, *where* we need to be."

"It *is* a lot to wrap my mind around," said Sal. "But there's a problem you *didn't* consider, Héctor."

Héctor watched as Sal walked up to the metal container and grabbed a giant silver padlock. They pulled on it, then let it fall back down, where it banged loudly on the metal.

"This container is locked," they said. "And none of us have the key."

Juliana placed a hand on Héctor's shoulder. "It was a good idea while it lasted."

But he squirmed away from her. "No, this could still work! Sal, who would have a key for this?"

"Honestly?" said Sal. "Well, I know that the janitor has one, since he was mainly the person who had to box up and store all the books. And Mr. Mbalia probably has one too. He's the head of security."

"I just want to state out loud that I think this is now turning into a bad idea," said Juliana. "Isn't there an easier way to solve this?"

"I don't know," said Héctor.

"Well," she said, "have you considered that maybe the Room won't let us *steal* something?"

Héctor frowned. "Actually . . . no. But it's worth a shot to see if we can get the keys." When Juliana raised an eyebrow at him, he added, "It's for a good cause! Maybe the two things cancel each other out?"

"That kinda makes sense," said Sal. "And it's not like we'll be stealing anything. We're just . . . borrowing them? Right?"

"See!" said Héctor.

"I'm not sold, but . . . we can try," said Juliana. "As long as we don't get in trouble."

"Then let me compromise: if the Room doesn't let us get the keys, we'll rethink this. Deal?"

After a moment, both Sal and Juliana nodded.

"Excellent," said Héctor. "Then phase two of Operation Save the Library is in effect!" He rushed back into the Room and beckoned for the others to follow him.

"So, now we giving these things names?" said Juliana. "What was *my* mission the other day called?"

"Well, it all happened so quickly," said Héctor. "So we didn't get to the naming part."

"Maybe Operation Sweaty Principal?" said Sal.

Juliana busted out laughing at that. "That's gross, but I accept it."

Héctor shut the door once Juliana and Sal crossed inside. "This won't take too long," he said. "Operation Save the Library will be a success very soon!"

He took a deep breath, hoped with all his might that this would work, and opened the door.

His heart leaped in excitement when he saw the dull gray walls of Sal's school, illuminated by sunlight.

"Well, we're definitely still at my school," said Sal. "And it's the right time!" Then they pointed. "And that's definitely the janitor's office."

Another door was directly across from the Room. The coast looked clear, so Héctor darted over to it, tried the handle, and—

Locked.

He rushed back to the Room and shut the door before

Juliana and Sal could leave. "Lemme try again," he explained.

Héctor looked upward, almost like he was praying. "Room, I don't know if you can hear me, but we *need* to get in that office. Cut us some slack?"

He waited a moment, then repeated himself . . . only to face the exact same results. He stomped his foot on the ground. "This has to work!" he whispered loudly.

After perhaps the fifth go at this, Juliana was frustrated. "Héctor, it's clear the Room won't take us inside the janitor's office," she said. "Can we just think of something else?"

"What about this Mr. Mbalia?" asked Héctor, turning to Sal. "Let's just assume that we can't make it inside his office either. Will he help us?"

Sal grimaced. "Oh, I don't think we should try that."

"Why not?" said Héctor.

"It's just that . . ." Sal paused and then shook their head. "Mr. Mbalia doesn't really like . . . anything. He's kind of . . . difficult?"

"Difficult *how*?" said Héctor.

"I'm pretty sure the only time he's ever referred to the word 'fun' was to say, 'Don't have it.' It's like he's allergic to the very concept."

Héctor rubbed his chin. "Hmm. So, he's not going to be easy, then."

"No," said Sal.

Héctor shrugged. "That's fine. It'll just be one of my more difficult roles."

Juliana sucked in air between clenched teeth. "I am not sure about this," she said. "Are you just going to *ask* him for the keys, Héctor?"

He flashed her a smile. "Why yes I am! You'll see."

"But we don't even go to Sal's school," she said.

"And I feel like I need to remind you that he's impossible," warned Sal.

"No one can resist my skills when I actually get going," said Héctor as the three of them moved back into the Room. "You'll see."

But quietly, deep down in his heart, Héctor was panicking. What if this *didn't* work?

Nah. It was going to. Héctor was in control! There was no way he'd let this slip out of his grasp.

"Y'all ready?" he asked.

Sal and Juliana looked nervous. They traded a quick glance at one another. "I think so," said Juliana.

"I *hope* so," added Sal.

"Good enough," said Héctor, and he opened the Room.

CHAPTER THIRTY-THREE

When Héctor opened the door to the Room again, a new sight greeted them: the closed door to the Saguaro Academy security office. There was a black nameplate tacked to it: K. MBALIA. Héctor took a deep breath, then stepped out into the hallway and knocked on the wooden door.

After a moment without a response, he tried the doorknob.

Locked. As he expected.

"Okay, no one freak out," said Héctor. "This isn't a dead end."

Juliana groaned. "I *really* think we need to reconsider this."

"Reconsider what?"

They spun around to face a tall Black man, his head bald and shiny, his beard cut tightly around his jaw. He raised a single eyebrow while frowning. "What are y'all doing outside my office?"

Here goes *nothing*, thought Héctor.

He cleared his throat. "Mr. Mbalia!" he said, his voice

pitching high in faux excitement. "Just who we were looking for!"

"Well, I assumed that, since you were trying to get into my *locked* office," he said. "Repeatedly. So you better have a good reason for that."

Héctor cleared his throat again. "Well, we were looking for you." He cast a quick glance at Sal, who had lost all the color in their face. *Okay, no help there*, he thought.

"You mentioned that. For what?"

"So," Héctor continued, "we wanted to . . . to ask you for something."

"Well, here I am," Mr. Mbalia said. "You gonna get to asking or just stand there all slack-jawed?"

Now Héctor looked to Juliana. She had pretty much the same expression on her face as Sal did on theirs.

"Well, I was wondering if . . . you would lend us the key . . . to the storage container out back?"

Héctor flinched. Not his best work.

Mr. Mbalia didn't really react. His eyebrow was still raised, and the frown seemed to be permanently stuck on his face. "You want the key."

"Yes."

"To the storage unit."

"Yep."

"The one with all the library books in it."

"That would be the one."

"Do you possibly have a reason for such a request?"

Héctor breathed out. "Yes, I do."

Mr. Mbalia crossed his arms over the front of his blue cardigan. "Are you going to *share* that reason with me?"

Unfortunately for Héctor, he had done virtually no prep work for this role. His confidence was fading.

So he was shocked when *Sal* spoke up and saved him: "It's for an extra credit project."

Mr. Mbalia's eyes went wide. "Extra credit?"

"Yes!" said Héctor, probably a little too quickly. "An extra credit project."

"And who assigned an extra credit project that would require you to get into a locked storage container at"— Mr. Mbalia looked at his watch—"nine fifty-five in the morning?"

This was now a complete disaster.

Thankfully, Sal was quick with another answer. "Oh, that would be Ms. Pérez, my English teacher."

"Perfect." And for the first time, Mr. Mbalia smiled. He pulled out a massive set of keys from his back pocket. "Thank you for telling me that. Now, if you'll excuse me, I'll just go into *my* office and give Ms. Pérez a call to verify what you've all told me."

Oh, Héctor did not like Mr. Mbalia's smile. It sent a chill down his spine, and the first words that popped in his brain came right out of his mouth.

"No, you can't!"

Mr. Mbalia turned. His smile was even *wider*.

"Oh, I can't, can I? Do you mean that I, the head of security at this fine establishment, am not able to call Ms. Pérez, or that you don't *want* me to?"

More words manifested in Héctor's brain, and just as before, out they came.

"We don't want you to because it's a surprise."

The smile disappeared. Genuine confusion replaced it, and Héctor felt Juliana gently slap the back of his arm, as if to say, *You've gone too far, bruh!*

"A surprise."

"Yeah," said Héctor, smiling and nodding. "For Ms. Pérez."

"A surprise extra credit assignment?"

"Yes."

"So Ms. Pérez assigned something she doesn't actually know about?"

". . . yes?" said Héctor, and he couldn't help the grimace that spread over his face.

Mr. Mbalia waved a dismissal at the three of them and went back to unlocking his door. "I don't have time for any jokes or shenanigans," he said.

"I told you!" whispered Sal.

"You should listen to your friend Sal there, and just go back to class."

"Won't you reconsider?" Héctor asked.

"Reconsider *what*? There's no way what you just told me is true."

"But what if it *is*?" he countered.

Mr. Mbalia sighed as if the sigh came not just from deep in his soul, but stretched back through time to every interaction he'd ever had with a difficult student. He turned back one more time, and Juliana said, in the lowest possible voice, "Oh, we're dead."

Mr. Mbalia's eyes went wide.

And that smile came *back*.

"Hello, Ms. Pérez," he said, and Héctor's entire set of insides dropped to the floor (or at least it felt like that). He turned back to see a brown-skinned woman with curly hair to her shoulders come bouncing over. "These students are here for an extra credit assignment you gave them! But it's a secret, so I'll understand if you don't know what they're talking about."

Then Mr. Mbalia smiled so wide, Héctor was sure the security officer's face would explode.

Yeah, Héctor thought. *We're dead.*

CHAPTER THIRTY-FOUR

The three of them did not speak as Ms. Pérez gazed from one face to the next. She narrowed her eyes when she looked at Héctor. Panic had now made a permanent home in his chest. *This is the worst*, he thought. There was no way he could keep up this act *now*.

"What are you talking about?" Ms. Pérez asked.

"These fine students were outside my office," explained Mr. Mbalia, "trying to get in without a key, when I happened upon them."

"Okay . . . ," she said. "And what for?"

"Oh, they're very creative, Ms. Pérez. Because you inspire such an active imagination in them, I assume!"

Sal cleared their throat. "Good morning, Ms. Pérez," they said. "We were just . . . it was just . . ."

Héctor reached down and squeezed Sal's hand, hoping he could send some courage through touch.

Sal took a deep breath. "We wanted to surprise you," they said finally.

Ms. Pérez gave them a smile that managed to look concerned, too. "Oh, that's sweet, Sal. But . . . what kind of surprise is in Mr. Mbalia's office?"

"You know, I had the same question!" Unsurprisingly, Mr. Mbalia's smile was directed right at Héctor.

But Sal kept going. "We wanted to do something for you and the whole school." Another deep breath. "And move all the library books from the storage container to the empty math classroom."

Ms. Pérez put a hand to her chest. "You *what*?"

Juliana jumped in. "It's not fair that there isn't a library, and the classroom is just *empty*. So . . . why not use it for something?"

Sal's English teacher looked to Héctor. He merely nodded at her.

"Well . . . okay," said Ms. Pérez. "That's actually not a bad idea."

"Really?" said Sal.

"Which classroom are they talking about, Ms. Pérez?" asked Mr. Mbalia. He had one of his eyebrows raised in suspicion again.

"On the north side of campus," she said. "It was that one that got shut down due to a gas leak? They fixed it and all, but it never got used again."

"And you think you could run a library out of that?"

Ms. Pérez was deep in thought for a moment. "I'd need some shelving," she said softly.

"We got some bookshelves in storage," said Mr. Mbalia.

"And it would need to be cleaned, of course," she continued.

Sal's eyes went wide.

"Which Mr. Hernandez could do in a day," Mr. Mbalia added.

Ms. Pérez grinned. "I really do think it could work, Kwame," she said.

Mr. Mbalia nodded his head. "I *do* hate that container a lot," he said, and relief rushed through Héctor.

"Mr. Mbalia, I think my students *maybe* got a little ahead of themselves, but their hearts were in the right place." She put a hand on Sal's shoulder, and their eyes went wide.

They'd caught it, too, Héctor thought. He didn't know why Ms. Pérez would cover for him and Juliana. But she'd just said they were *her* students!

"Perhaps," said Mr. Mbalia. "But next time, don't try to solve something like this entirely by yourselves, okay?"

"Yes, you could've just *asked* me," said Ms. Pérez, who then fixed her gaze on Héctor. "There was no need to try something so elaborate. Sometimes, you can just *ask*."

Juliana shot Héctor a look that basically said, *I told you so!*

Sorry, he mouthed at her.

"We promise," said Sal. "Thank you for listening to us."

"And thank you for the good idea!" she said. "I think it's worth us visiting the principal's office to see if we can get official approval." She beamed at Sal. "Would you like to come with me? Since it was your idea and all."

Sal's joy was infectious. "Yes, I'd love that," they said. "Can my friends come too?"

Juliana and Héctor exchanged a look of horror.

"Perhaps it should just be the two of us," Ms. Pérez said, and then she turned and *winked* at Héctor.

What did *that* mean?!

"We probably need to get to class," said Juliana.

"Right," said Héctor, his hands shaking as he tried to unlock his phone. He kept getting the password wrong. "Class."

"Which class do you need to head to?" asked Mr. Mbalia.

Oh no, thought Héctor.

"Um . . . ," said Juliana.

"Mrs. Caroline's art class," Héctor blurted out.

He saw Sal silently put their hand to their forehead and close their eyes. Juliana glared at Héctor.

And Ms. Pérez . . . oh *no*.

Her eyes were wide, and her head was tilted to the

side. "Did you say Mrs. Caroline?"

"I—I did," said Héctor, and he was certain he would never breathe again.

"Right," she said. "Well, off you go to class, then. Tell Mrs. Caroline to talk to me later if she has a problem with you being tardy."

Ms. Pérez turned and walked away, Mr. Mbalia at her side. Héctor felt like he was going to explode. "Did she just—"

Juliana shook her head. "We don't have time, Héctor. We need to get back home before Mr. Mbalia comes back."

She was right. Before they darted off, Sal gave both Juliana and Héctor a quick hug. "Thank you," they said softly. "I couldn't have done this without you."

"Of course," said Héctor. "Let us know if it gets approved; I'll come help you with the moving and setup!"

"Me too," said Juliana. "Promise!"

And then the two of them—who definitely were *not* students at Saguaro Academy—ran down the hallway. But Héctor sensed something odd behind him, and as he rounded a corner, he gazed back.

Ms. Pérez was at the end of the hallway, looking at him. Just *staring*.

What was that all about? he wondered.

This would have all fallen apart without Ms. Pérez. In fact, Héctor was now aware of just how *badly* his plan had gone. What if they'd been discovered?

They both sprinted into the Room, and Juliana immediately collapsed onto the couch, roaring laughter. "Héctor, I can't believe that just *happened*!"

"Me either," he said, plopping down next to her.

"Why did that teacher protect us?" Then she lightly hit Héctor's arm. "And why did you tell her *your* art teacher's name?"

"I don't know! I just panicked!"

"Well, it worked so . . . good job, Héctor. You helped pull this off. Not *perfectly*, but . . . you did it!"

"Maybe," he said. "But . . . I also should have listened to you. I made that way more complicated than it needed to be."

Juliana smiled at him. "Thank you for saying that, but there was no way we could have known that Ms. Pérez was down to move the library. So, you still set this all in motion."

"I guess," he said.

"Take some credit, Héctor!" she said, slapping him on the arm with the back of her hand. "You helped out Sal big time. We *both* did."

Warmth spread through him, as his phone vibrated in his pocket. He pulled it out to see a text from his mami:

> No te preocupes mijo, pero tu abuela se cayó. It
> wasn't a bad fall and she's fine, but I'm coming to
> get you. besitos xoxox

Despite his mother's request, a burst of fear hit him in the stomach. "Uh, my mom is coming to get me," he announced. "Family emergency."

"Go, go!" said Juliana. "I'll see you soon?"

"I hope so," he said.

Héctor popped back into his school, and the bell rang. He looked at his phone again: 9:34 a.m. Pre-algebra was about to start. He and Juliana had saved Sal's library in a whopping zero minutes.

Héctor was overjoyed by this, but as he made for the front office, fear began to creep in. He hoped his abuela was okay.

CHAPTER THIRTY-FIVE

Héctor did not like hospitals.

Truthfully, he didn't know anyone who actually enjoyed them, but they always gave him the creeps. The main hospital in Orangevale felt so lifeless; whoever had designed it had barely used a scrap of color *anywhere*.

He sat at the end of Abuela's bed, his phone in his hand. He kept unlocking it and then . . . nothing. He didn't want to look at his unread messages in his old group chat with Tim and Sophia. A game might have kept him distracted while he waited, but he wasn't in the mood. Abuela wasn't even going to be here very long— her nurse had said that they just wanted to check one X-ray before releasing her—but each second stretched out and seemed to last forever.

Abuela Sonia had a gown on over her regular clothes, but one leg of her jeans had been pulled up, and bandages were wrapped tightly around her ankle. He'd never seen someone's ankle so terribly swollen, and it worried him. This whole *place* worried him. His parents had told him that Abuela had just had a nasty sprain, and it wasn't anything serious. Yet being here, in a place so clean and boring and clinical . . . it made him nervous. What if it got worse? What if the doctors had missed something?

"Héctor."

He looked up to meet his abuela's eyes. She looked so tired, but she still managed to raise an eyebrow in concern. "You doing okay over there?" she asked.

He fidgeted in his chair. "Yeah. I guess."

Abuela winked at his mami and papi. "Give us a moment, will you?"

Mami kissed his forehead as she left, and Papi ruffled his hair. "Pull your chair up next to me, nieto," said Abuela. "You're too far!"

He scooted his chair up to the side of her bed. "Does it hurt?"

"Not right now," she said, and she took his hand. "They gave me the *good* stuff, so I'm feeling great."

"You sure? What happened?"

She waved at him. "Ay, it wasn't that bad, nieto. Took a wrong step in my kitchen, and down I went." She laughed at herself. "I'm mostly glad no one else was there. Can't have any of you thinking I'm not all suavecita." She brushed her hair back dramatically.

It made Héctor smile. He knew which side of the family had given him his flair for drama.

"Now there's that beautiful smile of yours," said

Abuela, and she reached out and brushed her fingers over Héctor's face. "You don't like it here, do you?"

"Not at all," he said.

"It's basically a sprained ankle," she said, patting her injured right leg. "What, did you expect something worse?"

Héctor wasn't particularly embarrassed by emotions; he channeled them all the time when he was performing. But when his eyes stung with tears just then, he turned his face away from Abuela. He didn't want her to see this.

But she did. "Ay, niño," she said, and she reached for him, and he fell into her arms. "It's okay. I promise. *I* am okay."

"I just got scared," he said, and it was like there was a stone in his throat. "I don't like it here."

"Maybe we shouldn't have asked you to come."

He pulled away from her. "No!" he said forcefully. "No, I'm glad I'm here."

Abuela let the silence grow. "Why does this place make you uncomfortable, Héctor? It's not like you've ever spent a lot of time in hospitals."

That was true. But he hated the smell. The way everyone avoided eye contact. The *plainness* of it all.

But it wasn't just that. Sitting there, staring at his abuela, he couldn't stop thinking of Mike. Héctor was nowhere near school, and that boy was now invading his *thoughts*. Sure, things had gotten better in many ways, and he was so happy about his growing friendships. But it was all still a secret, wasn't it? And here was the one person, more than anyone else, that Héctor wanted to talk to. About *everything*.

So why couldn't he bring himself to tell her the truth?

He realized it wasn't the right time. He had helped Juliana, then Sal, and now? Héctor wanted to make Abuela proud by solving his problem by himself, just like she'd done.

It all fell into place then.

"When Mami texted me, I was scared," he finally said, after an uncomfortable silence. "I just kept thinking that something worse would happen. That you weren't going to be around anymore."

Her eyes welled up with tears. "Oh, papito, I'm not going anywhere," she said, holding him tight. It was exactly the kind of hug he needed.

She pulled away from him. "I'm here for you," she said. "I don't want you to think I'll *ever* let you down."

Héctor sniffled and wiped his nose with the back of his hand. "I don't want to let you down either," he said.

"You never do," said Abuela. "And look, even if you *do* . . . I'm not going to stop loving you, okay?"

He nodded and fell back into her arms. He stayed

there until Papi came back in the room, letting them know that Abuela was being discharged.

Abuela must have given Papi a look, because he was gone as soon as he came. And Héctor was thankful that Abuela had made this moment last a little longer.

CHAPTER THIRTY-SIX

Mami dropped him back off at school right as the bell for lunch rang. Héctor fell into step with the other students as if he hadn't been gone at all. A terrible thought nudged its way into his brain: *Did anyone even notice that you weren't here?*

It didn't make any sense to him. He had helped Juliana stand up to her principal; he had helped Sal orchestrate a return of their library. So . . . why didn't he feel wonderful? Accomplished?

Happy?

Héctor wasn't hungry, so he wandered over toward his art class to take advantage of Mrs. Caroline's open-door policy. Unfortunately, when he got there, it swung outward and nearly smacked him in the face. He backed away quickly and—

Oh.

Great.

Mike scowled at Héctor. "What are you looking at, punk?"

How original, thought Héctor. He didn't answer. He

just looked down at what Mike had clutched to his chest.

It looked like a canvas.

Mike caught his gaze, then quickly shoved the canvas behind his back. "Mind your business, Hector!" he yelled, and then he darted off into the hallway. Héctor turned to watch him run away.

"Wonder what's gotten into him."

He jumped in his spot. He hadn't even heard Mrs. Caroline come up behind him. She saw the confusion on Héctor's face, then shook her head. "How are you this morning, Héctor? How is your *heart*?"

Mrs. Caroline had started asking this recently. She explained it by saying that asking someone how they were rarely inspired them to tell the truth. "And I *want* the truth!" she had said. "The truth is complicated, but the best art comes from a place of honesty."

How *was* Héctor's heart? He was wired after the morning he'd had and his last interaction with Mike, so he said the first thing that came to mind:

"Confused."

"That's an interesting answer," she said. "What confuses you?"

This felt reckless. Absurd. But at the same time, he was so tired of having to hide himself from the world. Mrs. Caroline was *not* Ms. Heath. Even if he wasn't going to snitch on Mike, he could say *something* to her, because . . . well, she'd listen to him.

"What do you do if someone's being cruel to you?"

She raised an eyebrow, then glanced at the door. She turned back and smiled. "Is someone being mean to you, Mr. Muñoz?"

He frowned. "Cruel."

"What?" she said.

"Not mean. *Cruel*. It's different."

She nodded. "Okay, I hear you. That *is* very different."

"It is." He ran a hand through his curls, uncertain if he should press on, but he swallowed down his fear. "What do I do?"

"I assume this is someone you can't just get away from."

He nodded back at her. "Yeah."

"And you feel trapped."

His eyes went wide. "Kind of, actually. Like . . . I can't escape them but I also can't ignore them because they're everywhere."

Mrs. Caroline moved closer to Héctor and sat on the desk in front of him. "Do other people *like* this cruel person?"

"Yes," he said quietly, his heart thumping. He had to be careful; he didn't want to make this worse than it already was.

"That's really hard, Héctor," she said. "You shouldn't

feel bad about how difficult it is. Even grown-ups deal with that, and we don't always deal with it well."

"Really?" he said.

She nodded. "There used to be another art teacher here," she said. "When I came to Orangevale, we worked together to teach different grades. He had sixth grade, and I had seventh and eighth."

"What happened?"

"The previous teacher got *fired*."

"Whoa. You serious?"

She sighed, and it was the first time that she didn't seem like a teacher to him. It was like she was wearing a different outfit and he was seeing a new side of her.

"Very serious. He didn't like me, Héctor. And I have my suspicions why, but he was cruel to me. He stole supplies, he sabotaged my classes, he said terrible things about me behind my back to other teachers."

"What?" Héctor's blood boiled. How could *anyone* have anything bad to say about Mrs. Caroline?

"It was shocking. No matter how many times I tried being nice, his behavior didn't change. He just kept getting *worse*."

This sounded too familiar to Héctor. He had also tried to be kind to Mike and the Minions. He'd even told Ms. Heath!

"So what did you *do*?" he asked. "Did you, like . . .

rumble with him in the parking lot? Because I kinda wanna do that right now."

She chuckled. "If only it had been that easy," she said. "No, I had to report him after he started destroying my students' art."

Héctor didn't know what to say to that, except, "That is *horrible*. How? How could someone do that?"

"Well, I don't know. I may not ever know, Héctor. And I imagine that might be what's hard for you. Not knowing *why* this person has singled you out."

"What if it's because you're different?"

Mrs. Caroline nodded as recognition spread on her face. "That's very perceptive," she said. "That's probably what it is. People can sometimes be afraid of difference. And rather than try to understand it, they just lash out and hurt people, hoping they'll change. Or conform."

"But I don't want to be the same," he confessed.

"Then don't be," she said, and a huge smile lit up her face. She stood and smoothed out her red tulle skirt. "Be yourself. Be over the top. Outlast them. Show them that no amount of fear will *ever* make you change who you are."

She drifted over to her desk, leaving Héctor with his swirling emotions. He wanted to do exactly what she'd said so badly. But then he remembered how Mike and the Minions had reacted to Héctor's originality. How did

Mrs. Caroline do it? How did she push past the doubt?

"Mr. Muñoz?"

"Yeah?"

"It doesn't have to be me, but . . . if you need help, I'm here. You can talk to me."

"Thanks," he said. "I'll think about it."

He pulled out his sketch pad, then rose to go to the supply closet to get some pastels. As he pulled out different colors and ran them over his canvas with a steady hand, his chest started hurting. It was a small thing at first, and then it was like his body weighed a million pounds.

It didn't make sense. Héctor had talked to someone, and their response had been really good!

So why didn't he feel better?

What's wrong with me? he wondered as he sat back down.

He wanted the Room.

No.

He wanted to *disappear.*

Héctor glanced up from his desk, the other kids dutifully working on their own pieces, and saw that Mrs. Caroline had moved. She was standing on the opposite side of the classroom in front of a drawing tacked up on the wall.

It was the one Héctor had done: a door opening into a bright, mysterious world.

•••

Héctor spotted Taylor and Jackson while on his way to gym class. He should have been overjoyed to see them, but dread crept through his chest. So he kept his head down, hoping the two of them wouldn't see him. He just wasn't in the mood to talk.

But then Taylor called out his name, and there was no way he could pretend *not* to have heard that.

"Oh, hey," he said, nodding at the two of them as they approached.

Jackson adjusted his frames. "'Sup, man," he said. "You doing anything interesting this weekend?"

"Me?" said Héctor.

"Yeah. Me, Taylor, and Aishah were gonna go to this new thrift store on the other side of town. If your parents are cool with it, you could kick it with us."

"My dad is driving," offered Taylor.

That sounded *perfect* to Héctor, the exact kind of thing he missed from his old home. And with three people he actually *liked*?

But Héctor's mood was growing into something dark, and he found himself shaking his head. "Ah, I'm sorry," he said. "I have family stuff to do."

"Okay," said Jackson. "Next time?"

"Sure," said Héctor, and he dropped his head and made a beeline for the gym.

"See ya!" Taylor called out.

Héctor didn't even turn back to acknowledge him. *Good job*, he thought. *Already pushing away the only people who actually talk to you.*

That thought pressed down on him all through gym class.

Héctor was exhausted by the time Papi pulled into their driveway, and he shuffled out of the passenger seat and into the house.

"¿Estás bien, mijo?" Papi asked.

Héctor wanted to answer:

No, Papi, I'm not okay.

No, I'm so tired.

No, something is wrong. Maybe with *me*.

But once more, it was easier to think of the words than to say them.

He smiled weakly. "I think so," he said. "I'm just more tired than usual."

Papi kissed the top of Héctor's head and guided him into the house. "You've been working so hard," he said. "I officially give you permission to take a nap."

"Come on, Papi," he said. "I got homework to do."

"Homework can wait," Papi replied, and he took Héctor's backpack from his son's hands. "Besides, you can't do anything truly good if your body is on empty. It's important to refill yourself, too. ¿Entiendes?"

He was grateful for the permission, but his father's words rang in his brain once he tossed himself onto his bed. Refill himself? With what?

The ache in his chest came back as he lay there, the one that had appeared after his conversation with Mrs. Caroline. It wasn't just a heaviness.

No.

Empty. That's what his heart felt like.

Héctor was torn. It was like he lived two lives, and he couldn't tell one side about the other. Earlier that day, he'd even turned Jackson and Taylor away, despite that he had *wanted* to spend more time with them. It was exhausting to think about coming up with a new story to explain where he'd been, or how he knew Juliana and Sal. It was exhausting to crave the Room in places he couldn't access it.

And it was exhausting to have to do all of this by himself.

Héctor felt terribly, terribly lonely.

CHAPTER THIRTY-SEVEN

Héctor wasn't all that surprised when his mami nudged him awake and he learned he had slept through the night. "Looks like you really needed that," she said, smiling.

He yawned and stretched, and the feeling was gone: that ache, that terrible emptiness he'd felt the night before.

"Yeah," he said. "I guess I did."

He rushed to get ready that morning. He was actually excited to get to school. He wanted to stop by the Room to get an update on when he could help Sal with moving the library, but he *also* wanted to find Jackson. He shouldn't have turned down the chance to go thrifting with his three new friends.

Maybe . . .

Maybe it was time to fix all this, this separation of Héctor's life. What would happen if he brought someone *into* the Room? Would it even let him do that?

As thrilling as that thought was, Héctor knew he had to deal with one thing at a time. As his mami drove him to school before heading to work, he asked her about hanging out with his friends.

"And Taylor's dad said he'll drive," said Héctor after explaining everything. "So I could make sure to get everyone's number for you so you and Papi could talk to their parents."

Mami grinned. "Look at you!" she said. "Making friends! Get their parents' numbers, and your papi and I will give them a call tonight."

She planted a big kiss on his forehead after pulling up in front of Orangevale Middle School. "Let me know if any of your teachers need a note," she said. "In case they give you grief about homework."

"I will, Mami," he said, and he climbed out of the car, then blew her a kiss. "Love you!"

His mood *was* better, that was for sure. He marched up the steps to school and was delighted to see the door to the Room as soon as he was in the hallway.

Today, the Room had a totally new vibe: it looked like the cute corner coffee shops that were all over the Mission and the Castro in San Francisco. Natural light spilled in from a couple skylights in the ceiling, and Sal and Juliana were sitting at a counter next to an automatic coffee machine, the kind with like ten buttons to press to make any type of hot drink you wanted.

Héctor immediately felt at home.

"So, I have the *best* news!" Sal exclaimed, raising up a mug.

"What's up?" he said, walking over to the counter.

"First of all," said Juliana, "I need you to try this latte."

He heard his papi's voice in his head, telling him he was too young for espresso. But . . . Papi wasn't here. And a latte wasn't *that* bad.

"Okay, a *small* one," he said. "What is it?"

"Oh, you gotta wait for it," Juliana explained. "Let the surprise happen, Héctor!"

She pressed one of the buttons on the machine, and it whirred to life. Soon, a light-brown liquid was pouring into a white mug, and Héctor smelled something . . . earthy. And a little sweet. It certainly didn't smell as strong as the coffee his parents had.

When the machine finished, Juliana handed him the mug while Sal watched eagerly. He took a sniff and—

"No," he said. "No *way*!"

He knew that smell. He'd know it anywhere.

He took a tiny sip to avoid burning his tongue, and the sweet taste of his abuela's horchata filled his mouth. Somehow, that machine had made a horchata *latte*.

"You were right," he said. "The surprise was worth it."

"Okay, so," said Sal, "I know it hasn't been long." They

wrung their hands together nervously. "But I just spoke with Ms. Pérez."

"And?" said Héctor, his heart flopping.

"She *already* got approval to reopen the library in the classroom you found!"

Héctor nearly dropped his latte. He set it down delicately on the counter, and then began jumping up and down and screaming at Sal. "Yo, that's amazing to hear!" he said, plopping back down on the stool. "Oh, wow, I'm so *happy* for you!"

"And it wouldn't have happened if you hadn't come to me with the idea," Sal said.

"It was nothing," he said. "Just an idea."

"Bruh, just take the compliment," said Juliana, laughing. "You did something *good*."

This time, he felt heat in his cheeks, and he hoped that his friends couldn't see him blushing.

"Anyway," said Sal. "A bunch of us are going to help Ms. Pérez and Mr. Mbalia move the books to the new location. You wanna come help?"

"I would love that," he said, smiling. "When?"

"Ms. Pérez said we can start after school, so I'll come back in here, and then take you two into my school."

"Wow," said Héctor. "I can't believe we're actually doing this."

"Me either," said Sal. "Do you ever feel like this place is a big prank that we're not in on? Like, one day we're gonna wake up and find out it's all fake?"

"I thought it was just me!" Juliana exclaimed. "I am *always* thinking that!"

"But it's *not* fake," said Héctor. "It's real. And it helped us get your library back."

He stood and raised his arms up. "Thank you, Room!" he called out. "Whatever you are, you are the BEST."

An image popped into Héctor's head then: his school's New Year's party last year, held in the gym. It was the first time he had ever stayed up to midnight, and it was worth it. As the clock struck twelve, streamers and balloons fell from the ceiling, raining down a colorful chaos on everyone's heads.

Standing there in the Room, Héctor felt his heart leap as the same kind of balloons and streamers and glitter fell from the ceiling, covering the three of them, and soon, Sal and Juliana were up on their feet, dancing, kicking balloons, and Héctor never, ever wanted this moment to end. It felt like the sign he needed: this was where he was supposed to be and who he was supposed to be *with*.

He did not feel empty. He felt incredibly, beautifully full.

• • •

The hallways were packed with other students, all rushing to their destinations, but Héctor was floating. Sometimes, it was hard being at Orangevale, but if he hadn't come here, he never would have met Sal and Juliana.

That was the thought that was occupying his mind when the first bell before homeroom rang, and Héctor dashed off so he wouldn't be late.

And then Héctor turned a corner and ran directly into Ms. Heath.

It wasn't very hard, but Héctor still froze and grimaced. "I'm sorry, Ms. Heath," he said. "I just didn't want to be late to class."

She held a hand out and placed it on his chest. "Just a minute, young man."

Héctor's heart fluttered.

"Where do you *go?*"

He frowned at her. "What?"

"Where do you go, Mr. Muñoz? I've been keeping my eyes on you since you arrived, and you just . . . aren't around."

"Um . . . when?" he asked, the panic building in him. "Like . . . in general?"

"You know that's not what I mean, young man," she said, her hands on her hips. "You keep *disappearing*. Every time I need to talk to you."

He gulped and looked around as other kids made their way to homeroom. "I don't know," he said. "I'm either in class or at lunch."

"Where did you just come from?"

"Uh . . . I was at home before this?"

She stepped back and sighed. "I don't appreciate you getting smart with me."

He frowned. "I don't get what you mean."

"Don't act like I don't know that you have been hiding from me," she said.

"I don't know what you're talking about," he said, and he stepped around Ms. Heath. There were only five minutes between the first bell and homeroom, so he tried to join the flow of kids going to class.

And Ms. Heath grabbed the back of Héctor's shirt.

The collar stretched out, and he froze again, worried Ms. Heath had just ruined it. *Yo, what is she doing?*

"You cannot seem to follow the rules," she said, still holding on to his collar. "And every time I try to find you, you are somehow *gone*. Where are you hiding, Mr. Muñoz?"

He twisted away from Ms. Heath and then spun to face her. "Nowhere," he said. "I'm not hiding at *all!*"

Héctor had not intended for his words to come out so forcefully, but his frustration got the better of him.

Ms. Heath's eyes went wide. "So are you calling me a liar?"

Once again, as was always the case, an audience began to gather around them. *Orangevale Middle School sure likes their drama*, Héctor thought bitterly. How ironic.

He sighed. "I never called you a liar."

"I found you covered in garbage last week. I left you to clean it up, but when I came back with a trash bag, you were gone. Nowhere to be found."

Héctor didn't know what to say. She didn't care about what had been happening to him, and he had no strategies left.

The silence was unbearable. There were now at least ten more kids *behind* Ms. Heath, all of them unsure whether to walk past this.

"I'm waiting," said Ms. Heath.

"For *what*?" he said.

"For you to tell me where you've been."

She pushed her fists into her hips.

He narrowed his eyes at her.

"I cleaned up after myself," he said. "And then I went home."

"I know you're hiding something from me, Mr. Muñoz," she said. "Ever since you got here to this school, you've acted . . . *suspicious*."

She hissed the word, like it was a curse cast upon his body.

He shook his head. There was nothing he could say to her.

The crowd had grown, and Héctor knew each person there was going to create their own story in their head: Here was the weird new kid. The gay one. The one who couldn't follow the rules. It didn't matter who Héctor *actually* was, did it?

And then Héctor saw the true source of this whole nightmare.

Mike and Frank, their smiles wide, their eyes alight with mischief, were slowly making their way through the crowd.

Mike snickered behind Ms. Heath, but it was like the world did not exist to her. It was just her and Héctor.

"I'm waiting, Mr. Muñoz," she said. "Where do you *go?*"

Héctor still did not reply. Fear began to bubble up in his chest. She had already decided that he was a troublemaker, that he came to this school to disobey her, and nothing would change her mind. Anything he said would be picked apart. Would be disbelieved. There was a terrible irony in it all. Ms. Heath was supposed to be the person he could go to for protection. Instead, she was *targeting* him, too.

"Is everything okay?"

Héctor's face fell as Aishah approached them through the crowd, Jackson following her. But they both stilled when Ms. Heath cast a terrible glare at them.

"Please go to class," she said loudly.

But no one moved. Not a single inch.

"I know where he goes," said Mike, sliding up next to Ms. Heath. "It's obvious, isn't it?"

"Be quiet, Mr. Kimball," said Ms. Heath without breaking eye contact with Héctor. "I want the *truth*."

So he took a gamble, and he pointed to Mike. "*He* is the reason I have to hide."

In the moments before Ms. Heath spoke, Héctor probably could have heard a pin drop.

"He's not telling the—" Mike began.

"Be *quiet*, Mr. Kimball!" Ms. Heath repeated, still not breaking eye contact with Héctor. "You tried that story before."

"Because it's *true*!" he insisted. "Mike and Frank are the ones who chase me around and call me names, and *Mike* was the one who dumped trash on me!"

Héctor's heart sank when Ms. Heath clicked her tongue against her teeth and shook her head. "You can't just make things up and expect me to believe them, Mr. Muñoz."

"But—"

"No!" she shouted. "Now please tell me the truth!"

He glanced at Aishah, who had her hand over her mouth. Jackson looked horrified.

"Can I *please* just go to class, Ms. Heath?" he asked.

"I'm not the one holding you up," she said. "You are. If you would just answer my question, we could *all* continue with our day."

Mike giggled again, but Héctor wouldn't give him his attention this time.

"For every minute you don't answer me, that's one day of detention."

Ms. Heath stared at her watch.

He said nothing.

He was *furious*. Why? Why was she so obsessed with him? Weren't there other things happening at Orangevale Middle School to occupy her time?

"One minute," she announced. "One day of detention."

Some of the gathered students gasped, but Héctor did not budge. Did not speak. Did not give in.

"Come on, Hector," said Mike. "Just tell the truth so we can go to class. You're holding us all up."

Ms. Heath said nothing to that, and it squashed the last bit of hope in Héctor. Couldn't she see that Mike was making this worse? That he had it out for Héctor? Rage boiled in him, not just because he knew Mike didn't care about going to class, but because of how *horrific* this performance was. This was an affront to the truth *and* to the art of acting.

"Two minutes," she announced. "Two days of detention."

The final bell rang. There was a commotion as some of the students rushed past Héctor and Ms. Heath. On Ms. Heath's left side, Frank and Mike remained; on her right, Aishah and Jackson stood clutching hands; and just behind them all, Carlos's face drooped.

All of them said nothing. No one came to his defense, either, but could he blame them? Who dared to contradict Ms. Heath?

"Three minutes," she said, but this time, she sounded disappointed. "Three days, Mr. Muñoz."

It was like Héctor stood on center stage, a bright spotlight burning him away. He could feel every set of eyes on him, judging him, pitying him. Sweat ran down his neck, and he just wanted this to be over.

He couldn't stand it anymore.

"The janitor's closet," he said, the defeat creeping into his voice. "I hide in the janitor's closet."

Ms. Heath let her left arm fall to her side. "Thank you for telling me," she said.

Héctor sighed, relieved that at least this was over.

"Now take me there."

His breath stopped.

What?

He shot a look at Aishah and Jackson, his own cry of help.

But Ms. Heath snapped her fingers. "To class," she said. "*All* of you."

Aishah placed a hand on Héctor's shoulder, a gesture of sympathy.

Jackson said, "Sorry, bro. Come see us at lunch, okay?"

Then the two of them scurried off, and he watched Carlos disappear down the hallway behind Ms. Heath. Mike and Frank said nothing as they went the opposite way, and soon, it was just him and the head of security.

Where was he supposed to go? The Room was rarely in one place, and he wasn't even sure it would appear for him now. What if Juliana and Sal were inside it when he opened the door?

If it doesn't show up, she's going to think I'm lying again, he thought.

Héctor's heart raced as he guided Ms. Heath down the hallway, and he decided to take her to the spot in the hallway near the front entrance. That's where he'd first found the Room, so maybe that's where it would be.

Ms. Heath's sneakers squeaked on the tile, and they echoed in the empty hallways. He was certain his heart was beating so fiercely that she could hear it, too.

It was there, just steps from the front entrance, tucked into the wall on their left side.

JANITOR.

Héctor stood next to it and said nothing. Hopefully, all she wanted was to see it.

"Open it," she said calmly.

So much for that, he thought.

He gripped the metal handle. It was now or never.

"I'm waiting," said Ms. Heath.

He took a deep breath.

I need you *to be a regular closet.*

He turned the handle, pulled on the door, and swung it open toward himself.

And was met with the sight of a janitor's closet.

Cleaning supplies stacked on the shelf. A broom leaning up against the wall. In the corner, still as ever in his web, was King Ferdinand. *So you* are *still alive*, he thought.

"You hide in *here?*" said Ms. Heath, disbelief coating her voice.

He nodded.

She lowered her volume. "Oh," she said softly. "It's pretty small."

"Yeah," he said.

"And kind of dark," she added.

"I guess," he said. "But I don't mind."

Then she turned to face Héctor, and she sighed. Her face had softened and she gestured for him to leave the closet. He did, his face flushed with embarrassment, his head ringing from all the adrenaline.

"I need to ask you something," said Ms. Heath. "And you don't have to tell me now."

"Okay," he said, looking up at her.

She fixed him with a pitiful gaze. "Are you having problems at home, Héctor?"

That . . . was not what he expected her to say. "What do you mean?"

"If things are hard at home, or if someone is making you feel bad . . ." She pressed her lips together. "You can talk to me. If you need a grown-up to talk to, that is."

Héctor's anger flared again. The irony was too much. The obvious was right in front of her, but this whole time, she was creating her own story for Héctor instead of seeing the *actual* one unfolding.

So he shook his head. "I'm okay, Ms. Heath. Really."

"I'm just concerned about you, Mr. Muñoz," she said. "Given your tendency to act out."

Héctor winced. "Yes, Ms. Heath," he said. "I'm sorry for being such a bother."

One side of her mouth curled up in a sympathetic smile. "Don't worry about the detention," she said. "You don't have to serve it. You told me the truth, and that's what is most important. Just . . ." She paused. "Just try to behave, okay, Mr. Muñoz?"

"Yes, Ms. Heath." He nodded at her, tried to seem as sincere as possible. "I will."

She pulled out a small stack of hall passes and signed one for Héctor so he wouldn't have a tardy on his record. Then she gave a curt smile and strolled off.

Héctor let out a long sigh and closed his eyes. He leaned back against the wall for support so he wouldn't collapse. But it wasn't over; there was a short squeak, and when he looked up, the boys' room across the hall was open.

And Mike was creeping out of it, fury on his face.

CHAPTER THIRTY-EIGHT

This was impossible.

Héctor froze. The door to the Room was right there, but there was no way for him to duck inside of it without revealing everything to Mike.

Mike smirked. "You trying to hide?" he said, and he stepped closer. "Just like the coward you are?"

"Please go away, Mike," said Héctor.

Mike was now inches from him. He reached down and tried to pluck the hall pass from Héctor's hand, but Héctor quickly stuffed it into his jeans pocket.

"Go hide in the closet where you belong," Mike sneered.

Héctor couldn't help it. He rolled his eyes. It was such an obvious insult, and Mike had said far worse to him.

"You got a problem with me?" Mike said, and then he was so close that their noses almost touched. "We don't snitch in this school."

There was another groan in the hallway, and Héctor expected someone else to come upon them and break this up.

But no one did.

"You *just* tried to snitch on me to Ms. Heath," said Héctor.

"You could have gotten me in trouble," he shot back. "Why don't you mind your own business?"

"Because you won't leave me alone!" Héctor cried out, and he was so tired of this boy that he didn't care that he had raised his voice. "I've never done *anything* to you. I don't know why you hate me so much!"

Mike rested his forehead against Héctor's.

"Yes, you do."

He pushed off.

And then *the* word dropped out of Mike's mouth and he walked away.

It was a word Héctor hadn't heard since he was nine, when an older white man yelled it at Héctor as he walked by. He was dressed up as a princess for Halloween, complete with a long dress, painted nails, and a face full of makeup. His papi had chased the man off; it was also the first time Héctor had heard him swear. His parents had sat him down that night and told him what the word meant and how cruel it was, how people who were gay or queer had been called that openly for a long time. His parents held him and said that no matter what, they loved their son completely and without conditions.

It had not stung when he heard it that first time. But

now, three years later, it felt like a knife to the heart.

Like a punch in the gut.

Like a bomb had gone off.

Héctor slumped against the wall. He couldn't bring himself to go in the Room. It wouldn't make him feel better. Nothing would. Because Héctor knew the truth:

He would never fit in here at Orangevale Middle School. *Ever.*

Maybe he was exactly what Mike had called him. Maybe he'd never be anything more than that.

Héctor slipped into a fog. He wasn't able to remember much of the day, just images and the overwhelming feeling that everything was wrong. He hid in the library during lunch and couldn't bring himself to eat. After gym, he saw the Room. Had it appeared earlier but he was too lost in his head to notice it? Maybe.

But Héctor made a choice. He didn't open the door to the Room and kept walking. It appeared again just a few seconds later on the opposite side of the hallway. He ignored it again. Then it sat next to the exit, almost like it was beckoning to him.

Héctor shook his head, walked out the front door of his school, and headed to the pickup area. His papi arrived soon after, and Héctor still said nothing as he climbed inside the car. He simply leaned his head against the window, watched the world of Orangevale rush by.

He knew he had probably disappointed Sal and Juliana.
He knew he had probably lost the only friends he had.
But this was what he deserved, right?
He didn't belong here. He didn't belong anywhere.

CHAPTER THIRTY-NINE

The next week of Héctor's life seemed to last forever, and yet it also passed in a blur.

He didn't go back to the Room once. He saw it every single day; it often appeared just ahead of where he was walking, anticipating his movements. It was next to the boys' room. It was adjacent to Mrs. Caroline's class Tuesday afternoon. It was across from the entrance to the gym on Wednesday. One morning, just before lunch, he spotted it by the big water fountain on the north side of school, the one that had such intense pressure that if you weren't careful, your face would get blasted.

He glanced at it, and the door opened all on its own.

Every time he considered it, he thought about having to tell his friends why he'd missed the library move. Even worse, though, he knew that while seeing Sal and Juliana would certainly make him feel better, he would still have to come back to Orangevale. He would have to deal with this nightmare all on his own.

So he drifted through the days, avoiding the Misfits, too, even though each of them tried to talk to him at one point or another. That meant he sat far from Aishah in Mrs. Caroline's class, and he ate all his lunches in the library.

Jackson came up to him while he was waiting for Papi to pick him up on Friday afternoon. He didn't say anything for a few moments and instead just scraped his shoe against the cement.

"Hey, Héctor, are you mad at us?"

Héctor turned his head. "At who?"

"Me. Aishah. Taylor."

He didn't *think* he was mad; mostly, he was embarrassed. So he said, "I don't think so."

"Did we do something to you?"

Emotions flooded Héctor's body: Anger. Frustration. Sadness. So he couldn't stop the words when they came out of his mouth.

"No," he said. "That's the problem. You didn't do anything."

Jackson froze. "What?"

"Why didn't you say anything? Or back me up? You just let Ms. Heath believe that I was lying."

Jackson's head drooped down. "I tried," he said, "but I was afraid."

"Well, imagine how I felt," said Héctor.

He knew it was mean and unfair as soon as the words came out of his mouth.

"I'm sorry," said Jackson, and behind his glasses, his eyes were red.

Papi pulled up in the car, and before Héctor got in, he put his hand on Jackson's arm. "I know. We'll talk. Just . . . not now."

Jackson nodded. "Word. See ya."

At home that evening, Héctor pulled out his phone and went to his old group chat with Tim and Sophia.

Neither of them had sent him a message in weeks.

Do they know what Mike said too?

It was an irrational thought. But he lay back on his bed, ignoring his homework for the third evening in a row, and he convinced himself that was what had *actually* happened. It was only a matter of time before everyone in his life started calling him that word.

Because that was all he was, here in Orangevale.

CHAPTER FORTY

That weekend, Abuela, who was still staying with the family while her ankle healed, took Héctor with her while she ran errands. She was very chatty, which was fine with him because it meant he didn't have to talk much. She gossiped about some of her friends in Orangevale. Her stories were an easy distraction. If Héctor could think about the lives of other people, he didn't have to think about his own.

At home, he kept to himself while he caught up on all the homework he'd put off during the week. He regretted ignoring his work, but it also kept his parents from bugging him about the plans he'd mentioned to go to the thrift store with his new friends. Sometimes, they were a little *too* perceptive, and he wasn't ready to talk to them yet about why it had fallen through.

(Or ever? He wasn't sure about that.)

Even after a weekend away from school, though, he still hadn't shaken the despair that held tightly on to his heart. He was terrified that he'd see Mike on Monday, but they never crossed paths in the hallways. He thought about talking to the Misfits at lunch, but he chickened out as soon as he entered the cafeteria, instead making a beeline to the library to eat the lunch Abuela had packed him.

Art class didn't bring him out of his funk either. Mrs. Caroline commented that his sketches lately almost seemed unfinished. "Are you sure you don't want to add more?" she said, tapping the still life of a bowl of fruit they'd been assigned that day.

He shook his head. He didn't explain himself further to Mrs. Caroline, either. In a way, he thought it was perfect unfinished. It felt more honest to him.

His Tuesday looked to be more of the same until lunchtime, when he realized that he'd left his food in the refrigerator at home. His stomach grumbled in response, and he was shocked at his first thought: *I should see if the Room has any food.*

No. He wasn't ready for that. Not yet.

So he stood in line, collected his unappetizing meal, and then had to make a choice: Where was he going to sit?

His eyes fell on his usual spot, but the Table of Misfits was empty except for Pat, planted in the same spot as always at the far end of the table. His face was buried in a book.

Empty was okay for the moment. He didn't see the rest of the Misfits anywhere, and he figured he could just leave if things got too weird.

He was by himself for a full minute before the bench across from Héctor squealed as it was pulled across the tile.

Jackson plopped down. "'Sup, Héctor."

Héctor forced a corner of his mouth to curl up, but that was it. "Hi," he said.

Aishah approached the table, too, and she sat to Héctor's right. "Hi, Héctor," she said.

"You guys don't have to sit with me," said Héctor. "I'll understand."

"I'll sit anywhere I want," Aishah said without hesitation. "Besides, you are not going to become Pat part two at this table."

"What?" said Héctor.

She gestured with a spork toward Pat. "Y'all are *literally* as far apart as humanly possible."

Taylor appeared behind Jackson. "What's good, Héctor? Nice to have you back!"

"*Is* it?" he said.

Aishah frowned at him. "Yes, Héctor, of *course* it is!"

"It's been so weird without you," Taylor added. "Well, plus, things have changed a little bit."

"Changed how?" said Héctor.

As if on cue, a new person sat at the Table of Misfits in between Jackson and Taylor.

Carlos.

Héctor's reaction was pure instinct: he pushed his tray forward and stood up.

"What is *he* doing here?" he said.

This wasn't happening! It didn't matter that Carlos had turned on Mike. How long had Carlos tormented all of them? Were the others forgetting that?

Carlos didn't flinch when Héctor stood up. He picked up the fresh-baked chocolate chip cookie off his tray and put it on Héctor's. "Consider this the start of an apology," he said. "A peace offering."

He felt a hand on his arm, and he looked down to see Aishah staring up at him, imploring him to sit back down. "It's okay, Héctor," she said. "I think you should hear him out."

He sat but continued shaking his head. "No, I don't think so. You *let* him go after me, Carlos!" He lowered his voice. "All of you did. You hung me out to dry."

"You're right," said Jackson. "Just like you said to me last week. We didn't do anything to stop him."

"And it probably doesn't help," added Taylor, "but we're all *terrified* of Mike."

Héctor's shoulders drooped. He couldn't be mad at that moment because he was just as afraid of Mike as they were.

"I know," said Héctor. "And I shouldn't have spoken to you like I did last week, Jackson."

"It's cool, I promise," he said, smiling. "I think we all get it."

"Because we've all been there," said Carlos.

That stopped Héctor. "*What?* What are you talking about, dude?"

Carlos's brown face turned a deep red. "Héctor, I'm so sorry," he said, his voice cracking. "I went along with most of it because . . . well." He wiped at his eyes. "I'm afraid of him, too. Last year, he started making fun of my dad. He works in landscaping, and Mike saw him working one day. He started saying the most awful things about me and my dad."

"Really?" said Héctor. "Like what he said to me? About the trash?"

"Worse," said Carlos. "But instead of standing up to him, I joined him. It was easier that way. If I made fun of the same people he picked on, then he would ignore me."

So, Héctor had been right about that part. But it still stung: Carlos had thrown so many people under the bus to save himself.

"That sucks, man," said Héctor. "But . . . what about us? You helped Mike!"

Carlos sighed. "I really am sorry for what I did. But I'll tell you the same thing I told Aishah, Jackson, and Taylor. We shouldn't have stayed quiet last week. We shouldn't have let that happen."

"None of us should have," said Aishah. "And we're tired of being afraid."

"Meaning *what*?" asked Héctor.

Carlos let out a long breath. "If you ever decide to confront Mike or Ms. Heath—and we totally get it if you don't—count me in. I'll help."

"Count us *all* in," said Jackson.

"It's okay," said Héctor. "I think I'll just do my best to avoid Mike."

"Well, for what it's worth," said Aishah, "we couldn't believe that you tried to stand up to Ms. Heath last week. That was *so* brave, Héctor. No one *ever* has."

Now Héctor's face burned. "Wait, really?"

Taylor nodded. "Bro, I don't think any of us have ever seen someone survive a double dose of Ms. Heath and Mike before. Like . . . ever. And here you are! You're like . . . like a dragon or something."

Héctor had to laugh at that. "A *dragon*? I wish I breathed fire."

"Maybe you could roast off Frank's terrible haircut," Aishah muttered.

Héctor's mouth dropped open. "Aishah!" he exclaimed. "That was mean!"

"But am I wrong?" she said. "Who cuts that boy's hair?"

Carlos laughed. "Actually . . . he does it himself."

"No!" said Jackson. "No *way* he does that."

Carlos nodded. "Yeah, he thinks it makes him look 'cute' for the girls."

"Ugh," groaned Héctor. "He's not even in the top one hundred cute boys at this school."

He didn't realize what he'd said until the silence spread over the table.

Oh no. What have I done?

But there were no expressions of horror, no shocked faces, no disgust anywhere at the Table of Misfits. Aishah was nodding her head; Jackson looked like he was about to leap over the table and give Héctor a hug; Carlos looked utterly pleased.

And Taylor was doing his best approximation of the heart eye emoji.

Héctor looked down the table.

Pat was staring at him, and he raised his thumb up and nodded.

"Well," said Héctor. "I'm glad that's out in the open."

"Me too," said Aishah. "You're not alone, you know that?"

"I guess," he said. "I'm sorry I never—"

"No, I don't think you understand her," said Jackson. "You're not *alone*." He tilted his head over toward Aishah, then pointed at himself.

Héctor's breath was caught in his throat. "Do you mean—?"

Jackson nodded. "Me. And Aishah."

"What?" Héctor felt like he couldn't breathe. "You're serious?"

"No, I'm queer," said Aishah, and the whole table— Pat included—burst into laughter.

"And I like boys," said Jackson. "I don't know what word works for me, so . . ." He put a hand over his heart. "That's me."

Héctor felt like his jaw was on the floor. "Whoa, I had *no* idea!"

"Well, now you know," said Aishah. "Two more members of the team—and two supporters in Carlos and Taylor."

"Most definitely," said Carlos. "We got your back."

Taylor flashed a peace sign, a toothy grin on his face. "Best friends, bro."

As the group fell into conversation and Aishah tried to get him to tell her who he thought the cutest boy was (he wouldn't tell her), Héctor felt like he could breathe again, like he could be himself, totally and completely.

It was the first time he'd felt that *outside* of the Room, and he clung to it tightly.

CHAPTER FORTY-ONE

Héctor left lunch with an odd feeling brewing in his stomach, something in between relief and a bubbling nervousness. He was lost in himself when he rounded the corner and found himself next to the Room.

He came to a dead stop and ran his fingers over the wooden frame. He'd ignored this place for a week, convinced that his friends would be disappointed in him. But . . . *he* was the one who had given up on them, hadn't he? And it was *Mike* who had put these dark ideas in his mind.

An announcement broke his silence. "Students," said Vice Principal Giles, "as a reminder, please head straight to the auditorium tomorrow morning instead of your first classes. The spirit assembly will start at eight forty-five a.m. sharp. Thank you!"

Assembly? He vaguely recalled Mrs. Torres mentioning it in homeroom, but the past few days had blended together into a haze.

No, he couldn't let Mike have this much control over his life.

It was finally time.

He wrenched the door open, and the Room appeared as Sal's cozy library, books lining the walls in tightly packed shelves. There were three majestic upholstered chairs in the middle of the Room, and two of them were occupied, one by Sal, who was eating some savory-smelling noodles in a flower-patterned blouse, and the other by Juliana, who had her nose buried in a graphic novel, her hair now in a set of box braids.

"Héctor?" she said, dropping the book to the floor, and then both of them were on their feet, and they rushed to Héctor, then wrapped their arms around him.

"Where you *been*, dude?" said Sal.

"We missed you so much!" said Juliana.

"And we're so, so sorry we couldn't help you," said Sal.

"Help *me*?" Héctor stepped back from them. "But *I* was the one who didn't help *you*."

"Bruh, what are you talking about?" asked Juliana.

"Moving books last week," he said. "I stood y'all up."

"That's okay!" said Sal. "Half the school showed up to help. It was amazing! You didn't really miss anything."

"Still, I feel terrible," said Héctor. "I couldn't be there for you."

"*We* should have been there for *you*, Héctor," said Juliana. "We should have said something."

He put his hands in his hair, frustrated. "Yo, I have no

idea what you're talking about."

The realization spread across Juliana's face first. "Oh no," she said. "Sal, he doesn't know we saw it."

Sal gasped.

"Saw *what*?"

Oh no.

No, no, no.

They *couldn't* have.

Juliana grimaced. "What happened to you."

His heart dropped into his stomach.

He was right back there: in the hallway. Mike was in his face. The groan he'd heard . . .

Oh. That was the door to the Room, wasn't it? And like it had hidden itself when Ms. Heath had forced Héctor to reveal it, it had cloaked itself from Mike.

"So you saw it," said Héctor.

"We saw everything," said Sal.

He groaned. "How much is 'everything'?"

"We were both in the Room when you opened it and that security lady was with you," said Juliana. "We didn't get it at first, but . . . Héctor, the Room prevented her from seeing us."

"And then, we were gonna go out and grab you," said Sal, "but that other boy showed up and . . ."

Sal didn't finish. And they didn't need to.

"Then we were both talking about what to do," said

Juliana, "and by the time we came to get you, you were gone."

Héctor wobbled for a moment. They *saw* it? *All* of it? He made for one of the chairs and sank into it. What was this feeling passing through him? Fear? Anxiety?

No.

He was *ashamed*.

Ashamed that he hadn't stood up for himself. Ashamed that a word had affected him so much. Ashamed that he felt so *useless*.

"Héctor, you all right?" Juliana asked. "We just missed you, that's all."

"I don't know why I let Mike get to me," he confessed. "I just keep hearing his voice in my head, calling me that word over and over again."

"You get to be hurt, Héctor," Sal said. "Just like Juliana gets to be hurt over what I said to her. What Mike did was awful."

"You saw how upset I was over my principal," said Juliana. "It's not fair to yourself to try and like . . . I dunno. Deny how you're feeling."

"He *hurt* you," said Sal. "He's been doing it since you got here, right?"

It came out of Héctor in a flood. He caught Juliana up on everything he had confessed to Sal: Mike and the Minions. The name calling. There was some of it that was new to Sal, too: How Héctor had told the truth to Ms. Heath—*twice*—and how it had backfired. The lack of relief that came from talking to Mrs. Caroline. How he was so worried about his family finding out what was going on at school. When he was done, he felt both exhausted—it was draining to recount it all—and *lighter.* It was as if some massive stone had been lifted out of his chest and cast away.

He guessed that this was what telling the truth felt like.

Héctor braced himself for what would come next: The guilt. He was certain that the two of them would ask him why he hadn't told them earlier. He could hear the questions in his head. *We told you about our problems! Why did you keep everything to yourself?*

But that didn't happen. Instead, Sal nodded, and then said, "What can we do for you?"

"I'm ready for anything," added Juliana. "You name the time and the place, and it's *on.*"

Héctor laughed at her. "I don't know that there's anything you all *can* do. I think I just have to ignore him until he finds a new target."

Juliana gave him a skeptical look. "And then just let *them* get bullied?"

"No, of course not," said Héctor. "But what *could* I possibly do?"

Oh. It hit him hard: he had asked his Orangevale friends why they hadn't stopped Mike, and yet here he was, unsure how to stop him himself.

"Maybe we use the Room to get revenge?" suggested Sal.

"Nah," said Héctor. "Something tells me that getting revenge would just make Mike madder at me, and then he would *never* leave me alone."

"What if we go after this Ms. Heath?" asked Sal. "Maybe that's the way we approach this."

"I appreciate that you want to help," he said. "But I don't want this to get worse than it already is. Can we just leave it be for now?"

Sal and Juliana traded a look, then nodded at him.

"Whatever you want," said Sal.

"And I'll stop keeping secrets," he promised. "From both of you."

"Perfect," said Juliana, and both she and Sal smiled at him.

He felt so much lighter, but his eyes were heavy, and exhaustion was creeping into his head. He wiped at his eyes.

He'd been crying and hadn't even noticed.

"Okay, okay, enough of this!" said Héctor. "I need to know what you've both been up to. And when is your dance, Juliana?"

"Friday!" she exclaimed. "I just finished my playlist, and I'm so excited. I got some Janelle Monáe, some Prince, maybe a little Beyoncé. One of her PG songs, of course."

"And how do you feel about going with *Sascha*?" asked Sal. "That's what we *really* want to know."

Juliana bit her lip. "I'm a little nervous," she admitted. "I just don't want anything to go wrong."

"You're going to be *perfect*," said Héctor. "You're gonna play the best set ever, and then you're gonna slow dance with Sascha, and all this will have been worth it."

"You sure?" said Juliana.

"Definitely," he said. "You're gonna kill it."

Héctor asked about the noodles Sal was eating. They explained it was a dish called pancit that their father made all the time. Sal promised to bring some for everyone to share. The promise filled Héctor with joy, but as he thought about going back to class, dread crept in. Was his life always going to be watered down by Mike and Frank?

Maybe it was time for him to do something about all of this.

CHAPTER FORTY-TWO

"¡Vámonos, Héctor!"

Abuela Sonia honked the horn a couple more times as Héctor raced down the front steps at school. "I'm coming, I'm coming!" he shouted back. He hadn't expected her to pick him up from school that day, but she was always a welcome sight.

He hopped in the passenger side of her sedan and saw her cane stuck between the seats. She had on another one of her colorful tops that she'd made at home. This one was covered in patterns of suns and flowers. She was como un jardín, all by herself.

"We got somewhere to be, nieto," she said. "Una sorpresa."

A surprise? Héctor's day had already been so very full of them. "Where are you taking me?"

She rolled her eyes dramatically. "What kind of surprise would it be if I told you?"

"Okay, fair," he said. "Take me forth, Abuela!"

Abuela Sonia was uncharacteristically quiet on the drive, so Héctor gazed out the window, watching

Orangevale pass him. The tall palms, the homes and businesses set so far-back from the street, the group of kids on their BMX bikes . . . all of it made him look at the city in a new light. It wasn't the same as the Mission. It never would be. But after the day he'd had, he began to feel hope that he could carve out his own life here.

"Are we going to that thrift store you mentioned?" he asked, breaking the silence.

Abuela tried to hide a smile. "Wow. You didn't ask me to spoil the surprise for five whole minutes."

He laughed at her. "Okay, okay. I'm giving myself over to you. And trusting you."

This time, Abuela's smile was infectious and she fidgeted in her seat. Oh, what was this secret? She looked like she was going to explode!

So even Héctor couldn't hide his shock as Abuela Sonia turned into a tiny strip mall, and there, at the very end of the building, was a bright and colorful sign: PANADERÍA HERNANDEZ.

"Abuela," he said, his voice cautious. "Is that a panadería? Here? In Orangevale?!"

She smiled ear to ear. "I found it last week online," she said. "I know you said you missed home, so I thought I'd find a tiny piece of home *here*."

"I can't believe it," he said.

"I don't know if it's any good, but . . . would you like to try it with me, papito?"

He could not imagine anything better.

Once inside Panadería Hernandez, Héctor was overwhelmed: By the yeasty, sweet smell that filled his nostrils. By the bright colors of the conchas and the galletas and the endless rows of sweet things to eat. By the gracious smiles on the faces of the man and woman behind the counter, who explained all the pan dulce that Héctor did not recognize, like the spiral-shaped novia, or the sweet muffin called a mantecada. The woman was named Zoraida, and gorgeous black curls fell on either side of her face. She pointed out her favorite pan dulce and described them, and Héctor deeply wished he could eat them all. He ended up getting a pink concha and pan de muerto, his personal favorite, which was usually reserved for El Día de los Muertos, but thankfully they had some left.

Abuela Sonia told him that he deserved to be happy now, anyway.

That was what he was focused on as he sat across from her at a wooden booth, sweet breads piled up in front of him. He had only stuffed a few bites in his mouth when she sat down, two Mexican hot chocolates in her hands, and said, "Héctor, I really do want you to be happy."

"I know," he said, crumbs tumbling out of his mouth. "Trust me. I'm *very* happy right now."

"I know," she said. "But are you *actually* happy?"

His hand froze, midway to his mouth, and then he put the mantecada back down. "What do you mean?"

She shrugged. "I don't know. You tell me."

He narrowed his eyes at her. "Are you trying to trick me with pan dulce, Abuela?"

"Maybe," she said. "But don't think I haven't noticed you moping around the house for the past week or so. All of us have noticed it. Me, your mami and papi . . . we know you're going through something." She put her hands up when Héctor made to speak. "Just telling you what I've seen."

He didn't respond to that, so she continued. "You know me. Straight to the point. And I've backed off to give you space. I just thought I'd try something new on you."

"Which is?" he asked.

"A panadería."

He groaned. "So this *is* a trick!"

She laughed. "Not really. I am happy to be here with you, even if you don't tell me what's going on. I promise that, nieto."

He took a tentative bite out of the concha, rolled the sugar around with his tongue. Being honest with the

Misfits had felt good. Telling Juliana and Sal everything felt *incredible*. So why was there still all this hesitation in him?

"I don't know where to start," he finally said.

Which was true!

"Try the beginning," she said. "Even if that's the day you moved here to Orangevale."

That wasn't *exactly* what he meant. How could he tell her about the Room? *Should* he even do that? He examined Abuela's face, and her eyes were soft and loving. He did feel safe with her, just like he did with the friends he'd made. All his worst anxieties—that he'd disappointed everyone, that no one would want to be around him anymore—hadn't come true. So, there was no reason to think Abuela would be any different.

But if he started telling his abuela about a magical room that allowed him to travel to other states, to defy the laws of time and space, she wouldn't be very happy. She would be furious with him for lying to her, for not taking this trip to the panadería seriously.

That *was* the beginning.

That *was* the truth.

But . . . the Room wasn't really the problem, was it? In fact, it never had been.

He took a deep breath.

Let it out.

Took another.

Abuela Sonia smiled, and there was no pity on her face. She just looked . . . proud. Proud to have a grandson like him.

So he started talking.

He chose the first day at Orangevale Middle School as the beginning, then traced his way from that to the taunting. The jokes. The Minions.

To *Mike*.

Halfway through talking about Mike, Abuela Sonia reached across the table with a napkin and wiped at the tears pouring down his face. "Don't want your pan dulce to get all soggy," she said, and he laughed—because it was funny, because it broke the tension, because if he didn't, he would have started bawling.

He found a way to tell her about Sal and Juliana by saying that they were students in eighth grade and had classes on the far side of campus.

He was surprised, then, that it was somehow more painful to tell Abuela the truth about the bullying than it had been earlier that day when he confessed it to his friends. He didn't understand that. Maybe it was because he'd known Abuela his whole life, and now, after twelve years, he was finally showing her a side of him she never knew existed.

So he pressed on, even though he hesitated when he

got to the garbage. He almost didn't tell her about the word Mike had used on him, but . . . he couldn't hold this part back. It was the worst of it all, and if he was going to conquer it, he had to face it.

Abuela Sonia was quiet for a while when he finished. She picked up an elotito, a miniature pan dulce shaped like an ear of corn, and she chewed on it a bit.

Then she pointed it at him.

"You and I, we are not so very different, nieto."

Héctor blew his nose on a napkin. "I don't know," he finally said, once he could talk. "How is this happening to me? I feel like I'm never going to escape this. I'll always be what he called me."

"But you made some friends, didn't you?"

"Huh?"

She named them.

Aishah.

Jackson.

Taylor.

Sal.

Juliana.

(She wasn't sure about Carlos, either.)

"And you wouldn't have made those friends if you weren't a good, interesting person," she said. "These people *want* to be around you, Héctor."

"I guess," he said, taking another bite.

"No 'I guess' allowed. I'm right." She pointed the elotito at him again. "I think this Mike and Frank have gotten in your head, papito. And you're starting to believe them."

He'd been so down on himself for a long, long time. Maybe his abuela was right.

She reached across the table and held his hand. "Just because Mike and his friends are mean and insecure doesn't mean they'll *always* have power over you."

"Insecure?" he asked. "Mike isn't insecure. He's so *confident*."

"Those don't mean the same thing," she said, shaking her head. "You can appear incredibly confident on the outside, but be consumed by insecurity on the inside."

"But how is *Mike* insecure?"

"Some boys are raised to believe that there are things they're not supposed to do as boys," she continued. "Like dance. Or wear makeup. Or do theater. Or be an artist."

"But . . ." He scratched at his head with his free hand. "That doesn't make any sense. I do all those things, and I'm still a boy."

Then he thought of Sal, of how brave and scary it was for them to do what they wanted and not be a boy or a girl, but who they really *were*.

This gender stuff seemed so complicated sometimes.

"I know, nieto," his abuela said. "That wasn't as big of

a deal back in San Francisco. But not everyone is as open about this kind of stuff."

"So why can't Mike just leave me alone? None of what I do affects him at all!"

"Oh, I can't explain everything about him," she said. "And I don't want you to think I'm trying to excuse him. He still sounds like un baboso."

"Abuela!" Héctor cried, nearly choking.

"I'm just saying. I don't like anyone who makes you feel that way about yourself."

"I just wish I had told you earlier," he said.

"Why didn't you?"

"I didn't want you to think I couldn't handle the hard stuff," he said. "You told me to do things by myself, remember?"

She frowned deeply. "¿Cuándo? No recuerdo eso."

"At the carnicería," he explained. "And I know you dealt with Abuelo leaving you all on your own and—"

She squeezed his hand tightly, then withdrew it. Silence fell, and Héctor watched as her face twisted up. It was a quick flash, and then she shook her head.

"What is it, Abuela?" he asked.

"Es nada," she said, dismissing him with a wave.

He snatched his abuela's paper plate from her. "I thought this was La Panadería de la Verdad," he joked. "Where's the honesty?"

But there was no humor on Abuela Sonia's face. She looked away from Héctor, and he recognized what was happening: She was ashamed. Bashful. Shy.

Was this what his face had looked like earlier that day, right before he told Sal and Juliana the truth?

What on earth did *she* have to be shy about?

"Héctor, that wasn't what I meant," she said. "At all. I was just talking about what hobbies you could have started."

"But . . ." Héctor sighed in exasperation. "This whole time, I thought you would be disappointed in me if I asked for help!"

"Oh, nieto, *never*!" she exclaimed. "I'm so sorry you thought that's what I meant. Héctor, you can *always* ask people for help. That doesn't make you a bad person, or weak, and it *certainly* would never disappoint me."

He put his head in his hands. "I've been so worried!"

"No," Abuela Sonia said, shaking her head, and now her eyes were watery and red. "No, this is my fault."

"What? No! I'll figure this out."

"It's not that," she said. "I just . . . I just thought that the world would have gotten easier for kids like you. I didn't expect my little Héctor to still be struggling with this sort of stuff, too."

He sat upright, put his mantecada down. "Struggling with what stuff?" he asked.

Abuela Sonia finally looked at him. Her eyes were red and glassy, and the lights of the panadería illuminated the tracks of her tears down her cheeks. "Oh, mi amor, why do you think your abuelo left me all those years ago?"

His heart thumped fiercely in his chest. "I don't know. I never really asked Papi about it. He just told me that Abuelo fell in love with someone else, and that divorce happens sometimes."

She smiled then. "He's not wrong. Eventually, Esteban *did* fall in love again, and he's married now. I'm very happy for him. Honestly."

Héctor took a sip of his hot chocolate. "Then what do you mean?"

She let out a long breath. "Papito, I was the one who fell in love with someone else *first*."

"Oh," he said, his eyebrows creasing together as he tried to comprehend what he'd just heard.

"With a woman," she added.

His mouth fell open.

His heart raced faster.

And his eyes watered up.

"So . . . you're like . . . ," Héctor began.

He couldn't even finish the sentence. He put his hand on his chest.

"Yes, Héctor," she said. "I am just like you."

His bottom lip quivered.

He thought of what Aishah and Jackson had told him at lunch. And here was his own abuela, admitting that she was *just like him*? It swallowed him whole. Aishah's words came back to him: *You're not alone, you know that?*

"Your parents wanted me to tell you for a long time," she said, the tears streaming freely. "You were too young when Esteban and I separated. Oh, Héctor, he was so supportive of me. He said he'd always suspected, and he wanted nothing more than for me to be happy. So when you came out, your papi begged me to tell you. He thought it would help you."

"Wait," he said, wiping at his cheeks. "I'm confused. Who was she? Why have I never met her? I thought you lived alone."

She pressed her lips together tightly. "You were five when it happened."

He frowned. "I thought you said Abuelo Esteban left you when I was like two."

"Her name was Rosa," she said.

"Was?"

Oh no, he thought.

Abuela Sonia gulped down some of her hot chocolate. "A drunk driver hit her," she said, then blew her nose on a napkin. "She didn't suffer."

"I'm sorry," he said. "I wish I could have met her."

"Me too, amor. Me, too."

She put her head in her hands for a moment, and Héctor stood up and squeezed into the booth next to her, so he could wrap his arms around her torso as her body shook.

"That's why I didn't tell you," she explained. "I wasn't ashamed of who I was. I wasn't ashamed of her. I wasn't ashamed of my marriage ending. I just . . . I didn't know how to tell you that the person I loved most in the world was no longer here. Every time I worked up the courage, the words seemed to evaporate."

"You tried to tell me," he said as it dawned on him. "Weeks ago."

She nodded. "I recognized what you were going through," she said. "But then I worried . . . what if I was making it about myself? What if I was wrong about what I thought was going on, and then you pulled away from me?"

"But Abuela, I would *never* leave you," he said, and he hugged her tight again.

"I guess I just got worried about someone I love leaving me. *Again*."

She told him how hard it was to deal with absence, to have a hole in your life that couldn't be filled by anyone or anything else, at least not at first. But slowly, over time, the hole began to shrink.

It reminded Héctor of something he hadn't told her. "You know my old friends from Alta Vista basically ghosted me?"

"Ay, no," she said. "That has to have made this hard."

"I guess," he said. "But I think you're right. I was so sad over losing those friends that I wouldn't accept that I had made *new* friends here."

"That's part of life," said Abuela Sonia. "You learn to surround yourself with people who make an effort to be in your life. Do these new friends make you feel like you matter? Like they actually care for you?"

"Yeah," he said, without hesitation. "They do."

"They sound like keepers," she said.

"Te amo, Abuela," he said. "Just the way you are."

She pulled him closer. "Just the way you are," she repeated.

It was a promise.

CHAPTER FORTY-THREE

The next time Héctor walked through the double doors into Orangevale Middle School, it was like he'd stepped into a new world.

He needed help.

And it was okay to ask for it.

Maybe that was why the Room had shown up in the first place. He had asked the universe for help, out of desperation and sadness and fear, and it had provided. He still didn't understand its magic or where it came from, but he couldn't deny what the Room had done to his life.

He passed by the door.

JANITOR.

It wasn't time yet, though. Héctor smiled at the Room. *I'll come back for you.*

Héctor picked up the pace. He'd been thinking about this all morning, and perhaps it was time to tell a sympathetic adult. His first instinct was Mrs. Caroline, and he made his way toward her art class. She would definitely listen to him, and she'd promised to help.

Yet he found his body slowing in the hallway. What if she took Mike's side? What if she took *no one's* side, and nothing got solved? Suddenly, this didn't feel like the right decision, and Héctor came to a full stop.

No. This wasn't right.

How could he end this? How could he make Mike leave him alone?

Héctor turned back from the art class, aimlessly walking toward the entrance. He passed Ms. Heath, who merely nodded her head at him. A brief flash of nerves shot up his spine as he remembered what she last said to him.

He was done trying to tell people what had happened to him. And that's when the first spark of an idea hit him: he had to *show* everyone what was going on.

He needed help for this, and he knew who he needed it from, but . . . where were the Misfits *outside* of lunch?

"Think, think," Héctor whispered to himself. "Where would you hang out before school if you weren't popular?"

It didn't take him long to figure that one out. He rounded the nearest corner, and seconds later, he pushed the doors and walked into the library. The librarian, Mr. Reynolds, a tall Black man with thick locs to his shoulders, nodded a greeting, then went back to organizing a stack of books.

Gathered around one of the desktops at the computer station were the Misfits: Aishah, Jackson, Taylor, and the newest member, Carlos.

Aishah was the first to notice that he'd arrived. "Héctor!" she said. "Whoa, we've never seen you in here in the morning."

"I know," he said. "I've spent some lunches here, though."

"It's pretty nice," said Taylor. "And I can do all my alien research here on the computers."

"Right," said Héctor, scratching his head at that. "Aliens."

"You all right?" asked Jackson, who rose from the chair in front of the computer. "You came in here all quick."

"Yeah, you look like you're *vibrating*," said Aishah.

"I got an idea," he said. "I changed my mind."

"About what?" said Jackson.

Héctor gave Carlos a pointed look. "I am glad you apologized, but . . . would you like to *do* something to make it up to me?"

Carlos nodded his head furiously. "Yes," he said. "*Anything*."

"What's on your mind, bruh?" said Jackson.

Héctor had never smiled this big since he'd gotten to Orangevale Middle School.

"It's time to finally expose Mike for who he is."

Aishah actually whooped out loud. "I told you he'd come around," she said, laughing.

"We're there, bro," said Carlos. "Whatever it is."

Taylor jumped up and down. "Oh, this is *great*. I can finally use all my training."

"What training?" said Héctor.

"Oh no," groaned Aishah. "Don't get him started."

"I've been watching YouTube videos," Taylor explained. "I'm pretty sure I'm at *least* a black belt by now."

"That's . . . wonderful," said Héctor. "Wait—a black belt in *what*?"

"Yes," said Taylor, smiling.

"O-okay," said Héctor, shaking his head. "But it's not that kind of plan." The details were forming in his mind. "Okay, you know that janitor's closet near the front of school?"

"Sure," said Carlos. "It's not far from where Ms. Heath hangs out."

"That's the one," said Héctor. "After homeroom, meet me there before you go to the spirit assembly."

"We'll be there," said Jackson.

"Okay, I got one more thing to do," said Héctor. "Thank you!"

When Héctor left the library, he looked both ways to make sure Ms. Heath wasn't around.

The coast was clear.

I need you, he thought, closing his eyes. *I need you to be there, and I need Sal and Juliana to be inside.*

This had to work. Héctor was certain he'd never needed anything like this in his whole life.

He got his answer when he opened his eyes. The door was directly across from the library.

JANITOR.

This was it.

This could be exactly what he needed.

He tore the door open.

There was the couch.

The fridge.

The television.

The video games.

There were Sal and Juliana, a couple glasses of horchata between them.

They turned to look at him.

"Héctor?" Sal said, worried. "Everything okay?"

"I know that I told you that I wasn't going to do anything about what's been happening to me," he said, coming into the Room and letting the door slam behind him.

"Yeah, of course," said Juliana, standing up. "It's unfair of us to try to *force* you to do anything about Mike."

"Well, you don't need to. Because I'm ready."

Sal got up too. "Ready for *what*?"

Héctor started laughing. He couldn't control it. The idea was so dramatic, so over the top, so very . . .

Him.

It was the most Héctor plan of all time.

"Y'all want to help me get a little revenge?"

CHAPTER FORTY-FOUR

When Héctor told them the plan, Sal laughed so hard at it that they started crying, and Juliana simply stared at Héctor, slack-jawed.

"Oh, you really *thought* about this one," she finally said. "This is . . . this is almost *evil*."

"But it's not," said Sal. "And it's exactly what Mike and Frank deserve."

"The others are about to be here any second, so you need to go take your places," said Héctor. "And that's why I need *you*, Juliana. I don't know anything about this auditorium and how it works. I only know the theater at my last school."

"That's fine," she said. "Most sound systems are the same, and Sal can help me set up."

"And you know what you have to do?" Héctor asked Sal.

They nodded. "I am *ready* for this."

"I can't thank you enough," he said.

Then Juliana and Sal rushed in for a hug. And at that

moment, Héctor felt like he was going to conquer the world.

After homeroom, Héctor was out of breath from taking a risk and running back to the Room, but thankfully, Ms. Heath hadn't spotted him. His timing was impeccable, too, because maybe ten seconds later, there was a knock at the door.

As many times as he'd been in the Room, it had always changed when he wasn't looking. But there was no time for that now, and he gasped as the transformation began.

The back wall of the Room rushed toward the door, and the furniture sank into the floor as if it were made of quicksand. As the sides of the Room shrank, one of them swallowed up the refrigerator. Héctor quickly moved back until he bumped into the door, and then the shelving units *grew out of the wall*. They sprouted forth, and all the supplies were on them, too: the bottle of hand soap. The bleach. The floor polish. The broom popped out of another wall, then came to rest upon it.

Héctor looked up into the corner.

King Ferdinand crawled out of the darkness, and in a matter of seconds, he wove an intricate web, one that looked like it had been there for years.

He smiled. "Good morning, King Ferdinand," he said.

And then he turned and opened the door.

Carlos, Aishah, Taylor, and Jackson quickly stuffed themselves into the closet, lit only by a single bulb above them. "Wow, it's pretty snug in here," said Jackson. "You hide here sometimes?"

"Yeah," said Héctor. "And before you say it: yes, I'm aware of the irony."

They all looked at him with blank faces.

Héctor pointed at his own chest. "Get it? Me? Hiding in the closet?"

Jackson was the first to laugh, then the others followed. "Yo, that's a good one," said Aishah. "You're funny, you know that?"

He beamed.

Since the assembly was starting soon, he told them everything as quickly as he could. When he finished, Carlos looked like he was going to explode. "Yo, I got you," he said. "It's perfect. Mike will be so easy to rile up."

"All you have to do is make sure they get backstage, okay?" said Héctor. "In case they don't take the bait."

"And we're the bait, right?" said Aishah, smiling. "We can say *anything* to him?"

"The worse you can come up with, the better," replied Héctor. "As long as you get them to where they need to be."

"This feels too good to be true," said Taylor. "You think this is gonna work?"

"I do," said Héctor.

"We won't let you down," said Carlos. He put his hand on Héctor's shoulder. "And *I* won't let you down again either."

The first bell rang, which meant they had only a few minutes left to pull this off. The Misfits gathered in the hallway, and Héctor stood just inside the Room, which was still disguised as the janitor's closet.

The only problem . . . they had to find Mike, and *soon*.

"Hey, buttface! Out of my way!"

Héctor could recognize that voice from a mile away. *How nice of Mike to walk right into our trap*, he thought.

"Now's your chance," Héctor whispered. "Let Mike get a little ahead, and then—"

"Oh, don't worry," said Jackson, who rubbed his hands together like a supervillain. "He'll never know what's coming."

The group waited for a few seconds, and then . . .

"Hey, Mike!" Aishah screamed.

Héctor moved to the side of the doorway and gazed down the hall. Sure enough, Mike spun around.

"What do *you* want?" he spat.

Frank appeared behind him.

"Ugh, it's Aishah," he said. "Does she even wash her hair with that thing on?"

"Funny you say that, Frank," she shot back. "Do you wash that peach fuzz you call a mustache, or is that just left over after you drink from the toilet?"

Héctor was pretty sure that his spirit exited his body at that moment. A couple kids who were walking by stopped to stare at Aishah.

"What did you say?" Frank stalked forward, but Mike put his hand out, stopping him.

"I got this," said Mike.

"Do you?" said Carlos. "Or are you gonna ask your dad to do your homework again?"

Mike's jaw dropped. "Bro," he said. "What are you doing with *them*?"

"I think the better question is what I was doing with *you*," Carlos shot back. "They're way better friends than you ever were."

Héctor watched as Mike shook his head. "Whatever, man," he said. "I don't need this."

And then Mike turned around and started to walk away.

There were no more taunts or threats; just the sound of shoes on tile as everyone shuffled toward the auditorium.

No! Héctor thought. This wasn't supposed to happen!

But before he could panic further, Jackson started cackling. "I always knew you were actually a *coward*," he said, drawing out that last word. "A wimp. A *loser*."

Mike spun back around. "Never," he said. "You're going to regret that."

"Am I?" said Jackson. "I'm not the one here who looks like a giant Cabbage Patch Kid."

That was it. Without another word, Mike and Frank sprinted toward the Misfits and the chase was on.

Héctor really hoped this would work.

He took a deep breath. The next step: he had to will the Room to let him out backstage in the auditorium. He *needed* it; he wasn't sure he could sneak backstage in time.

You can do it, he thought.

He opened the door.

And stared at Mrs. Caroline, who sat at her desk.

His heart leaped into his throat. *What?* Why had the Room sent him here?

Mrs. Caroline looked up and smiled. "Good morning, Héctor," she said. "Shouldn't you be heading to the spirit assembly, though?"

"Ummmm."

That's all that came out of his mouth. Just a *sound*. So

he slammed the door and leaned against it. *No*, he told the Room. *That is not what I need.*

He opened it again.

Mrs. Caroline was standing up now, and she started to approach him. "Héctor?" she said, her tone worried. "Everything okay?"

"No!" he shouted, which was probably the *worst* possible response to give, and he shut the door forcefully again.

What was happening? This was a disaster!

"I need to be backstage," he said out loud. "Please."

This time, he inched the door open slowly.

And was face-to-face with Mrs. Caroline.

She stuck her hand out and held the door. "Mr. Muñoz," she said. "You cannot keep interrupting me, and you should be on your way to the auditorium."

Her gaze drifted above Héctor's head.

And behind him.

Into the Room.

Which, to Héctor, still looked like a closet.

Which, to Mrs. Caroline, would be *literally* impossible.

He held his breath.

But she just looked back down at him. "Do you need anything?" she asked. "Anything at all?"

"No," he said, the word rushing out with the air he'd been holding back. "I'm sorry, Mrs. Caroline. I'll leave you alone."

She stepped back, confusion on her face, and he closed the door.

He was sweating. This was worse than he could have imagined. The Misfits were supposed to lead Mike and Frank to *Héctor*. If he wasn't there at the end, this would fall apart in a second. Should he just run for it? Oh, God, how would that *work*? The second any teacher saw him trying to get near the stage, he'd be caught.

"Please," he begged. "I need to be backstage."

He opened the door.

Ms. Heath's office was across the hall.

Shut.

Opened.

Mr. Giles's office—the vice principal?

"Stop it!" he screamed, his voice echoing in the hallway.

Shut.

Opened.

Home. HOME?!

The Room had brought him *home*.

He stared at his own bedroom, his colorful cobija beckoning to him, some clothes spread at the foot of his bed.

"Héctor?"

No.

Abuela Sonia's voice.

"¿Eres tú, Héctor?"

Why was this happening to him?

He slammed the door one last time.

When Héctor turned around, there was just a small gray couch in the middle of the Room. No TV. No fridge. No games. But he didn't even make it there; he collapsed on the ground where he stood and began to cry in frustration.

"This isn't what I want!" he screamed, and he pounded a fist against the floor. "Who are you? Why won't you give me what I need?"

He looked up.

He was met with silence.

Because of *course* he was.

This was just a room. Not a person. Not a living thing. It might have been magical in ways he could not understand, but . . . it was still a room.

He stood up and wiped the snot away. He placed a hand on the door.

"Please," he said. "I can't do what you want me to. I can't talk to those people."

He sniffled. "I have to do this *my* way."

Héctor gripped the handle.

"Please. Let me do this."

He opened the door to the Room.

An expansive darkness greeted him.

He took a step forward, and he found himself laughing.

Backstage.

He was backstage.

CHAPTER FORTY-FIVE

Héctor had very little time to appreciate this turn of events before Juliana appeared from the shadows to his left. "It's so dark back here!" she whispered. "Are you sure we can't turn on some lights?"

"Not yet," said Héctor. "We don't want anyone to suspect there's someone back here. Just turn on the single spotlight once they're here."

Sal sidled up to Héctor on his right side. "Well, at least I figured out how to open the curtain," they said.

"What about the sound system?" Héctor asked Juliana. "Is it like the one at your school?"

"Yeah," she said. "Same brand and everything."

"Then you know when to turn it on, right?"

"Most def," she said. "This is gonna work, Héctor. I know it."

I hope so, he thought.

They each crept to their places: Juliana went back into the shadows to the control panel for the microphones. Sal crossed the stage and stood in the wings, waiting for their cue.

And Héctor stood in the middle of the stage.

Waiting.

A door inched open on the same side of the stage as Sal.

Héctor held his breath.

Aishah snuck in, followed by Jackson. Héctor wasn't sure they could see him, so he cupped his hands around his mouth. "Pssst!" he whispered, then waved them over. Once they found him, he asked, "Where are they?"

Jackson was out of breath for a moment. "We lost them," he wheezed out.

"*What?*" Héctor said.

"Frank started chasing us," he explained, "and Mike went after the others. But we should be fine. Taylor . . . he . . ."

"Oh *no*," said Héctor, hitting his forehead with an open palm. "What did he *do*?"

"Oh, it was amazing," said Aishah. "He did this flying leap off a corner and collided with Frank, and he got Mike *and* Frank to chase *him*."

"I respect his energy," said Héctor, trying not to laugh. "Even if I don't understand it."

"Don't worry," said Aishah. "They'll be here."

Aishah and Jackson snuck back out of the stage doors.

Héctor's heart was racing, and he nearly jumped out of his skin when those same doors burst open. Carlos and Taylor stumbled through.

"Go!" hissed Héctor. "Get out of here!"

They could all hear footsteps in the hallway, so Carlos and Taylor took a risk and snuck out from behind the curtain to get to their seats. *Please don't let them get caught,* he begged. He couldn't have this fall apart now.

The doors opened one more time.

Héctor's targets arrived.

And immediately froze.

The noise from the other side of the curtain continued to grow; the rest of the school was getting settled in the auditorium. Héctor watched as Sal tucked farther into the shadow by the wall to stay hidden from Mike and Frank.

This has to work, Héctor thought.

He stepped forward and walked to center stage.

A single beam of light popped on above him and showered down, casting a perfect circle around Héctor, illuminating him and his outfit.

He had the red flannel tied around his waist, the same one he'd stuffed back into his closet weeks ago. His black denim cutoffs looked perfect with his brown boots and the black tank top.

Héctor's two bullies crept toward him, glee and hunger on their faces.

He was done dressing how *other* people wanted him to. He had tried so hard to be what these boys wanted: Quiet. Obedient. Small. *Normal.*

No more.

It was time for Héctor to step into a starring role.

And it was the role of a lifetime:

He was going to be *himself.*

Héctor raised his hands up. "You got me," he said.

Mike stalked up to him, his face just inches from Héctor's. "Why you gotta be so *dramatic*, Heck-tor? Is it because you just can't help it?"

Frank snickered.

"Yes," said Héctor. "I truly can't help it. This is who I am."

"We don't like your kind around here," Frank said, and it was like the words slithered out of his mouth.

"What kind would that be?" Héctor asked. "Just . . . humor me."

Mike squinted at Héctor, then looked to Frank. "What? What are you talking about?"

"Well, I just don't understand what my 'kind' is."

Mike began to circle around Héctor, confusion spreading over his face. "Yo, this is *gay*," said Mike.

"Yes, it *is*!" exclaimed Héctor. "Is that what you mean? You don't like *that* kind of person?"

"I don't," Mike said forcefully. "You're weird. Unnatural."

That stung Héctor a bit, but this improvised play was just getting good. He had to go further into the role, to let the harmful things Mike and Frank said slide off him.

Frank hovered behind Mike. "Yeah," he said. "Do you have a crush on us? Is that why you're so annoying? I bet you do."

"I bet when he goes home, he dreams about us," added Mike.

"Freak."

"Loser."

"Weirdo."

Then Mike put his nose against Héctor's, as he had done before.

Héctor tried his best not to back up, not to show Mike how terrified he was.

"I know exactly what you are," said Mike.

He smiled.

And then he said the word.

Again.

He said it with confidence. He meant both syllables.

His smile grew wider.

Mike was so sure of himself that he didn't notice the hush that fell over the auditorium on the other side of the curtain.

So Héctor went in for the kill.

"Why do you call me that?" Héctor asked. "Why can't you two just leave me alone?"

Mike actually laughed. "Why not? I can do whatever I want to you."

"Not anymore," Héctor said, and he slowly stepped back, out of the light. "I won't let you."

"How are you going to stop us?" Mike asked. "Everyone is *always* going to believe me over you. Ms. Heath. Mrs. Caroline. And anyone who doesn't . . . well, what are they going to do?"

Mike stepped into the center of the beam of light.

"I run this school," he declared.

"No, you don't," said Héctor.

He looked over to Sal.

"*Now!*"

It all happened so fast. Sal pulled furiously on the lever that activated the curtains, and light burst onto the stage as they were wrenched open.

There was a collective gasp from the people in the auditorium.

And Mike—who looked back to Héctor with fury on his face—leaped forward, his hands on Héctor's chest, and Héctor hit the stage hard. Fire bloomed in his right leg. He struggled to breathe, to cry out in pain, but the wind was knocked out of him. He watched in horror as Mike raised his arm up, balled his fist and—

"Don't move another muscle!"

Mike froze.

Both Héctor and Mike looked in the direction of that familiar voice. There, at the edge of the stage, was the shadowed form of Ms. Heath, her fists dug into her hips.

Héctor couldn't see her face, but she sounded *furious*.

"Mike Kimball, what do you think you are *doing*?"

Mike sat upright, and the pain flared again up Héctor's leg.

"And don't you go anywhere, Mr. Thomas!" Ms. Heath barked.

Héctor saw that Frank had been trying to sneak away.

Steps pounded up the stairs on stage left near Frank, and Vice Principal Giles stormed into view, burly like a linebacker, the light from the auditorium shining off the dark skin on his shaved head. "Did I hear what I *thought* I heard?" he bellowed. "Mr. Kimball, Mr. Thomas, you will *both* meet me in my office *right now*."

Mike finally stood up, and he sputtered out a few guttural sounds. "I didn't do anything!" he finally screamed. "It was *his* fault!"

"You expect us to believe that?" Ms. Heath shouted

back. "After what we just heard?"

"Heard?"

Mike looked from Ms. Heath down to Héctor. Héctor let the grimace wash off his face and smiled.

"The stage microphones were on the whole time," he said.

The color drained from Mike's face. "That's not possible," he said.

"Really?" said Mr. Giles. "Because I just heard you tell the entire school that *you* run it. Which was a surprise to me as vice principal."

"But I—I didn't mean—"

Mike couldn't finish the sentence. He glanced back at Frank, who wore a similar expression of shock.

"I am so disappointed in your behavior, Mike," said Ms. Heath. She stepped forward, closer to the stage light, and Héctor could now see her face, twisted in frustration. "I can't believe you would do something like this!"

There was a flare within Héctor. Not in his leg, which still throbbed from where Mike's knee had dug into it. No, this was a flash of anger, one that hit Héctor square in the chest.

This was not part of the plan.

He wasn't playing a role anymore.

Héctor lifted himself from the stage floor and hobbled forward. "That's the problem," he said to Ms. Heath. "You always believed him. *Always.*"

"Mr. Muñoz," said Vice Principal Giles. "I don't know what you're referring to, but perhaps this isn't the best time for this."

Héctor stared out at the crowd beyond the stage.

Every seat was full. His fellow students sat mostly with their hands clapped over their mouths, their eyes wide. He was looking for the Misfits, though. He spotted them on the far right, sitting together.

"Mr. Giles," Héctor began. He gulped. "I think it's the perfect time."

"What are you *talking* about?" he said.

It was now or never.

"How many of you have ever been bullied or picked on by Mike or Frank?"

Héctor shouted it to the audience as terror rose in him. He had never done something like this.

He raised his hand.

Then . . .

Aishah did.

Then Jackson.

Then Taylor.

Then Carlos.

And then . . . it was like a wave. A few students near those four raised their hands. Then more on the opposite side.

Then: more than half the audience.

Off to the left, he saw a hand raised in the air, shaking. It belonged to Carmen. And right then, Héctor couldn't find the energy to be angry with her. They might never be friends again, but the reason she'd behaved as she did?

It was *Mike*.

Héctor turned back to Ms. Heath, whose expression had drooped in horror. "Oh my God," she said. "I'm sorry. I didn't know."

"Because you didn't *want* to know," Héctor said, his voice much quieter than before, and for a moment, the sadness returned. "I told you the first time you asked me. I told you *everything*. And you said Mike"—Héctor pointed to Mike, who still stood motionless in the spotlight—"would never do something like that."

A voice rang out from the audience.

"He *was* doing it the whole time," said Carlos, who had stood up. "And I know because . . . because I was right there with him."

His head dropped down. "I'm sorry, too," he added. "I didn't want Mike to pick on me and my dad anymore, so I joined him." Carlos's voice broke on the last word.

He looked back up at the stage. "Ms. Heath, Héctor isn't lying. This has been going on as long as I've been here."

Héctor's eyes brimmed with tears. Carlos had finally thrown *himself* under the bus, rather than someone else.

Mr. Giles turned back to Héctor. "I can't apologize enough for what happened to you. If what I heard was any sort of indication . . ." He shuddered. "That behavior is not tolerated here at Orangevale Middle School."

He addressed his final words to Ms. Heath. "You will meet me after school," he said. "We're not finished either."

Mr. Giles waved at Frank and Mike, who trudged off like wounded puppies. He picked up Carlos on the way, and Ms. Heath followed all of them. She did not look back at Héctor, though, and he couldn't ignore his lingering disappointment. *That's it?* he thought. Ms. Heath apparently had no other explanation for why she'd done what she did, and for some reason, that stung.

But there was no time to consider it. Héctor stood on stage alone, and there was a horribly awkward silence in the auditorium. The thrill of getting to expose Mike was wearing off and . . . well, who was he *now*?

He had no idea what to do next. He limped to the edge of the stage in that silence but froze when he heard the clapping.

It was slow at first, and when Héctor looked out into

the crowd, he saw that Aishah was standing, pride on her face. Then Jackson rose quickly and did the same. It spread. The applause was scattered, then haphazard, then *thunderous*.

Mrs. Caroline drifted down one of the aisles until she was at the edge of the stage, and she reached an arm out. Her dress was particularly colorful that day, too. It looked as if flowers had bloomed all along her body, growing forth from her dark skin and illuminating her presence.

She smiled at Héctor.

"Take a bow, Héctor Muñoz," she said over the applause. "You've earned it."

CHAPTER FORTY-SIX

It was hard for anyone, let alone Héctor, to pay attention during classes that day. The teachers had not known what to do about the spirit assembly, so everyone went back to their regular schedule. Lunch was overwhelming, and for the first time, *everyone* wanted to sit at the Table of Misfits. But Héctor spent the time with his friends, nodding at people when they came over or shaking a few hands with kids who thanked him. Even Mr. Holiday sat Héctor down during gym class to ask him how he pulled it off.

It was a little fun making up *that* story.

His day had been jam-packed, so he'd had no chance to look for the Room until after gym. But he had no problem finding it, and even better? His friends were inside. Sal and Juliana immediately began to jump up and down and shriek at him.

"Oh, Héctor, you were *amazing*!" exclaimed Juliana.

"That was a *performance*," added Sal, hugging him. "I was so lost in it that I almost forgot I don't go to your school. Are you in trouble?"

"Did anyone get suspended?" said Juliana.

Héctor laughed. "I don't think I'll know until next week."

"Are you, like . . . like a local *hero* now?" said Sal.

"Is your leg okay?" Juliana blurted out.

Héctor laughed. "One thing at a time!" he said. "And it's just a sprain. I'll be fine."

"We've been *dying* to know," said Juliana. "We had no idea what happened after we left! Do you know how hard it was to go through a whole school day after that?"

"Well, I can't thank you two enough," he said. "I could not have done this without you."

"What*ever*," said Juliana. "You helped us, too."

"Don't forget that," said Sal. "We were just returning the favor."

Héctor looked around the Room. It appeared as a combination of all three of their rooms. There was the fridge. The couch. The TV. The beanbag chairs. The expansive library in the back, with shelves that seemed to stretch into the darkness forever.

Héctor's stomach dropped.

"So," he said, uncertain he wanted the answer, "now what? What happens to this place?"

"What do you mean?" Juliana asked.

"Well, I still think my theory is right," he explained. "I don't understand where this room came from or anything. But if it gives us what we need, what happens when we don't need it anymore?"

"Who says we won't need it again?" Sal said.

"Well, you have your library now," he said. "And Juliana, you got to come out to your mom and got your DJ gig back."

"And the dance is *tonight*," said Juliana. "I'm so nervous. But excited!"

"You're gonna be *amazing*," said Sal. "I know it."

Héctor smiled at both of them. "Maybe I'm overreacting. Maybe this will be here tomorrow, and we'll just laugh at how paranoid I am."

A silence fell over the Room as the three of them looked at one another.

"We should exchange phone numbers or something," said Juliana. "Just in case."

"Yes!" said Héctor. "I thought of that before, but I keep forgetting to bring it up!"

They all traded their contact information. But as soon as they'd done that, the silence returned.

"Is this it?" Sal asked. "I'll see you two again, won't I?"

Héctor scoffed at them. "Of course! I'm sure of it."

Sal rushed into Héctor's arms for a hug anyway. If this really was the last time Héctor was going to see Sal, he would miss them. Their hugs. Their voice.

Sal hugged Juliana before heading to the door. "Don't

be a stranger," they said. "I know we didn't get off on the best foot, but I promise to be a friend to you."

"Thank you, Sal," she said. And then: "I believe you."

They opened the door.

Closed it.

And when Juliana and Héctor turned back to the Room, the library was gone. No more shelves, no more books, none of the comfy high-backed chairs either. *Wow*, Héctor thought. *Sal is really gone.*

He didn't want to believe it, but he still felt a lump forming in his throat as he looked around the Room.

"I think you might be right, Héctor," said Juliana. "I guess this is it."

"We have our phones," he said.

"True." She sighed. "Still. This all feels so sudden. This can't really be coming to an end, can it?"

He shook his head. "Nah," he said. "I think it's the start of something new and exciting. At least I *hope* so."

The two of them hugged long and hard.

"Thank you," said Juliana. "For everything."

"Right back at ya," said Héctor.

He watched her open the door.

Step out.

Close it.

As he moved forward, he heard the Room shifting behind him. The light dimmed until the closet was illuminated by a single bulb that hung from the ceiling. He turned back.

It was nothing more than a janitor's closet.

A single closet, full of cleaning supplies, an intricate web in the corner . . .

And him. One boy, who had somehow changed his life for the better.

Héctor waved goodbye to King Ferdinand.

He reached for the door.

"Thank you," he said aloud. "I don't know if there's a person behind this, or if it's just some weird magic, but . . . thank you. You gave me friends and a place to feel safe."

He grasped the handle.

"You gave me what I needed."

Héctor pushed the door open and hobbled back into the hallways of his school. There was an echo as the door shut, and Héctor glanced back at it.

It wasn't there. He was staring at a blank wall.

He pulled out his phone and composed a message to Sal and Juliana:

> Yo yo yo. Sup friends.

Seconds later, Juliana replied:

> I think the door is gone for me.

Then, Sal:

> Me too.

Héctor shook his head. It was too strange to wrap his mind around. He sent off another message:

> Then this group chat is perfect. We can stay in
> touch across time and space lmao.
> **Juliana:** Like our own magic.
> **Sal:** But we gotta have a good name for the chat.
>   Can't leave it plain.

No, that was unacceptable. But Héctor wasn't sure what to say. Something about a squad? Nah, no one really said that anymore. Something referencing the Room? Maybe. What had they done? Infiltrated each other's schools. The Infiltrators?

No.

No, he had it.

He edited the chat name and sent it out to the group.

> **The Insiders.**

He sent another text:

> I know it's cheesy, but that's who we were.
> Insiders. And we changed our lives because of it.

Seconds later.

> **Juliana:** Oh, I love it. Because it's the opposite of
>   being an outsider.
> **Sal:** It's perfect, Héctor.

Yes. It was.

• • •

When he got home that afternoon, his papi was eager to know why his son was limping around, but Héctor asked if he could wait until Mami was home before he explained. Abuela Sonia waved off Papi. "Let him be," she said. "He'll tell us when he's ready."

"It's nothing bad, I promise you," said Héctor.

Well, he thought. *It doesn't* end *badly*.

To kill time, Abuela sat Héctor down at the table and urged him to try his hand at a tamale again.

He grabbed a ball of masa.

Spread it out against the husk.

Laid some pork on top of that.

Rolled it.

Abuela Sonia examined it. She turned it about in her hands.

"Perfecto," she said, and a burst of relief spread in Héctor.

She winked at him. "Otra vez."

Again.

He made another one. This one was not so perfect, but it wasn't a disaster. His abuela made one small correction, and then he moved on to a third one. And a fourth. And soon, it just clicked. It was like he'd *always* been able to make them.

Over dinner that night, he told them everything. Not

just because it was only a matter of time before Vice Principal Giles gave them a call—but because he finally *wanted* to tell them what he'd been through.

Abuela Sonia held his hand tightly while he spoke, and every time he slowed down or hesitated, she squeezed. It was her way of encouraging him, of reminding him that this wasn't his fault.

His parents cried. They burned with rage. Mami said she was ready to march down to the school the next day and give them a piece of her mind. Then Papi said *he* wanted to do it, and soon, they had decided to go together and were strategizing who would talk about what. Immediately after that, Mami started convincing herself that if she'd followed up on her idea to find an after-school drama program, maybe none of this would have happened, but she just got so busy and—

Abuela Sonia had to shush them. "There will be time for that," she said when they had quieted down. "But Héctor needed to solve this and to decide for himself to ask for help when it got to be too much. Let him *ask* you to take charge if he needs it."

She looked to Héctor and smiled.

He didn't know what he would do without her.

Unlike his old Alta Vista group chat, the Insiders chat stayed active all week. He simply couldn't get enough of it. They traded jokes and memes. Sal and Héctor freaked out when Juliana sent over photos of the dance, complete with one of her locked in the arms of Sascha, the two of them slow dancing under a sparkling disco ball.

Is it weird that I ship you two? texted Sal. **Because I do.**

Juliana sent back like a hundred hearts.

The chat admittedly distracted him, too, and a week after the events in the auditorium, he was caught texting during lunch. Ms. Heath was no longer around, and the new head of campus security was a Black woman named Ms. Clayton. While Héctor had appreciated Ms. Heath's consistent style, she had *nothing* on Ms. Clayton. She had on a white dress with small cherries all over it, and he loved how it looked against her brown skin.

Ms. Clayton tapped Héctor on the shoulder. "No phones during the school day," she reminded him.

"Sorry," he said, stuffing it back in his pocket.

She smiled at him.

"I'm sure whatever you're doing is exciting," Ms. Clayton said, "but please keep cell phone usage to after-school hours unless it is an emergency."

He saluted her. "Yes, ma'am."

"Oh, we don't need to use 'ma'am' on me," she said, grimacing. "Got me feeling like I'm a thousand years old. Ms. Clayton is fine."

Héctor's friends arrived shortly after. Aishah scooted

next to him; Jackson sat across the table, like he always did, and was then joined by Taylor.

Then Carlos, freshly returned from his four-day suspension, stood at the end of the table. Héctor gave him a genuine smile, and Carlos sat.

The five of them ate their food, which still wasn't that good. They talked about relatively normal things: Video games. Music. The odd smell in the gymnasium that Mr. Holiday never seemed to notice. Taylor even told Héctor about how he had decided that Twinkies would be the currency of the future. "You know, since they last forever," he said.

It was strangely brilliant, and Héctor told him so.

"So, this weekend," said Aishah. "Thrifting?"

"It'll be fun!" said Jackson.

"And my dad can still drive us," said Taylor. He paused for a moment and looked at Carlos. "He's got a big truck, so all of us could go."

Carlos visibly gulped. "We could also get helados out by Lake Natoma."

"What are helados?" asked Aishah.

Héctor's eyes went wide. "Oh, you're in for a treat!" he exclaimed. "They're like these ice cream bars—"

"—and they're like super creamy and good?" finished Carlos.

"They're life-changing," said Héctor.

"One hundred percent," said Carlos.

"I'm down," said Jackson. "It is unfortunately still eight billion degrees out."

"I'll ask my parents," said Héctor. "But . . . yeah, I'd love to."

Aishah punched the air. "Perfect."

When the bell signifying the end of lunch rang, Héctor felt calm. At peace. And he didn't know what the future was going to look like, but he knew then that he could *imagine* a future with these people by his side.

That felt like a victory to Héctor Muñoz.

EPILOGUE

Miles and miles away.

Another country.

Another state.

Another city.

Another school.

Hafsah adjusts her niqab while staring into the mirror in the bathroom. The door is locked, and someone is pounding on it, telling her to hurry up. A voice in her head says to take it off. It says to keep it on. It says that she will never escape their judgmental eyes. It says terrible things.

It overwhelms her and she starts to cry. She just wants to be herself, but the people in her rural school do not understand her. They call her names. They ask her demeaning questions. She just wants to escape some days. To disappear and feel safe.

But she can't have that, can she?

She takes a deep breath and turns to the exit, but her breath catches in her throat.

There's another door. It is ornate, made of some sort

of dark wood, etched with a ridiculous pattern. Leaves, vines, and blooming flowers. Like the garden Hafsah wishes she had, where she could grow orchids and tomatoes and poppies and everything colorful and alive.

She drifts over to it, puts her hand on the wood.

Is it calling to her?

She pushes.

On the other side of the door, light trickles down between the vines that crisscross over a glass ceiling. The warmth hits her next as the humidity escapes from the greenhouse. An *actual* greenhouse. *How is this possible?* she wonders.

Is that music? Because she's sure it sounds like her favorite Beyoncé song . . .

Hafsah steps forward . . .

Another town.

Another campus.

Another crosswalk.

Samantha stands on the other side of the street. Ridgewood Junior High is just a few steps away, but she can't seem to make her feet work.

She looks down.

Her jeans—faded, stained, full of holes—are too tight.

What will Rachel say to her *today*? What mean joke will she make at Samantha's expense?

She takes a deep breath, though, and lifts her chin up. "Head up high," her mother told her that morning. "Don't ever let them see you down."

Samantha crosses the street. People giggle at her, badly hiding it behind their hands. She ignores them. She pays no mind to Ethan, who asks her if she stole her outfit from a thrift store, or to Rachel, who quips back, "They wouldn't even take Sam's clothes if she *paid* them to."

She knows that she can hide in the bathroom until the homeroom bell rings, and she knows how to time it exactly so that she is the last student, so that Ms. Tremaine will start her lecture and no one will be able to make any more comments. Before she can get there, though, someone yells something crude at her, and she picks up the pace, trying to outrun the comments about how it looks like she rolled in mud, and she is so flustered that she pulls open the wrong door. It *must* be the wrong door, because she finds herself in a massive walk-in closet.

Racks and racks of clothes line the walls. The room is gently lit so that it's not too bright, not too dark. In the center are a giant standing mirror and a couple empty racks.

Samantha peeks back into the hallway, then into the

closet again. What *is* this place? The teachers' lounge? No, that doesn't even make *sense*.

She lets the door close behind her as she approaches a rack. There is an adorable pair of dyed lavender jeans on the end, and when she looks at the tag . . .

It's her size.

So is the maroon shirt next to it.

As is the sparkly dress that she immediately wants to wear, to twirl around in, to feel like she's a star at the center of the universe.

It's all her size—as if this place was designed *perfectly* for her . . .

Another place.

Another time.

Another.

DeShawn shoves his way past his teacher, past the other kids who are yelling at him, their voices grating in his head. How can a sound hurt so much?

The lights are too bright.

A locker slams shut, and it feels like his brain is going to explode, like he is a circuit set to overload any second. Every sound, every flash of light, is like a flood, and he's going to drown.

He doesn't even know where he's going, but he knows

it is another attack. His therapist calls them "episodes," and he likes that word. It makes it sound like a television show. But more importantly, it means that it has an ending. And that's what he needs more than anything: an end to this torrent of overstimulation. He can barely keep his eyes open, and he just *runs*.

DeShawn does not even remember passing through a doorway. He only hears the soft click of a latch finding its place.

Then *all* the sound is gone.

He freezes, then opens his eyes.

He is in a room. The walls are a dark red, almost black, and they look so soft. He reaches out and touches the one nearest to him; it's like velvet. The sensation sends a shiver up his arm, and his mind quiets down.

There's a beanbag.

There's a steaming cup on a table.

He approaches it.

Is that . . . *chamomile*? His favorite tea?

There's a bowl there, too, and tears spring to his eyes when he sees it is full of tiny marbles. He plops down on the beanbag, relishing how comfortable it feels, then sticks his fingers into the bowl.

It's a sound he likes, the way the marbles strike one another.

It calms him.

Fills him with nothing but a sound that he *can* control.

He smiles.

DeShawn does not understand it, but somehow, this room is exactly what he needs.

ACKNOWLEDGMENTS

Thank you.

To my agent, DongWon Song, who has watched this manuscript take shape from an idea that came from the very first book I wrote in 2003. You encouraged me to pursue writing a middle grade book, and I am forever in your debt because of that.

To Stephanie Stein, my editor extraordinaire. Throughout this process, you pushed me to make this more queer. More ridiculous. More heartfelt. This book doesn't exist in its final form without you, and I hope I have a long, long career making books with you.

To the entire Harper Collins team, for your loving, thoughtful, and detailed support of *The Insiders*. You've made this nonbinary queer Latinx writer extremely, extremely happy. Shout out to Louisa Currigan, Jon Howard, Jessie Gang, Meghan Pettit, Allison Brown, Jacquelynn Burke, and Robby Imfeld.

To Helder Oliveira, whose show-stopping illustrations make up the cover for this book. I cried when I saw your first draft, and my heart swelled up a million sizes when I saw the final one. Thank you for bringing Héctor, Juliana, and Sal to life.

Throughout this book, you may have caught a number of cameos and references to some wonderful young adult and middle grade authors. There are approximately 25 of them, some far more subtle than others. While you have fun trying to figure out who they are, I wanted to thank these people in an interesting way. All of them appear in the book as a reference to the main theme of *The Insiders*: at one point or another, each have made me feel safe and accepted within this community. Thank you to these people. You changed my life forever.

Thank you, Baize White, for helping me with this manuscript before you left this world. I miss you, and I wish you were still alive to see it become a book.

And finally, for all the queer and trans kids out there! Whether you know who you are or you're still discovering yourself or whether you come to the truth later in life, I want each of you to know:

No one is ever really alone.

Much love,
Mark Oshiro

DON'T MISS...

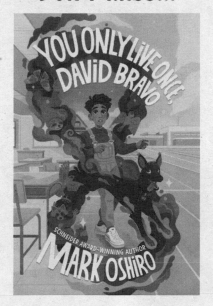

When David Bravo wishes for a do-over after a disastrous first week of middle school, he's surprised to summon a talking, shape-shifting dog who claims that a choice in David's past really *did* put him on the wrong timeline . . . and she can take him back to fix it. But when his first attempt (and the second, and the third) is a total disaster, they're left scrambling through timeline after timeline—on a quest that leads to answers in the most unexpected places.

TUESDAY, SEPTEMBER 5
8:10 A.M.
The (first) first day of middle school

"What if we just *don't* go to school?"

I'm standing next to Antoine Harris, who's got his thumbs looped behind the straps of his backpack. His mom left the two of us here, staring at the steps that lead up to the entrance of Mira Monte Middle School. Other kids are rushing up them before the first bell rings, but the two of us? We're not moving at all.

"That's a really good idea, David," says Antoine. "But what are we going to do all day?"

I scratch at my chin. "We could walk to Target."

Antoine's raises an eyebrow at me. "Target?"

"I already came up with the perfect cover story," I say. "We were hired by LEGO to assemble the display models."

"Okay, but I get all the *Star Wars* ones."

I put my hands up. "They're all yours. I'll be busy assembling that huge fire station set they have."

"That's a good plan," says Antoine, smirking, but then he turns back to those daunting steps. He sighs. "It can't be *that* bad, can it?"

"We don't have any classes together!" I whine.

"And we have *classes*," Antoine says, frowning. "I don't get why we can't still have the same teacher all day."

"Whoever made up the idea of middle school is evil," I say. "We should turn around right now and head straight to the LEGOS."

Antoine hesitates, then scratches his scalp between two of the intricately braided cornrows he just got a few days ago. "I think my parents would be mad if I didn't show up to the first day of school."

"Well, of *course*," I say. "But think how excited they'll be to find out we've been hired by Target to put together all their LEGO sets."

He laughs at that. "How about this?" he says. "Let's regroup at lunch. At least then we don't have to become clichés and worry about where we're going to sit."

"Excellent plan," I say. "No after-school specials about us."

And then:

The Handshake.

We slap the back sides of our hands against each other's twice.

"Crisscross," we say in unison.

A dap, mine on top first, then his.

"Always floss."

(Because we both care about dental hygiene, okay?)

We grip each other's hands but only at the fingers.

"Always friends."

Then we pull our hands apart, so fast that it makes a little snapping sound.

"To the end."

Antoine bumps his shoulder against mine as the two of us ascend the stairs to Mira Monte Middle School. I don't know what our first day of seventh grade will hold, but at least my best friend is at my side.

And then, for the first time since we met in first grade when his family moved here from Virginia, Antoine veers off, waving, and heads to a different class than mine.

I have this urge to chase after him, but I don't. *No, David*, I tell myself, and I stop walking just short of the front gate. *You just have to make it to lunch.*

I can do that.

I think.

But maybe not. I don't like new things, like surprises or anything that interrupts my routines. Starting at this new school feels like a million surprises and interruptions all wrapped into one giant mess.

I breathe in. I breathe out. A part of me wants to give in to the sensation sneaking up on me and just *freeze*. I do that sometimes, especially when I'm overwhelmed.

There's also a bigger part of me that doesn't want to be the weirdo standing outside the school when the first bell rings.

So I make myself keep going, past the iron front gate, and I join the stream of students at Mira Monte Middle School, walking into the uncertain and the unknown.

TUESDAY, SEPTEMBER 5
8:15 A.M.
First class (not the fancy seats in an airplane, unfortunately)

I reach into my pocket and pull out the folded piece of paper I stuffed in there earlier. I have all six of my classes marked in color-coded ink, but somehow, I forgot to include classroom numbers. So I know I have SOCIAL STUDIES first but absolutely no idea where it is.

Oh, this is going to be fun.

I move to the side as a river of more kids pours into campus. Mom and Dad brought me here a week ago for orientation, but they didn't give us a tour, and this place is like a never-ending maze. At least I'm not going to the other middle school—La Sierra Junior High—all the way on the other side of town. That has to be the ugliest campus I've ever seen.

I'm already sweating as I rush up to the closest building. It's always so warm here in California that our schools are made up of several buildings, spread out from one another. Antoine told me that his old school out in Virginia was a single building because it got snowy and cold during the winter. To be honest, the design of our schools here makes no sense to me. Who *wants* to be outside when it's super hot?

Like right now. The sign on the side of the building reads MATHEMATICS. A drop of sweat runs right into the side of my eye.

This is the worst.

I turn around and thankfully spot a sign that says HISTORY AND SOCIAL STUDIES on the building across the way. I unfortunately have to cut through a bunch of kids to get there, which earns me numerous dirty looks. Relief floods me when I see a paper tacked to an open door with the name of the teacher I'm looking for.

I walk into Mr. Bradshaw's class—room 213—and am immediately faced with another choice to make.

Where do I sit?

"Welcome, students," says Mr. Bradshaw, a tall white man with a shiny bald spot in the middle of his gray-and-white hair. "Please choose where you sit carefully. That will be your seat for the remainder of the year!"

More students shuffle in—tall, brown, Black, white, Asian, short, chubby, awkward, loud—and desks are disappearing quickly. I think about sitting next to the girl in the front row with the freckles and pigtails, but the empty desk beside her is claimed while I hesitate. Do I quickly make a decision before desks are occupied? Oh, absolutely not. Finally, I dart over to the rear corner and sit next to an Asian girl who slams a notebook shut as soon as I turn to her.

"Hi," she says, a nervous edge to her voice. "Gracie. I wasn't doing anything."

I blink a few times at her. "Okay," I say. "I'm David."

She smiles but turns away.

Well . . . that happened. I put my backpack on the floor to my left, then pull out my own notebook and a pen. I don't actually know what I'm supposed to be doing. Antoine's older brother, Isaiah, told me when he visited over the summer that middle school was going to be a big change for me. "You'll have homework all the time," he explained. "And be prepared to have to take notes."

I'm not really sure what that actually means. What am I supposed to "note"? What the teacher is wearing? The things he says? *Everything* he says? Everything I'm thinking?

Wow. This is a lot already, and class hasn't even started.

The bell rings, and right as it does, the last two kids come tumbling into class. I don't need to be a middle school expert to know that I will *not* be friends with them. They're slugging each other in the shoulder repeatedly.

The taller and browner of the two—who honestly looks like he's at least in high school—sneers at the other. "Man, you're *weak*," he says.

"Please take a seat, gentlemen," says Mr. Bradshaw, gesturing to the only two open seats . . . which are of course right in front of me.

"Where should we take our seats?" says the other kid, then grabs the back of an empty chair and lifts it up. "Should we take them outside?"

He's the paler one, and he's got this long, stringy blond hair that looks like what happens when the grass dries out in the fields behind my house. *Should I take notes on that?* I think.

"Yeah, let's go sit right outside the windows," says the tall kid.

Mr. Bradshaw's mouth curls up on one side. He doesn't exactly look happy. I glance over at Gracie, and she slams her notebook shut again and smiles.

O-okay.

As Mr. Bradshaw calls out our names and marks us down on his "map" of the classroom so he can do attendance more easily in the future, I learn that the almost-late kids are Tommy Rodriguez and Walter May. Tommy flashes two peace signs when Mr. Bradshaw calls out his name. "That's me," he says. "What are you gonna teach us, Teacher?"

Mr. Bradshaw frowns. "This is social studies, Mr. Rodriguez."

"Dope," says Tommy. "You gonna teach us about Twitter?"

Our teacher narrows his eyes at Tommy. "What?"

"You know," says Tommy. "Like . . . social media?"

This . . . this is going to be a long year.

There are so many other kids in the room. I don't catch all the names, but I know I'll remember Wunmi Onyebuchi because hers is so great. She's got this gorgeous dark skin and her hair is shaved down short all over. She even has on a *Julie and the Phantoms* shirt, so I'm pretty sure she's cooler than me. Gracie's last name is Lim, and Mr. Bradshaw smiles at her. "Good to have you here, Gracie," he says. "I've heard a lot about you."

Gracie goes red in the face. I have no idea what that means.

Finally, after Tommy and Walter interrupt about forty-five more times (I am guessing, because I didn't *actually* take notes), Mr. Bradshaw introduces his class to us. He tells us that we're going to learn a little bit of history about the world, but we're also going to spend time "expanding our horizons."

"It's my job to teach you about this wonderfully diverse and complicated world," he explains. "And I can't imagine a better way of doing that than assigning you homework."

I can't lie; like everyone else in class, I groan when Mr. Bradshaw says that.

"Homework *already*?" says Tommy.

"Yes, *already*," says Mr. Bradshaw. "But it's going to be an easy A. I believe everyone here can start the year off with a perfect score."

Gracie flips a few pages into her notebook to find a blank one, and I realize this must be it. It's time to take notes. I ready myself, my pen in my hand.

"Each of you is going to introduce us to the cultures of your home," says Mr. Bradshaw.

My heart leaps.

"You will give a short presentation—all oral, under two minutes—explain what cultures make up your home and make you *you*."

Wait. *Wait.*

"Tell your fellow students about where you and your parents come from! Do you have interesting cultural practices or traditions in your home that you'd like to share?"

My throat tightens, and I try to gulp down all the spit in my mouth, but I have to choke back a cough.

Oh, no. No, I don't want to do this.

"I'll start," continues Mr. Bradshaw. "My family is originally from Boston, and I was born outside Cambridge, Massachusetts. But my grandparents are actually from a place called Rotterdam, which is in the Netherlands, just

south of Amsterdam! Have any of you been to Amsterdam?"

There are a lot of head shakes, and a few kids softly
mutter, "No." I want to blurt out that most of us haven't
even left California before. The Netherlands?! I don't even
know where that is on a map!

That's not why my skin feels like it's being shocked with
electricity, though. As Mr. Bradshaw talks about having
Dutch heritage and all the kinds of food he ate growing up,
I realize just how hard this is going to be. I'm not like any
of these people because . . . well, because I was adopted
when I was an infant.

And I don't actually know what I am.

I've always known I was adopted. I mean . . . I would
have figured it out if my parents hadn't told me. My mom
is Japanese, born in Okinawa but raised in Hawai'i. So
she's got a dark brown hue to her skin, and long black hair
that's as straight as can be. Dad's parents are from Mexico
and Brazil, and his skin tone is a lot like Mom's, though his
hair is intensely curly.

Then there's me. I don't look like either of them. My
skin is a lot lighter, though I tan superfast whenever I'm in
the sun. My hair is black, but it's wavy rather than curly.
I don't resemble my parents, either, so I usually get lots of
weird looks when we're out in public.

Mom and Dad sat me down before I was ever in school
to tell me that they loved me very much, which is why they

chose to have me be a part of their family. They've been pretty open about it, too; Mom said I could always ask her questions about my adoption if I wanted to.

But what was there to ask about? The only question I had—all the way back in kindergarten, when Ms. Wells asked me if I knew anything about my birth parents—had already been answered. I was part of a "closed" adoption, meaning that no one but the adoption agency knew anything about where I came from. My parents were told that my birth parents were Latinx, but that's it. They knew exactly what I did.

Yet it didn't seem to matter when I told other people that. They *always* had questions, like Yasi in fourth grade, who wanted to know if I'd ever met my birth parents. Or Ms. Gull, the substitute in fifth grade, who asked me what it was like knowing my past was a "mystery."

Oh, god, was I going to have to go through all of this again? I just don't like thinking about this stuff.

I haven't taken any notes or heard a single thing our teacher has been saying when I realize that my fellow classmates are staring down at textbooks. And there's somehow one on *my* desk. When did that show up?

I don't like this feeling, like there's an avalanche waiting around the corner and it's only a matter of time before it crashes down on me. I look to Gracie in panic, and she mouths, "Page six," to me. I thank her silently and turn to it, desperate to catch up, but I still can't escape the growing panic inside me.

Why do I have to start my first year of middle school with this?